Regency Romance Box Sets
A Very Regency Christmas
Three Wicked Rogues

Standalone Christmas Books
Christmas in the Duke's Arms

Paranormal Books:

The Siren Saga
Echoes in the Silence, Book 1

Highlanders Hold Grudges

Wicked Willful Highlanders, Book 1

by
Julie Johnstone

The best way to stay in touch is to subscribe to my newsletter. Go to https://juliejohnstoneauthor.com and subscribe in the box at the top of the page that says Newsletter. If you don't hear from me once a month, please check your spam filter and set up your email to allow my messages through to you so you don't miss the opportunity to win great prizes or hear about appearances.

If you're interested in when my books go on sale or want to be one of the first to know about my new releases, please follow me on BookBub! You'll get quick book notifications every time there's a new pre-order, book on sale, or new release. You can follow me on BookBub here: www.bookbub.com/authors/julie-johnstone

Dedication

To all those who hold grudges, may you release them and fly with the freedom of a bright spirt and light heart, because grudges often lead to trouble, and that, my friend, cages your soul behind invincible bars.

Prologue

The Year of Our Lord 1257
The Highlands, Scotland

*H*e'd been following her for weeks now.

It had started accidentally, innocently, chivalrously even, when he'd happened to spot her hunting near twilight. That a lass would be alone at such an hour in such a place had caught him off guard. He'd started to call out to her to offer her safe passage out of the treacherous woods, but before he could, she'd amazed him by felling a deer with one shot of her bow. In that moment, he'd judged her capable of taking care of herself, and he'd turned to make his own way home in the opposite direction.

Then some sort of fate had intervened. Or he supposed it was such a thing. His mother was always yammering about fate, so there was a part of him that entertained the fanciful female notion, though he'd never admit it aloud.

Whatever it was, the lass's scream rent the air before he'd managed to take ten steps. He'd swiveled back around, and his jaw had fallen open. She'd been racing in circles, the green skirt of her fine gown swirling about her ankles in the wind, fiery hair swishing about her delicate shoulders. From a distance, she looked like a frightened fairy sprite flailing her slender arms and screeching. He'd started back toward her when she stopped and slung a black snake to the ground. Then she'd whipped out a dagger, flung it at the slithering creature, and lopped its head right off with the one throw.

Amazed, Alasdair had returned his gaze to the lass as a satisfied smile pulled up her full lips, and by the gods, what a bonny smile it had been. It had lit up her face, transforming it from beautiful to unforgettable. It had done something to him he still couldn't truthfully explain. Her smile had warmed him through better than his plaid, or the quilt upon his bed, or even the fire that dulled the cold in his bedchamber. The heat her smile created went deep into his bones to thaw the chill of winter within him. But that magical smile alone had not been the thing to make him start following her. After all, he was supposed to be training with the men his da had assigned him, not idling his time following a lass. It was the talking she'd done to herself after the snake was dead that had set him on his course. Her husky voice had beckoned to him as if he were a starving man and she were a goose cooking over a fire or fresh bread baking in the pit. But as tempting as her tone had been, like a full pitcher of mead after a hard day training in the blistering sun, it was what she'd said that had lured him in.

Dunnae be a quitter.

And then she'd set her dainty hands on her nicely rounded hips as if she was lecturing herself. That had been the thing to make him notice just how touchable her hips were. At first glance in the woods, he'd noticed her hair. He'd had to have been a blind man not to, what with it being fire spun with gold. It blazed around her face in a halo.

"Kill the Black Boar," she'd muttered. She'd bitten her plump lip, and that had been the thing to make him really take note of her lips and then her face. Wide eyes, dark-blue like the deepest part of the loch where he swam, and the gaze there looked to be as turbulent, too. Alasdair had stared at those well-framed eyes while calling up the legend of the Black Boar. It wasn't a secret. She wasn't the only one trying to find it and kill it. Most clansmen who lived in the Kintail lands wanted to claim the victory of slaying the boar that had ended the lives of many a Highlander. But she was a lass. She was meant to be by a fireside with a needle and thread, or in the kitchens ordering the staff, or with the bairns, whatever her lot was. At least all the lasses he knew did such things anyway, and at seventeen summers he knew plenty of lasses. None of them hunted, which made her instantly intriguing.

His forehead had crinkled in contemplation when she'd said, "Find the boar, kill the boar, prove yer worth." He recalled nodding absent agreement. He'd understood desiring to prove yerself. He was the laird's eldest son. He wanted to be worthy in his own right, not just because his father was laird.

"Ye'll come back tomorrow, Maeve," she'd said to herself. "Ye'll come back tomorrow, even if ye're scairt. Nay." She'd given a shake of her head, and her hair had swayed around her shoulders a bit more. An errant question had run through his mind then, one that now repeated itself every time he saw her. Would those fiery strands singe his skin if he slid his fingers into her thick mane, or would her hair feel like the finest thing he'd ever touched?

"It dunnae matter the danger. Ye'll return, and then they will see."

She'd marched off in the opposite direction, and he'd stood there only a breath or two before he'd followed. It was to ensure she made it out of the woods safe, he'd told himself. She'd made it out, and before he could decide if he also needed to ensure she got safely home, a rider had appeared before her. Alasdair had recognized the emblem emblazed on the cloak before he recognized Colin Fraser.

Alasdair's muscles had twitched at the sight of a Fraser. No Fraser was a good one, but the Fraser laird's son had been an especially unwelcome sight. Where a Fraser ventured, nothing good followed. Alasdair had moved his attention off the blond-haired, double-weapon-wielding man back to the lass. She hadn't appeared tense, nor had she tried to run or scream, which meant she likely knew Colin Fraser. That should have lit an instant dislike for her in Alasdair, yet it hadn't. Perhaps it had been because the boy looked to be lecturing the lass. Mayhap she disliked the Fraser, too. But then the lad had reached a hand down to her and she'd taken it quickly enough, then swung up into the saddle behind him. Alasdair had turned away before they were out of sight. He'd done his duty, and he'd intended to forget her.

Then he'd dreamed of her, or rather, her death. The Black Boar had killed her in his dream, so he'd gone back to the woods the next day. His intentions had been honorable. He'd simply wanted to ensure she was safe. Someone needed to. She was taking all sorts of unspeakable risks with her person. She hunted alone, searched for the Black Boar, and did both near dark. It made him taut as a bowstring whenever he watched her. And yet, he understood it, and he was even fascinated by it, by her. But he knew if she saw him, she'd quit, and he wanted her to get the boar and to change the minds of whomever she was attempting to impress.

So here he was several weeks later when he should be training. He'd been lying lately to come here, too. Saying he had to see to tenants. His mother would fall on her knees and offer a prayer for his soul if she knew he'd lied, and his da would be rightfully vexed that he was ignoring his duties. Even if she was uncommonly lovely.

She paused on the meandering trail through the thick woods, and Alasdair dropped to his haunches behind a tree. She took out her bow. He'd seen her do this enough times now that he started looking around for the deer she intended to shoot or, if luck had finally found her, the Black Boar. It was a deer.

She raised her bow. She was a good shot, felling more deer than she missed. This buck was no exception. It went down with one arrow, and she strode toward it with purpose, her head held high and her slender shoulders pressed back. She kneeled in front of the deer, and hair slipped across her forehead to veil her cheek and eyes. Sunlight glinted on her head, making his fingers curl with the desire to slide his hands into her tresses.

He knew she'd leave the deer. It would be too cumbersome and heavy for her to attempt to take back by herself to wherever she lived, but he also suspected she'd send someone after it, or come back herself with help, because he'd found nary a trace of the deer she'd shot previously. He wasn't surprised when she rose because this was what she did every time. She'd kneel before whatever animal she had felled and stay motionless for a moment, staring down at it. He suspected she was offering some sort of respect to the fallen creature. Just as she started to turn toward the west, the direction she always took, she froze.

In that instant, Alasdair's senses, which had been dazed by her, crackled back to awareness. The deep low growl of a wolf filled the silence before he located the gray and brown furry beast, but it was not so for the lass. She was already nocking an arrow, even as he was reaching for his own and running toward her to aid her. As she loosed her arrow, she looked in his direction. He must have made a noise in the brittle fallen leaves. Her arrow flew toward the large creature that was now charging her, but her aim wasn't true. Fear slammed Alasdair. He'd distracted her in his attempt to aid her.

Her arrow skimmed past the wolf. It was almost upon her, and Alasdair's heartbeat banged in his ears as he let loose his own arrow with a prayer that it reached the wolf before the beast reached the lass. The arrow whistled through the air as he ran and let out a war cry to try to distract the wolf, but the beast was on a mission, one that included ripping the lass to bits. Her mouth formed a shocked *O* as the creature advanced, her eyes widened, and she threw her arms up over her face as the wolf let out a ferocious growl and leaped at her.

Alasdair's arrow pierced the creature in the side mid-leap. The growling beast fell upon the lass, and she flew backward with a thud to land flat on her back with the beast on top of her.

Five more steps to reach her.

The beast had been slowed but not killed. It reared its head, sharp teeth bared, and she screamed. Alasdair grabbed handfuls of fur as the wolf snapped his jaws toward the lass. Alasdair jerked the animal back with one hand and plunged his dagger into the animal's neck. The wolf went limp in his hands while blood seeped from the dagger wound. He dropped the wolf to the ground and turned his attention to the lass, not sure whether he'd get hysterics, fainting, or anger that she'd been followed.

But to his amazed disbelief, she wasn't even looking at him. "Watch out!" she screamed right before a loud piercing keen burst from behind him. He turned, and there was the Black Boar some ten paces away. It grunted and growled and showed its pointy teeth. The animal's short ears went back, and its coarse black hair raised upon its back.

Alasdair pulled out his other dagger to throw it and kill the beast when the lass said, "Wait! Please let me fell it."

"What do I get if I let ye fell the Black Boar?" He was only teasing, but she answered before he could let her know.

"Anything ye want," she said.

A grin split his lips. That was too tempting of an offer for him not to take her up on it. "Go ahead, then." He kept a firm grip on his dagger just in case the boar was persistent. It was far enough away that Alasdair would have time to throw it.

Her answer was a grunt, followed by the distinct click of her bow being pulled taut, an arrow being nocked, then whistling by his ear. It plunged into the boar's head right between its eyes. The beast let out another shrill squeal before it fell sideways with a *thunk* to lie motionless. He swiveled around to face the lass once more and found her focus on him. Her russet eyebrows rose high over those deep-blue eyes, and she swept her gaze over him from head to foot. Her full lips pressed together, and he almost laughed. He knew what he currently looked like.

He still wore the old, tattered braies he'd had on since that morning when he'd trained alone at the edge of the loch. His hair was pulled back at the nape of his neck, and he'd allowed his little sister to paint his face with red berries as a trade to keep the secret that he was venturing into the woods when she'd seen him headed that way.

"Take this coin," she said, holding her hand out to him. "I imagine yer family needs it."

She thought him a poor servant, did she? Well, coin had been harder to come by lately what with the Frasers and the

MacKenzies raiding his family's lands, but it wasn't so hard to come by that he'd accept coin over what he truly wanted from her. "I dunnae want yer coin."

She frowned, and the action caused a pretty little pucker between her brows. "What then?" she demanded.

"A kiss."

Maeve's jaw slid open at the lad's request. But, no, he wasn't a lad. Was he Colin's age? Her dearest friend wasn't yet a full man, but he was near to being one. She squinted at the stranger, trying to decide his age, but with the berry stain all over his face it was hard to tell. "How old are ye?"

"Old enough to kiss ye."

Her cheeks heated at his bold words. She'd never been kissed, but lately she'd imagined her first kiss would come from Colin. She expected to wed him. Their fathers were both lairds and friends, and she'd known Colin all fifteen summers of her life.

"That's nae what I asked," she said, attempting to give him the cross look Beitris always gave her when she stole a sweetmeat from the head cook's kitchen. She pursed her lips, turned her head to the side, and gave him her practiced side eye glance. "How old are ye?"

"How old are ye?"

"Fifteen summers," she said, throwing a look over her shoulder. She could not get caught in these woods by Colin again. He'd threatened to tell her da when he'd discovered her hunting in the woods several sennights ago. She'd had to plead with him not to and vow not to hunt anymore—a harmless white lie. In truth it had irked her that she'd had to bargain with Colin at all, though she understood that he thought he was looking out for her.

The stranger grinned, and two dimples appeared in his cheeks. Those dimples made her stomach go tight in a way she'd never experienced before, and that strange feeling is what made up her mind to let him kiss her. She'd been having needling in her heart that she didn't feel for Colin like a lass should for the man she meant to wed.

"Step closer," she said, boldness coming over her.

"Why?" he asked, crossing his arms over his chest. Those were no lad's arms. They had a bulge of muscle at his bicep that made her want to run her fingers over the swell. And his forearms were thick as well. Her gaze fell downward, taking him in. His chest and stomach were bare except for two leather straps that crossed in an X over his torso. The straps held his weapons, of which he'd already used two daggers, but he still had two swords sheathed.

"Do ye always have so many weapons attached to yer person?" she asked, wondering if it was cumbersome to carry so many weapons at once.

He laughed. "Ye dunnae stay on one topic verra long, do ye?"

The blush that had been just in her cheeks flushed down her neck and heated her chest. Her da teased her that she was just like her mother, who had been unable to stick to one subject for more than a breath. Colin called her "squirrel brain," which she detested. "If ye're going to make a jest of me, then I hardly think ye'd want to kiss me."

"I'm nae making a jest of ye," he said, his tone so serious that she believed him. "I find it endearing."

She snorted at that. "Are ye one of those lads who uses honeyed words to try to tumble the lasses?"

He frowned. "Nay. I dunnae have to use honeyed words to get lasses."

"Oh." She rolled her eyes. "My, my, ye do fancy yerself handsome, then?"

"Well, nay. Or maybe, aye?" He shrugged, and she laughed.

"Which is it?"

"Well, if I say nay, I sound like I'm lying, and if I say aye, I sound like I'm full of myself, but it's nae either."

"Maeve!"

Colin's call made her jump nearly out of her skin. She bit her lip and glanced around the woods, not seeing him yet.

"He's coming from the west," the stranger said, tilting his head in the direction of her home. "Who is he?"

She stared for a moment, transfixed by the way his dark locks glistened with the rays of sun filtering through them.

He hefted up one eyebrow in question, making her realize she'd been staring. She cleared her throat, but her cheeks burned with embarrassment. "My dearest friend. Mayhap my future husband."

The stranger frowned at that. "Betrothed, are ye?"

Here was her chance to retrieve the senses she'd lost and get out of kissing him, and she really did need to disappear before Colin saw her, but she found herself shaking her head truthfully for some reason. "Nae yet."

He grinned, opening up a flood of heat within her. "In that case," he said, "close yer eyes."

"Why do I need to close my eyes?"

"Because when ye dream of me at night in the years to come, I dunnae want ye recalling me with all this berry stain on my face."

"Ye're all sorts of prideful," she said, her foolish lips pulling into what felt like a ridiculously large smile.

"Aye, I am at that. Now close yer eyes. We've about

thirty paces afore yer almost betrothed is upon us."

She glanced over her shoulder and frowned. Colin stood off in the distance at the top of the hill that led down the path toward them. She faced the stranger once more, her heart now racing. Whether it was from the kiss to come or the fear of Colin discovering her, she was unsure. "Get on with it."

"Are these the honeyed words ye use with all the lads?"

"I dunnae use honeyed words with lads."

"How do ye expect to catch a husband, then?"

"I dunnae need to catch a husband," she said, smirking at him. "A man should be so lucky as to catch me."

His gaze swept her from head to foot and back, and heat unfurled in her belly. "Likely ye're right, lass, but I'll nae be certain until after the kiss."

Before she knew what was happening, she found herself gathered in his embrace and being tugged toward him, toward warmth and the earthy smell of burned wood, soil, and fresh grass. Her chest brushed his—soft to hard—and caused her to gasp with the shock of the contrast of their bodies. He hooked a finger under her chin and brought his face toward hers, and she did close her eyes then because, though she didn't really think she'd recall this stranger two breaths after he left her, just in case she did, she'd rather the memory not be with berries smeared on his face.

His fingers slid into her hair, surprising her, and when he cupped the back of her head, his touch was so gentle, the pressure and heat of his hands so reassuring, that a little sigh escaped her. And then his lips brushed hers like a whisper of a breeze with the power of a storm wind. That touch jolted through her and caused her to rock backward on her heels, but since the stranger was still cupping her head, she stayed firmly in place.

His other hand came to the back of her neck, and his fingers met the tender flesh there, causing her to inhale sharply just as his lips came to hers once more. But this time his touch was firmer, and the strong hardness of his lips sent the pit of her stomach into a wild swirl. She'd never been kissed before, but this, this heady sensation was all she had hoped it would be. She wanted more, and she rose on her tiptoes to get what she wanted. Her hands found his shoulders, and she grasped him, trying to tug him toward her as he had done to her.

A satisfied grunt came from him as his kiss grew stronger, sending shivers of something wonderful and new racing through her. Her entire body pulsed to life with an intensity that scared her. She broke the kiss and stepped back from him, relieved that he let her, yet also oddly disappointed that the kiss had to come to an end. But it had to, and quickly.

"Maeve!" Colin called, and she'd never been so grateful for the thick brush in this forest as she was at that moment.

"Ye best be going," she said, shocked at how husky her voice sounded. When had that happened?

He nodded, looking slightly bemused, which pleased her greatly because it wouldn't quite be fair if she was the only one affected by their kiss. When he reached for her, she thought for a moment he was going to draw her to him once more, and she wasn't at all displeased at the notion. Her brain had been turned to mush by one kiss! But he didn't slide his strong fingers into her hair as he had done moments ago. Instead, he gave a gentle tug to the ribbon at the end of the braid that hung down the right side of her head, and it released easily for him.

She opened her mouth to protest because the ribbon had been her mother's before she passed away, but then he spoke. "To remember ye by, if ye'll allow me?"

"Well, since ye asked so nicely," she said, the heat that swept over her surprising her as much as her agreement.

His grin caused her heart to thump uncomfortably. Mayhap she wouldn't wed Colin after all. "What's yer name?" she asked.

"Liked the kiss, did ye?" he said, smirking.

She knew he was simply teasing her, but her pride was a great big beast of a thing. It would likely be her downfall one day. "Forget I asked," she said, her tone sharp as her prickly pride. "Go on with ye."

He grasped her hand and placed it against his heart. The thundering in his chest made her eyes go wide. His gaze was riveted on her face which made excitement dance through her. He smiled slowly, and it widened in approval as he stared at her. "My name is Alasdair. Alasdair MacRae."

Her mouth slipped open at the news, and her heart took a plunge toward the ground. Well, this was ill luck indeed, and probably what she deserved for being so eager to throw Colin over.

Alasdair's dark perfect brows knitted together. She wanted to groan. Of course he had to be so temptingly handsome. "What is it?" he asked reaching for her elbow, but she jerked backward out of his grasp.

"Ye're a MacRae?" The question came out as a suffocated whisper, and no wonder! She was having trouble believing what she'd just heard.

"Aye." The word was cautious, as if Alasdair instinctually knew he'd entered dangerous territory, and indeed, he had. "I'm the eldest son of Torac MacRae."

The ground shifted under her feet, tilting her world for a moment.

He glanced over her shoulder, a scowl settling on his

face. She knew without looking that Colin was approaching. "What is it?" he asked again, but now urgency laced his words.

Before she could answer Colin's voice rang out behind her. "Maeve MacKenzie. What the devil are ye doing cavorting with the son of yer father's greatest enemy?"

Chapter One

1262

The winter storm had picked up such force Maeve feared that if the battle her father had ridden out for didn't kill him, the weather would. From where she stood on the rampart, she normally would be able to see across the bridge to where her father and his men would return, but the snow was falling so hard, she could barely see the castle courtyard below, and all she could make out of the bridge were the torches that burned at the guard station. She normally loved the snow but not tonight. The white blanketed everything and suffocated the light of the moon and the stars, as well as setting a dark mood inside Maeve. She could not shake the growing tightening inside her. Something dreadful was on the precipice of occurring. Her bones ached with the oncoming trouble. That's why she was still standing in the cold, even though she could no longer feel her feet or hands. The layers of animal skins she had draped over her shoulders were no match for the brutal cold of the wind that blew so hard her ears rang from the whistling and her face was numb.

The other wives and daughters of the warriors who'd ridden out with her father earlier that day had long since gone inside to the warmth of the hearth and the food and wine that Beitris and the other kitchen servants were sure to be providing. If anyone could soothe a worried soul, it was

Maeve's former nanny. When Beitris had served as Maeve's caretaker after Maeve's mother had died, Beitris's soft voice and gentle touch had helped drive away many nightmares and tears. And when Maeve had no longer needed a full-time nanny and Beitris had moved to the kitchens, Beitris's stew had filled the hollow that would sometimes pop up in Maeve's belly when she watched other girls with their mothers. Beitris had a way of always knowing just what to do. When Maeve had wanted to persuade her father to teach her to hunt, Beitris had aided Maeve by fixing his favorite berry pie. Maeve would be eternally grateful for the lesson that excellent food was often the way to sway a man to one's desires.

But just now, food held no appeal at all, nor did sitting in the great hall surrounded by the women who would talk constantly of their worries for their men. It would only make Maeve's fear greater. She squinted into the night as the wind whipped her damp hair around her face. Where was her father? Why had he and his men not returned yet from their mission to relieve the MacRaes of their horses so they could not make any more late-night thieving runs to steal from Maeve's clan.

A tap on her shoulder made her jump, and she turned to find Beitris standing there with no more than her upturned nose and dark eyes visible underneath the heavy cloak she wore. But even in the dark, there was enough light from the torches on the rampart that Maeve could see the concern in Beitris's eyes.

"Come in," Beitris said. Maeve shook her head, and Beitris's chin jutted out determinedly at Maeve's refusal. Maeve chuckled, glad for the moment of levity, and Beitris glared at her. "Ye'll nae think it's all so amusing when ye lose a finger or a toe."

Beitris slipped her arm through Maeve's and pulled the woman close to her to rest her head on Beitris's shoulder as Maeve had done so many times in her life. "Where is he, Bee? He should have returned by now."

Beitris patted Maeve's cheek with her free hand. "He'll be back, child. The MacRaes are thieves, nae killers."

"And Da has Colin and his da with him, along with some of their warriors," Maeve said, more to reassure herself than Beitris, but when Beitris made no reassuring comment, Maeve glanced to her friend once more and found Beitris looking out into the distance but with a scowl upon her face.

"Bee, why do ye nae like Colin?"

"I like him just fine. The problem is, ye only like him just fine, too, and I promised yer mama the day ye were born that I'd ensure ye wed for love as she had done with yer da."

"Tell me the story again," Maeve said. She never tired of hearing the tale of when she was born. It made her sad because her mother had died birthing her, but it also filled her with warmth to know her mother had immediately loved her so much that she made Beitris, her dearest friend, and Maeve's father promise that that they would try to ensure Maeve wed for love.

Though Maeve's father had betrothed her to Colin upon her sixteenth birthday, to get the much needed support of an alliance with the Frasers to fight off the MacRae thieving, her da had stood behind her decision not to wed Colin yet, but she knew well her time was running short. Colin was more than tired of waiting for her, and she understood that. Her da had not rushed her, but she knew the Frasers were grumbling that they should have made a marriage contract with a more biddable lass. And she was no fool. She knew the only reason Colin's father did not break the contract was because Maeve would one day inherit Eilean Donan, which was the most strategic fortress in the Highlands.

"Tell me the story of my birth," Maeve said again. "Please."

"I will if ye'll come to the great hall."

Maeve opened her mouth to protest, but Beitris went on. "Just for a light repast and to warm yer hands and toes." Beitris swept her gaze over Maeve's face. "Yer cheeks are so red from the cold, I'd nae be surprised if yer delicate skin cracks. And ye need to don yer fur-lined cloak, and besides all that, ye kinnae even see yer da coming in these conditions. The men in the watchtowers will blow their horns when they spot yer da and the other men, and ye'll be able to reach the courtyard quicker from the great hall than up here from the rampart anyway. Come with me, child."

Maeve was about to say no, but the wind blew extra hard, setting her teeth to chattering and making her cheeks burn. She stomped her slippered feet to keep them from numbing further as she considered Bee's words. Bee was right. Maeve's worry kept her out here, but it was much smarter to wait in the great hall, so she nodded. Beitris didn't waste time taking advantage of Maeve's relenting to her request. Beitris grabbed Maeve by the hand and had her down the rampart and inside the castle hall in no time. Maeve had to admit, the moment the heavy wooden door shut behind her to block out the cold, a sigh of relief escaped her. But even before she was done expelling it, the horn announcing her father's return began to blow.

"He's returned!" Beitris gave her such a grin and yelped out loud, tugging on Maeve's hand as they raced through the shadowy corridor, laughing and running. They took the stairs down to the first floor at such a pace that Maeve more tripped down the last three stairs than descended them with actual purpose. Beitris was surprisingly spry for being fifteen years Maeve's senior. Bee had the door that led to the courtyard flung open even before Maeve had righted herself from her near tumble.

Maeve made it into the courtyard, where servants and clansmen and women streamed out in droves to see the returned warriors, and immediately the sound of pounding horse hooves hit her. Underneath her slipper-encased feet, the courtyard vibrated with the thundering of the horses carrying the MacKenzie men home. She darted in and out of her clanspeople, dodging running children, and sidestepping servants carrying large jugs of mead and wine for her da and his men, all the while looking toward the long bridge her da would have to cross to reach their home. Up ahead, Beitris ran toward the bridge. Her hood had fallen back from where it had been gathered around her face and her long hair, now a much duller shade of brown than it used to be, streamed down her back to nearly touch her behind.

Maeve's da appeared first at the far edge of the bridge, holding the MacKenzie flag with a pole, as he always did when he led his men home. She slowed her steps to a walk now that she saw him and knew he was safe. Her pulse still beat furiously from her running, but the fear that had plagued her all morning subsided instantly. Beitris still raced toward Maeve's da, appearing seemingly unaware that people were stopping to watch the woman's progress and were noting it with gapes.

Maeve found herself staring now, as a realization stirred within her. Beitris ran toward Maeve's father like a woman greeting her husband or lover. Maeve tracked Beitris's progress onto the snow-covered bridge, and as the woman slowed a little—due, no doubt, to the icy wood—Maeve glanced toward her father.

Her da was the bravest man she had ever known. He could have traveled surrounded by the safety of his guards with another appointed guard leading their journey, but he never did. He always chose to be the first to lead them into battle and the first to lead them home. He was good and true and brave, and she wanted a husband much like him. Colin was all those things, and yet, she had been unable to shake the reluctance to wed him. If only Colin's kisses would give her the same tingling as the one she'd gotten so many years ago from Alasdair MacRae. That was a feeling a girl simply did not forget, no matter how much she wanted to, given he was the enemy.

Maeve shook off the unwanted memory and concentrated on her father and Bee. Even from this distance Maeve could see the smile upturning Bee's lips. Why, she almost looked to be a woman in love! Maeve gasped. Had Beitris developed a tendre for Maeve's father? She blinked in surprise to find he had dismounted and moved well ahead of his men to stride toward Beitris. The closer they drew, the more shocked Maeve became. She watched slack-jawed as her father and Beitris collided. It was as if they were two bodies pulled together by some invisible force. Her father lifted Beitris off the ground and kissed her fully on the mouth. For a brief moment, they stayed locked that way before he set her down, and they separated, each looking around them, as if they had only just realized what they had done, what they had revealed and were hoping no one had taken note of.

But clapping erupted around them, and Beitris's sister came to stand beside Maeve. "Mayhap this means yer da will finally acknowledge his love for our Bee."

Maeve turned to look at the woman. "My da loves Beitris?"

Ulta faced her and smirked. "Aye, Maeve. Yer da has come to visit Bee in the kitchen every single day that he's at the castle for some fifteen years now. Sometimes they even slip away together," the woman said, giving Maeve a wink.

Heat singed Maeve's cheeks at the realization that Ulta was implying her da and Bee had been intimate. It couldn't be true, but then Maeve thought of the kiss and embrace she'd just witnessed, and she knew it most definitely could be.

"I dunnae understand," she said, thinking aloud.

"Well, dunnae look to me to explain it. Ask Bee why a man and a women may wish for some privacy."

"Nay," Maeve said with a mortified laugh. "I ken that part, but if they love each other, why would they hide it? Surely they dunnae think I'd care."

Ulta pursed her lips. "They've hidden it, Maeve, because if ye dunnae wed Colin and keep the needed support of the Frasers for yer clan, then yer da will need to wed a woman who can bring a strong alliance to yer clan, and that is nae my sister. But it looks like Bee may be accepting her fate."

"What fate?"

"Mistress," Ulta said, with a ringing note of disapproval. Her probing gaze pierced Maeve. "She would do anything to give ye the life ye want. Including, it finally seems, forsaking her good name, and it appears yer da has finally agreed to the same. I hope ye appreciate that and find the match yer heart desires."

"I did nae have any notion," Maeve protested, feeling Ulta's anger directed at her.

Ulta arched her eyebrows. "Ye're blind, then. Those are the two people closest to ye," she said, waving a hand toward Maeve's father and Bee. "Ye mean to tell me ye were so consumed with yerself that ye did nae see their longing to be together? They've waited and waited for ye to wed Colin Fraser, or to meet another, but ye just take yer time, aye?"

Heat raced from her cheeks to her neck and chest, and her focus went back to her father and Beitris. They walked side by side now, a respectable distance between them, but every few steps, they would turn to look at each other and a small smile would briefly appear on one of their faces. Her da and Bee had sacrificed their happiness for Maeve, and she had been blind to it. She felt terrible knowing they could wed, could be together, if only she would set aside the silly notion that she had needed to feel something extraordinary when Colin kissed her. Why had she even allowed her mind to linger on a thieving MacRae? No more!

"I'm going to fix this."

"I certainly hope so," Ulta said before walking away from Maeve.

Maeve weaved her way through the crowd toward her da and Beitris, who stopped as she approached. Her da opened his arms to her, and she walked into his loving embrace and buried her cheek against the soft wool of his plaid. She stood for a moment wrapped in the safety of his arms, and the knowledge of how much he had sacrificed for her hit her. She swallowed the sudden large lump in her throat and pulled back to look up at her father's face. His guards moved past them now, some on horseback and some had dismounted and were leading their horses as he had. His stable boy had hold of her father's mount and paused by them.

"Laird, do ye want me to take Gaillean to the stables?"

"Aye," her da said, stepping back from her but bringing

her to his side to put his arm on her shoulder and give her a squeeze. "I'm to the solar with Maeve—"

"And Beitris," Maeve interrupted, determined to fix what was her fault.

"And Beitris," her da said slowly, his face reddening.

Before Gaillean had moved on, they became surrounded as they walked by her da's men, who began to speak of the mission to their wives who had joined them in their walk to the castle.

"Was the mission successful?" one of the wives asked.

"Aye, our part," came a response from one of the warriors.

"Yer part?" Maeve asked, looking to her father to explain.

"We released the horses from their stables, which should stop the MacRaes from raiding us for a while, but Fraser wanted to take their sheep and goats."

Maeve frowned. "But ye argued to the council that such an action would leave the MacRaes in a desperate situation for the winter. I thought it was decided."

Her father gave her a stern look. "Were ye eavesdropping again, Maeve?"

"What is *eavesdropping* anyway?" Maeve said, trying to avoid admitting she'd done what she'd vowed to quit doing.

"Maeve."

"Fine, but I dunnae see why I kinnae sit in on council meetings," she replied, her tone defensive.

Her father patted her arm. "I would let ye, lass, but ye ken those old council men dunnae approve of women having input on council decisions. It is simply nae done."

"It is nae done *yet*," she countered. "Mayhap my future husband will be so inclined."

"I dunnae think Colin would be inclined to that,

Maeve."

She didn't, either, which was another reason she was reluctant to wed Colin. He was fine for a friend, but a husband was another matter. A husband would have control over her by law, which meant she needed to ensure the man she wed wanted her to be his equal, but now, with the new information that had come to light about Bee and her da, how could she not agree to wed him? She bit her lip as she thought about her problems and her da's troubling words about the raid against the MacRaes. "I ken the MacRaes are thieves, but I hate to think that innocent women and children will starve this winter just because the MacRae men are barbarians.

"They will nae. I reminded Fraser that we agreed he would only take the sheep, nae the goats."

That made Maeve feel a bit better. As they walked across the courtyard and into the castle, she asked, "So what was yer part of the mission for that?"

"We drew the MacRae guards away from the sheep by providing a distraction, and while they were dealing with us, the Frasers were supposed to take the animals."

"But ye dunnae ken if they were successful, I suppose?" she asked, falling into step beside Beitris, who had been walking silently beside Maeve's da.

"Nay, I dunnae, but it should have worked. They had plenty of time to complete the task."

"Laird," her da's right hand said. "Do ye wish to call a council meeting afore supper?"

Her da looked between Maeve and Beitris and then back to his men. "Nay. Go be with yer families. We'll meet in the morning." He focused on Maeve and Beitris then. "Come, let us speak in my solar."

Her da started up the stairs, and Maeve and Beitris fell

into step behind him. Maeve's mind turned to her new discovery about her father and Beitris again, what they had been sacrificing for her for all these years, and what she needed to do for them.

When she closed the solar door behind her and Beitris, she opened her mouth to speak, but her father beat her to it. "Lady MacLean's husband has died," her da said with his gaze locked on Beitris's.

To her right, Beitris gasped, and Maeve immediately understood why. Lady MacLean would be in need of a new husband, and the woman's sons would no doubt want her wed to a man who could bring them a beneficial alliance. Her da was intending to wed Lady MacLean. Maeve swallowed any hesitation to wed Colin. Her happiness was not the only happiness that mattered.

"I'm ready to wed Colin." She hoped she sounded more convinced than she felt.

Undeniable relief flooded her father's face, and then he grinned. "This is excellent!" he exclaimed.

"'Tis only excellent if yer the sort of man willing to trade his daughter's happiness for his own," Bee snipped.

"Woman," Maeve's da said, plopping down in a chair, "Ye ken what sort of man I am." He kicked his feet out in front of him and crossed them at his ankles before cocking up an eyebrow while a surprising half smile pulled one side of his mouth up. Maeve almost gasped at her father's flirtatious display.

"I thought I did," Bee said, stomping across the room to the sideboard where she picked up a jug of wine and filled three goblets. She took a long swig from one of the goblets and then said, "I find it awfully convenient after seeing our display a moment ago that Maeve here has miraculously finally decided to wed Colin Fraser after all these years."

Bee paused and glared at Maeve's father. "And ye should, too, *laird*."

Maeve had to bite the side of her cheek not to smile. Bee and her father were like an old married couple. It made Maeve's heart stretch and get warm. She had worried through the years that her father would never find love again, since he'd loved her mother so desperately, but he had, and Maeve had been too absorbed in herself to see it. She felt like the worst sort of daughter in the world. She had to get hold of this situation right away.

"I assure ye both, I had made up my mind to wed Colin afore I realized the two of ye have an, umm, tendre for each other," she lied.

"See there!" her da exclaimed. "The lass had already come to her senses."

"Mayhap ye need someone to knock ye in the head because ye've lost yers," Bee grumbled at Maeve's father. Then she strode to Maeve and handed her a goblet of wine before she said, "Ye twitch yer mouth when ye lie."

"I dunnae!" Maeve protested.

"See!" Bee exclaimed. "Ye just admitted ye lied.

"Nay," Maeve said, scrambling to correct her mistake. "I meant I dunnae lie, Bee."

"Quit trying to find trouble where it dunnae exist," Maeve's da grumbled. "And am I nae to get any wine?"

"Nae from my hands," Bee replied. "At least nae while ye are ignoring the truth to suit yerself.

"She said she'd made up her mind," Maeve's da said, glancing hopefully at her.

"I'd made up my mind, too, about ye," Bee grumbled, "but now I'm thinking I'm changing it." Maeve's da opened his mouth to speak, but Bee continued, focusing her attention on Maeve. "We both—" Bee cut Maeve's da a side glare "—want ye to wed for love, as we promised yer mama we would see that ye did."

The situation would have been depressing if not for the clear love between Maeve's da and Bee. Maeve pulled her fortitude up around her, determined to win this battle with Bee.

"I love Colin," she said, which was not a lie. She did love him, though it was not the passionate love her mother and father had shared, nor did it look to match the feelings her father and Beitris had for each other, but it was comfortable, safe, and would endure. That would have to be enough. She refused to allow her father and Beitris to sacrifice their love for the sake of her possibly finding a love like that or possibly not. "I'm tired of waiting," she added because Beitris still looked wholly unconvinced. "Da, I wish ye to go to the Fraser and tell him I'm ready to wed and set the date."

"I'll leave in the morning and—"

"Maeve wedding Colin Fraser is nae the solution, and if ye'd stop thinking about yerself, ye'd remember that!" Beitris blurted. "There's still time for Maeve to meet a man who will steal her heart."

Her da shoved out of his chair, stalked to where his wine goblet still sat, picked it up, downed it in one swig, and then glared down at Beitris as she glowered at him. It was as if they'd forgotten she was here. Never had she seen such a display from either of them, and it brought her such joy.

"Bah!" her father said.

"Dunnae *bah* me," Beitris replied. "Why, mayhap Maeve has already met the man of her heart and she just dunnae ken it."

Maeve gasped but quickly clamped her jaw shut on making any other sounds as her father turned to look at her and asked, "What's this, Maeve? Is there something ye have nae told me?"

Maeve glared at Beitris. She never should have shared with Beitris the kiss in the woods with Alasdair. She couldn't understand why Beitris would bring that up now after all this time, except she *could* understand it actually and her heart swelled. Beitris loved her as if Maeve were her own daughter and would do just about anything for Maeve to find happiness, even at the expense of her own happiness. Well, Maeve would not have it. Anyway, Beitris knew as well as Maeve did that the MacRaes were a dishonorable lot. One kiss that had made Maeve's knees weak did not change that fact.

"Nay, Da. Ye ken how Beitris is—fanciful." Maeve eyed Beitris and hoped the woman understood the look Maeve was shooting her, which was meant to convey that she should drop the ridiculousness she was about and allow Maeve to do her duty, as she should have done years ago.

"Ye heard her, Beitris. Maeve dunnae love another, nor does she have any other prospects. Why, it could be years, and that would be too late. I'll go to the Frasers in the morning."

Beitris harumphed and threw up her hands. "Go on then with ye, *Laird*. Who am I to give ye my opinion? Take yerself to the Frasers and sell yer daughter's future happiness for yer own selfishness. But dunnae expect me to be—" Beitris's words jerked to a halt, and she pressed her lips together before inhaling a sharp breath, which she blew forcefully out, making the brown strands of hair dangling in front of her face flutter. "I'll just take myself back to the kitchens, *Laird*. If ye have need of me, Maeve, ye ken where to find me," Beitris said with a quick glance Maeve's way.

Maeve didn't have time to even acknowledge Beitris's

words before the woman strode out the way they had come, grumbling loudly under her breath all the way. Maeve watched her, slack-jawed, until the solar door slammed shut behind the petite woman. Maeve turned to observe her da, who was also staring with his mouth hanging open. He clamped his own jaw shut and turned to Maeve with a surprisingly resigned look upon his face. "That woman cares for ye as her own, Maeve. And she's the most selfless woman."

Her father sounded positively choked up. It was the loveliest confirmation that she was doing the right thing for these two who had done so much for her. "Da," she said, fighting her urge to grin and failing. She could not choose a better woman for her da. "Is there something ye wish to tell me?"

He opened and closed his mouth like a fish caught on a line, and then he began to sputter. "I—That is...ye see— Och, Maeve. Let us have a goblet of wine first, aye?" One goblet turned into two as they sat in silence. Maeve did not speak because she could see by her da's drumming his fingers, shifting restlessly, and alternately scowling and staring into the distance that he was trying to find the words to express his love for Beitris. She wanted to give him time. It was the least she could do after all the time he had given her. He stood, strode around the room, sat back down, and stood again. Then he repeated the entire process but sat once more at the end.

Just as he finally took a deep breath and seemed as if he would speak, the solar door swung open and Father Dorian came in with a jug of mead in his hand and a frown upon his face. "I've been sent to tell ye by Ulta that supper will be late this night. Beitris burned her hand—"

Maeve's da cried out at the news and passed Maeve at a

fast clip toward the kitchen, which sent him skittering around Father Dorian who looked taken aback by his laird's reaction. Maeve stared at her da's back as a grin once again tugged at her lips. As if her father sensed Maeve was thinking about him, he turned and glanced toward her. "Maevie—"

A swell of warm emotion gripped her. Her da had not called her Maevie in ages.

"I—" He shoved a hand through his peppered hair. "I'm going to see to Beitris and then head out to make my way to the Fraser's."

"Now? But ye just got home, and—" And well, she was prepared to sacrifice herself, but honestly, she'd not expected it to happen tonight.

"Aye," he said, his jaw taking on that set look it got when he had settled upon something of which he'd not be swayed. "I wish to settle this matter once and for all. I expect I'll return home in four days' time. Let's talk then, aye?" A frown of worry added extra lines to his forehead.

"Da," she said, wanting to ease his worries about her happiness. "All will be well. Ye'll see."

Her da stared at her a long moment and then finally nodded. "Aye, it will. I'll speak with ye when I return. In the meantime, dunnae go hunting on yer own. Dunnae make the guards worry for yer safety when they need to be focused on protecting the castle and lands from the damnable MacRaes. Promise me."

"I vow it, Da. I will nae leave the castle grounds to go hunting on my own."

Chapter Two

"*I* failed ye," Brodick said.

Alasdair MacRae looked to his right hand and closest friend before he turned his attention back to the empty land far below him. From where he stood on the rampart of his family's castle he could finally see beyond the gates. The snow had quit and the white mist that had blanketed the land had lifted, but what he saw now made his fists curl.

"I'm sorry, Alasdair," Brodick offered. "If ye wish me to step down as yer right hand—"

Alasdair dismissed the ridiculous notion with a wave. "I would have made the same mistake if I'd been here." He'd not uttered the words to soothe his friend's feelings. They were true. He would have done exactly as Brodick had done had a fire started burning where the sheep were penned. He would have taken a hefty portion of the guards to see who or what had started the fire and try to save the sheep so that the clan would not be faced with yet another disaster. He would have left Darby in charge of a contingent of warriors to guard the castle grounds from thieving Frasers and murdering MacKenzies, and therein lay the two problems. After years of attacks from the Frasers and MacKenzies, Alasdair's clan did not have enough warriors to properly guard the castle anymore, and the men who were now in charge had been proven too green.

"Who trained Darby?" Alasdair asked, referring to the warrior who had been appointed head of the gate guards before this latest raid.

"Yer cousin did," Brodick said.

Alasdair nodded. Athelston had trained many men for him since Alasdair had taken over as laird, and thus far the men had done a good job, as far as Alasdair knew. But that was another problem: Alasdair was spread so thin that he was certain he was missing things. He thought about the fact that Darby had taken all the remaining men he'd been left with to guard the gates, which had left the stables vulnerable. All the horses not ridden by men had been taken. Darby should have known better than to leave the stables unguarded, and yet, it was hard to find fault when the man likely had believed he needed all the warriors with him to man the gates leading to the castle. Alasdair sighed and scrubbed a hand across his face.

"Do ye wish me to demote Darby?" Brodick asked.

"Nay. Nae yet. I'll train him personally, and if he proves he still kinnae handle the position of head of the gate guards, then I'll demote him myself." He hoped it didn't come to that. Darby had not had an easy life what with his father forced out of the clan five years prior in disgrace. The stigma of Darby's father being named a coward after abandoning his place in the front line in the first attack from the MacKenzies and Frasers had followed Darby for a long time, but the man had been a hard worker, training to learn the sword and bow and arrow on his own. It had been Athelston who had first pointed this out to Alasdair, and Alasdair had the utmost respect for any man trying to better himself, especially when the other men had not wanted to allow him among their ranks of castle warriors. For a moment, Alasdair considered speaking to Athelston about it, but his cousin was busy himself as the head of council under Alasdair. No, Alasdair would add this duty to his own burdens.

"I miss yer da."

Alasdair's throat tightened painfully at Brodick's words. He missed his da, too. His da would not have overlooked the fact that Darby needed more training.

"What did the king say of our accusations against the MacKenzies?"

"The king was ill, so my audience was with Robert Fraser," Alasdair explained, his neck muscles bunching at the memory.

Brodick snorted. "I dunnae need to ask any more to ken that the king's right hand said the scrap of plaid was nae proof that the MacKenzies murdered yer da."

Alasdair glanced toward Brodick. The jagged scar that ran from Brodick's lip to his right eye was white. It blanched that way whenever his friend was in a temper. Alasdair set a hand on Brodick's shoulder and squeezed. "We will have retribution for my da's death. Robert may deny it was the MacKenzies who pushed my da from the cliff, but we both ken it to be true. There is nae another explanation for why he was clutching the scrap of their plaid in his hand when we found him."

"Ye sound so calm now."

"Aye," Alasdair replied, nodding. "I am. I had a long journey back from the king's Court to get ahold of my anger and think upon vengeance. If Robert will nae give us justice against the MacKenzies, we must take it."

"Ye dunnae fear the king's retaliation upon us?"

"Aye," Alasdair said on a sigh. "I do, which is why we must be canny about how we get justice. It kinnae be a life for a life, but there are other ways to strike at the MacKenzie and bring an end to his clan's thieving and raiding us with the Frasers."

"What's the way ye speak of?"

"Alasdair!" came his sister's voice from behind him.

He turned to find Lara standing at the door to the castle. The wind whipped her dark hair all around her shoulders. "Mama wants to see ye. A fever has set in from Tavish's wound, and she's fretting."

"Damn the MacKenzies!" Alasdair swore before turning on his heel to follow Lara off the rampart and into the castle to see about his younger brother. The moment the castle door closed behind them, the strong smell of smoke that had been in the air from the fields the MacKenzies and Frasers had burned lessened. He fell into step beside his sister as Brodick came to his other side. "I thought Anise said the wound was nae so terrible?"

"Anise would say anything to please ye, Alasdair. She's a fancy for ye that ye stoke by bedding her. But Anise dunnae think it dire. Still, Mama is fretting."

Alasdair nodded at the news. Their mother was a worrier, but she had not always been wrong in the past to fret more than everyone else, so he'd go to her and see for himself. Lara was looking at him expectantly with a half-smile upon her face, an almost challenging one, which reminded him of her comment about Anise. "I dunnae stoke any fancy," he grumbled, irritated that his younger sister was speaking of such things. If she knew about Anise, then the entire castle likely did, and that meant he needed to end their relationship.

He'd been thinking of doing so of late anyway. They'd come together in grief—his over the loss of his father, hers over the loss of her husband to an illness around the same time as Alasdair's father had died—but lately his time with her had felt more like a habit than anything else. And he did not want Anise's reputation to suffer. She needed a husband, and it could not be him.

As Alasdair and Lara made their way through the corridor and then up the winding stairs to the third floor where his family's bedchambers were located, Alasdair asked, "How has a fever already set in from Tavish's wound? It seems quick for such a thing."

Lara paused at the top of the steps and patted a hand against his chest. "Ye missed supper, Alasdair." He blinked in surprise. Lara gave him an understanding look. "Ye've been putting out fires all day and tending to the men that were injured when the MacKenzies and Frasers attacked. 'Tis nae quick for there to be a change in Tavish's condition. He was struck by the arrow in the raid last night. That's plenty of time for fever to set in."

Alasdair nodded as Lara turned to continue to Tavish's bedchamber. His sister was right. That was plenty of time, and he could hardly believe he'd not realized the night and an entire day had passed since he'd returned home from Court to find his lands burning, their sheep and goats gone, his brother shot in the leg by an arrow that Tavish swore a MacKenzie had fired at him, many of the guards injured, and the women and children scared nearly witless.

Lara bit her lip, a thing she did when she was fretting, and she said, "Mama wants to wed me to Laird MacDougal because he's offered a hundred men as a wedding gift. I'll do it, but—"

"I'll nae let my younger sister be the sacrificial lamb to save our clan," Alasdair interrupted. "I ken well ye dunnae wish to wed MacDougal, and I kinnae say I blame ye."

"Me neither," Brodick added. "The man is older than ycr own da was. Ye need someone without one foot in the grave."

Lara pursed her lips at Brodick. "Oh, aye? Why is that?"

Brodick turned a deep shade of red. "'Tis nae the sort of thing I can put into words in front of ye. Yer ears are too delicate."

"Nae anymore, Brodick." She gave him a pointed look. "I ken all about what a younger man can do for a lass."

"What?" Brodick and Alasdair thundered at the same time, to which Lara laughed.

"How could I nae!" she said. "Between Brodick and ye taking lasses to yer bedchambers and mine being between the two of yers, all I hear half the time is, 'Oh, Brodick' or 'Oh, Alasdair, faster, harder, flip me o—'"

Alasdair slapped a palm over his sister's mouth. "That's enough out of ye." Her eyebrows arched high as merriment danced in her eyes. "Ye should have told us this sooner," he said.

"Aye," Brodick agreed with a vigorous nod. "Ye surely should have."

Lara peeled Alasdair's hand away from her mouth and looked between the two of them. "Well, I told ye now, so the two of ye need to tell yer women to—"

"I dunnae have a woman," Brodick said.

Lara snorted. "I'm nae surprised ye kinnae get a lass to stick to ye. From what I've heard, ye dunnae ken what to do in the bed." Alasdair laughed, but it died on his lips as Lara smirked at him. "Ye dunnae have room to chuckle. I heard ye being ordered about, as well."

"Ye should nae have listened to such a thing."

"Then ye should nae be so loud with yer lass," Lara said.

"Anise is nae my lass."

Lara's eyebrows rose even higher than they had been.

"And does Anise ken this?"

"Aye. She kens well I have a duty to wed for the clan's benefit, and I've a lass in mind."

"Do ye now?" Lara exclaimed.

"This is the first I'm hearing that ye're ready to chain yerself to a lass for life," Brodick said.

"I'm ready for the clan to be stable. That's what I'm ready for."

"What does ye taking a wife have to do with the clan being stable?" Lara asked, her nose now wrinkled.

"I overheard Robert Fraser speaking to another Fraser at the king's Court. He said the wedding of Colin Fraser and Maeve MacKenzie would be occurring within a sennight and that once the two of them are wed, those two clans would have an unbreakable bond because the MacKenzie laird dunnae love anything more than his daughter. Whoever weds her will have his undying support."

"I dunnae follow," Lara said.

Brodick grinned at Alasdair. "I follow, and I like it. Ye dunnae want to risk the king's wrath by taking a life for a life over something that kinnae be proved, but ye will take a wife for a life."

"Aye." Alasdair tried and failed to keep the grimness invading him over the choice he was being forced into out of his voice. He felt guilty about his plan, but he couldn't afford to.

Lara stomped her foot. "Speak plainly!"

"I mean to take Maeve MacKenzie to wife."

Lara rolled her eyes. "And I mean to be the next Queen of Scotland."

"'Tis enough sass from ye," he replied, his neck warming.

"'Tis enough delusion from ye," she shot back with a

smirk. "Maeve MacKenzie will nae ever agree to wed ye. The MacKenzies despise us just as much as we do them, I'm certain. And why would ye take to wife the daughter of the laird who gave the order to murder Da? Have ye gone daft?" Lara demanded, outraged. "Do ye nac despise her?"

"Just because I take her to wife dunnae mean that I have to like her, Lara."

"That should make for a happy union," Lara replied, sarcasm dripping from each word.

"I'll be happy to save the clan from starving this winter."

Realization swept his sister's features. "Ye think by taking her to wife her da will quit raiding us?"

He nodded. "He'd nae ever chance putting his beloved daughter in danger, and he will be forced to aid us in getting back the livestock that he and the Frasers stole."

Lara's dark eyebrows dipped together. "I like it, except the part where ye force her to wed ye."

"Who said I'm going to force her?" he replied, with a wink. "I can be verra charming when I wish to be."

When Lara burst out laughing, he served her a scowl. It took her a moment to quit her chuckling, and when she did, she grabbed her side with one hand and wiped her eyes with the other. "Ye gave me a pinch in my side what with yer thinking ye can make the lass want to wed ye after ye take her from her home by force. Are ye listening to yerself?" she demanded, not laughing anymore.

"I think it's a brilliant idea," Brodick said.

"Ye would," Lara snapped.

"What do ye mean by that, ye tart-tongued—"

"Ye both think that ye simply need to flex yer arms and the women will swoon," Lara interrupted Brodick, "but nae all women are the same, ye clot-heid. Nae all women will be dying for yer attention."

"Well, the MacKenzie lass certainly did nae mind yer brother's attention afore, so—"

"What do ye mean afore?" Lara gasped.

Alasdair glared at Brodick. He'd not planned to reveal that.

Brodick spoke before Alasdair could. "Near five years ago now—"

"I can explain it myself," Alasdair bit out. "Ye've helped enough."

Brodick threw up his hands. "Fine. I'll keep my mouth shut."

"That would be a damned fine change," Alasdair snapped.

"Oh, aye?" Brodick grumbled. "Fine then. Next time ye need aid ye'll have to beg me afore I help ye."

Lara snorted. "That's a lie. Yer one good quality is that ye always have my brother's back."

"I've two good qualities," Brodick replied, a smirk turning up his mouth.

"Name the other," Lara demanded.

Alasdair guessed by the amusement in his friend's eyes it would have something to do with a subject Alasdair would rather not stand around discussing with his sister, like lasses and beddings. "I saw her hunting in the woods some years ago," he interrupted.

Lara stared at him blankly.

"Maeve MacKenzie," he clarified, surprised his sister seemed to have forgotten the topic at hand. Normally, she was not the sort to be thrown off by another.

Lara's cheeks reddened. "Aye, of course. I kenned that."

Alasdair could tell Lara was lying, but he let it go. He didn't know why she felt the need to cover up that she'd momentarily forgotten, but he'd let her.

"How did ye seeing her in the woods years afore make ye think ye could get her to turn her skirts up for ye?"

"Good God, Lara," he thundered. "Must ye speak so plainly?"

"Aye," she said with a snicker. "It does please me to bother ye."

He shoved a hand through his hair. "I may have kissed her."

"Explain yerself."

"Ye ken I'm laird?" he bit out.

"Ye ken I'm yer sister?" she shot back.

He sighed. He was too soft on Lara and Tavish, too, for that matter, but he could not help it. He didn't want them to ever feel as if they were not his equals. "I started to follow her to ensure her safety."

Lara snorted at that. "I've seen Maeve Mackenzie with her fiery hair and ample figure. Lust made ye follow her."

He wasn't going to argue that point or speak of how she had intrigued him with her determination and skill. Yes, she had been beautiful—likely still was—but he'd known many beautiful women. There had been something about her. Mayhap it had been the proud, self-assured way she carried herself or the radiant smile that would grace her face even though she'd been alone in the woods. "Whatever it was," he continued, "we met, and I do believe I could woo her with time. Then after we are wed, I will gain a powerful albeit reluctant ally. I will keep my enemy's greatest treasure close, and that will bring him to our side. With MacKenzie as our ally, Fraser will be forced to back down, as I've been forced to do with them."

"Let me see if I ken ye," Lara said, tilting her head in thought. "Ye are going to snatch the lass from her home."

"The woods," he corrected. She undoubtedly still hunted alone. He'd just made a habit of not going into the woods near her home since the day he'd discovered who she was.

Lara nodded. "Oh, aye, the woods." He did not miss the sarcasm in his sister's tone, as it was the same that had been in his moments before. They were very alike that way. "I'm certain she will be verra happy with ye after ye do that, and she will be beside herself to wed ye." Lara arched her right eyebrow almost to her temple. "I think yer plan is foolish."

Alasdair's temper stirred. He had made it a point to listen to his sister's and brother's opinions on matters of the clan since their father had died. He wanted to be the sort of leader his father had been—a fair one who respected people's opinions—but that did not mean he had to agree with Lara's opinion.

"I believe ye are wrong, and it is the only plan that can save us. I will take her, and then I will convince her I want her, kinnae forget about her kiss—"

"Have ye thought of the daughter of our enemy since ye kissed her?" Lara asked, eyeing him.

"Nae a once," he lied. "Now back to my plan. I'll convince her that I am desperate to wed her."

"So ye'll lie?"

It wasn't all a lie. He hadn't forgotten Maeve's kiss, but it was yearning for what he'd never had that had kept her kiss in his memory. "I'll bend the truth to save the clan."

His sister frowned, opened her mouth, closed it, and opened it again, but did not speak for a long moment. She bit her lip, her cheeks reddened, and then she said, "Ye may be right." He started to smile, but she shook her head and held up her hand. "It may be the only thing that can save us, but even if ye do manage to persuade this woman to wed ye, have ye thought how the clan will treat her? How Mama will treat her?"

"What care do I have how the clan treats our enemy?" he demanded, thinking how her da had killed his.

Lara snorted. "Oh, the lies ye are telling yerself. They will circle back upon ye to nip ye in the arse. Ye're nae so cold and hard as this one," she said, jerking her thumb toward Brodick.

"I'll ask ye to keep yer opinions of me to yerself," Brodick bit out.

"Ye may ask it," Lara responded, "but that dunnae mean I'll acquiesce. Even if yer clot-heided plan works, Mama will nae ever agree to this."

"Mama will," came the voice of their mother from at the top of the stairs. Tears streamed out of puffy, red eyes and down her face. She swiped a hand across the tears, then gripped blindly for the banister. "Anise says she must take Tavish's leg, or he will lose his life," their mama said, and her own legs seemed to give out as she said the words.

Shock slammed Alasdair in the chest and took every bit of breath from his body, but he managed to lunge forward and catch his mother right before she hit the stairs. She landed hard in his arms, and an *oof* escaped her. Then she let out an animalistic wail that Alasdair felt deep within his bones. She turned her face to his, and her grief for Tavish's fate was like an arrow in his heart. He had failed to protect his brother. He had failed to protect his clan. He shoved any lingering guilt about Maeve MacKenzie away, along with the memory of how sweet her lips had felt under his. She was a means to an end and the enemy. He would woo her, and wed her, but that was where it would end. What happened after he got what he needed to secure an alliance with her clan was no concern of his.

Chapter Three

"*M*aeve!"
Maeve wasn't certain what actually woke her from her sleep—being shaken by Beitris or the horns that blew in what should have been the silent night. "Beitris!" she groaned, while pushing her friend's hands away from her shoulder and then rolling over as she tugged the coverlet over her head to block out the incessant horns.

"Maeve MacKenzie, that is the returning horn being blown!"

Maeve frowned under the warmth of the covers as she tried to sift through the thick mist in her mind to remember why Beitris's words should matter to her.

The distinct sound of a foot being stomped by her bed made her sigh. Beitris was not going to leave her be, but Maeve was equally determined to stay abed until she absolutely had to get up and leave the delightful warmth found under the weight of her coverlet.

"Maeve, I swear I have nae ever kenned a body that took as long to throw off the confusion of sleep as ye do."

"I'm a deep sleeper," Maeve murmured, even as a pleasant heaviness started to grip her again. Sleep was just in her reach. "Ohhh!" she cried out as her coverlet was ripped off her and a blast of cold air hit her. "'Tis freezing!" She scrambled to sit up as she opened her eyes. In the moonlight she could make out Beitris standing beside the bed with

Maeve's coverlet bunched in her hands. "Whatever are ye doing?" she demanded, reaching for her coverlet only to have Beitris take a step away from the bed.

"I'm waking ye up! That horn is for yer father's return!"

"Oh! Oh!" Maeve said as the last of the sleep mist finally rose. "Why did ye nae say so sooner?" she demanded, scooting to the side of the bed and then standing.

"Och, I did. Ye're still just as horrid to awaken as ye were when ye were a child."

"'Tis a gift," Maeve replied, winking at Beitris. She did so love to tease Bee. "Oh, Bee!" Maeve cried and, reaching out, grasped her friend by her arms and tugged her toward her. The woman wrapped Maeve in her loving embrace. "Da is home, and the two of ye can wed—"

Beitris pulled back from Maeve. "Wed?"

Maeve had tried to talk to Beitris about it multiple times after Maeve's father had left for the Fraser stronghold, but Beitris had refused to enter into the conversation with her, saying she was too busy every time. Maeve nodded. "Aye. Now that my wedding will be set to Colin, there's nae a need for—"

"I might as well tell ye now afore we go down to greet yer da," Bee said on a sigh.

"Tell me what?"

"Yer da decided afore he left to tell the Frasers ye were nae going to be wedding Colin Fraser."

"What?!" Maeve exclaimed, rushing to retrieve her gown from the chair where she had discarded it the night before. As she dressed, she said, "I told Da afore he left that I would wed Colin. Ye two deserve to be together, and I wish ye to be my family." She turned toward Beitris after getting her head and arms into the gown. Beitris had a suspiciously shiny look in her eyes, as if she might cry.

"We're already family, Maeve. I dunnae need a wedding to make me feel as if ye're my daughter and yer da is my husband."

That was the first Bee had acknowledged her feelings for Maeve's da. Though, of course, Maeve had known since their embrace the day he'd returned home that last time.

"Yer da and I made a death vow to yer mama to see ye wed for love. Ye dunnae love Colin Fraser."

Maeve leveled Beitris with, she hoped, an uncompromising look. "I love him in a sense." And she did. She had known him all her life. Their families had been friends for as long as she could remember. She had grown up playing chase with him in the forest and racing horses with him. She had a strong affection for him. The only thing that was missing was the funny tightening of her belly when he kissed her, the tilting of her world when he hugged her, the pounding of her heart when she spotted him across the courtyard. "He makes me feel safe," she said because it was true. He did make her feel safe, though slightly suffocated with the way he hovered around her and did not like her doing any activities he believed would endanger her, such as hunting. But his actions were born of concern, so she would tolerate them.

"Well, my dagger makes me feel safe, but I dunnae love my dagger, and I nae ever will," Beitris said, giving Maeve a dry look.

"Ye ken that is nae what I mean," Maeve said, bending over to put her slippers on. When she came up, Beitris held out Maeve's cloak to her. Maeve took the cloak, donned it, and said, "Deep love will grow."

"What of the passion ye felt with—"

Maeve slapped her palm over Beitris's mouth. "I should nae have ever told ye about that. Forget that man, Bee. I have. It dunnae matter if he tightened my belly with his kiss or nae. He is our enemy."

Beitris bit her lip. "Aye, but—"

"Nay. Nae more objections. I am a grown woman, and I ken well what choice I am making. I will nae ever be happy kenning that ye and Da lost yer chance to be husband and wife because of me." Beitris looked like she was wavering so Maeve pressed on, knowing it was Bee who would ultimately be the one to persuade Maeve's da to go back to the Frasers and undo what he'd done. Or if not, Maeve decided determinedly, she'd do so herself. Maeve started for her bedchamber door and waved Beitris to follow her. "I ken ye would do anything to ensure I'm happy, but Bee, I'd do the same for ye and Da. How would ye feel if Da remarried and ye had to watch him with his new wife every day? It would kill ye!"

Bee didn't have to answer. When Maeve glanced over her shoulder at her friend, the positively stricken look upon her face was answer enough and confirmation that she was indeed doing the right thing by wedding Colin.

"It would kill me," Beitris said, "to see ye unhappy as well, though."

Maeve slung her arm over Beitris's shoulder as they proceeded down the corridor toward the steps. "Dunnae fret, Bee. I will be perfectly happy with Colin. He is good and true."

Silently, they made their way down the stairs and through the door to the courtyard. The courtyard was teeming with her father's men, and they seemed to have formed a circle around someone. Maeve assumed it was her father, but even with the glowing torches that lit the courtyard, whoever was in the circle could not be seen.

An unusual hush seemed to have a hold of the men in

the courtyard, and Maeve and Beitris exchanged a concerned look as they picked their way through the crowd. A man holding a burning torch came from the other side of the way, and Maeve could have sworn she saw a flash of red and green in his plaid, which were Fraser colors, but that could not be correct, unless her da had wisely changed his mind about breaking her betrothal to Colin. As they passed men and received looks that seemed to border on sadness or pity, the hairs on the back of Maeve's neck prickled and her stomach grew tight as her breaths became shorter. Something was wrong. She felt it.

A murmur went up in the crowd of men, and she caught snippets of her name and Bee's on the lips of several, and suddenly, men were moving out of their way to make an easier path through the courtyard to the circle. That sent gooseflesh prickling down Maeve's back. It wasn't that the MacKenzie warriors were not always polite to her but rarely were they overly accommodating. She had grown up in their midst, thanks to her da allowing her to learn to hunt and to go on hunts with his men, so they tended to treat her more like one of them at times than like a lady to be shown extra niceties. Something was not right. Her palms began to sweat, and she shivered, and then the circle parted and there in the middle sat Colin upon his destrier, and beside him was her father, but he was not sitting upon his horse. He was face-first with his head dangling off one side, and his feet dangling off the other. He was perfectly still. He was, her mind registered with shock and then refused to believe it, as still as if he was dead.

A scream found its way from her twisting gut and ripped out of her, shredding her insides as it went. Beside her, Beitris moaned and fell to her knees in the dirt. Maeve glanced down at Bee. She should comfort her, except she had no comfort to give. Her heart was shattering in her chest, and a horrible coldness was sweeping through her.

"Maeve," Colin said, dismounting and coming to stand before her. The sadness in his gaze made her eyes fill with tears, and a terrible trembling overtook her. He scrubbed a hand across his face and said, "Yer da fell from his horse on a hunt to celebrate our upcoming joining of families."

"That kinnae be!" Beitris screamed as she scrambled to her feet and charged toward Colin. Maeve couldn't seem to lift her arms to stop Bee as she started pummeling Colin's chest with her fists. Maeve stared, feeling her mouth slip open as her father's guards and Colin's men began to move toward Bee, but Colin raised his hand and shook his head to stop them as his gaze held Maeve's.

"'Tis true, Maeve. Yer da gave me and my da the happy news that ye were ready to wed, and we went on a hunt to celebrate, and—" He paused, swallowing, as if choked up with emotion. A terrible ache gripped her chest, and she found her gaze leaving Colin, even as he began to speak again, and going to her da's still form. "He fell, and…and there was naught to be done for him."

"Liar!" Beitris screamed from behind her, but then Bee was pushing past her and moving toward Maeve's father.

Maeve glanced to her men for confirmation of what Colin said, though she believed him. She had no reason not to, except that her father had been the best horseman she knew. But even the most skilled horsemen had accidents. Her father had drilled that fact into her head, which was why he did not like her riding alone in the woods.

Her eyes locked with her father's right-hand man, Alfred, and he shook his head. "I was nae there, my lady. Yer da ordered us to stay back at the castle grounds."

That wasn't an unthinkable request. They hadn't been

hunting in dangerous territory. Her da had been with friends, so there had been no need for his men to accompany him. She nodded and willed herself to move toward her da. Her feet were almost as heavy as her arms had been, but she took one trodden step at a time.

"Maeve." Colin was beside her, lightly touching her elbow. "I'm so sorry, Maeve, so sorry."

She paused and turned toward him. "Why are ye sorry? Ye did nae kill him." Her words came out harsh, and she winced, seeing Colin's eyes widen and his lips part with obvious surprise, yet she could not summon an apology. She turned away from him, wanting to dismiss him and what his presence here represented, but turning from him only put her face-to-face with her father's still form and Beitris, who was shoving away the Fraser man who was trying to aid her in removing Maeve's father from the horse.

"Murderers!" Beitris yelled, and it was the desperation, the utter despair, in her voice that snapped Maeve out of her own trance.

"Alfred," she said, the word an order for his attention.

"Aye, my lady."

"Come and aid us." She closed the distance between herself and Beitris in a few short strides. Alfred was beside her even as she reached Beitris, as was a score of her father's guardsmen. Maeve pulled a still crying Beitris away as the men removed her father from the horse. His head lolled forward, then backward, as they flipped his body to lay him on the ground. Maeve sucked in a sharp breath as she took him in. The color of his skin reminded her of the ashes in the bottom of the fire grate. Gone was the pleasant rosiness of his cheeks. His eyes had been closed, but his mouth was slightly open.

Her throat tightened near painfully, and tears stabbed at

her lids, threatening to come, but she willed them back. She would not cry here, now, in front of all these people. She needed to be strong for Beitris and her clan. Maeve was her father's heir. Fear swept through her at the thought and all it implied. She was to inherit her clan's coveted fortress, Eilean Donan, but she was to have been wed by this time and have a husband to rule her men as well as his. She was no fool. This was a man's world, whether she liked it or not, and her clan council would never vote for her to lead this clan. And honestly, she wouldn't want to, not alone.

She stole a glance at Colin under her lashes and found him staring at her, his eyebrows raised in question. He wanted to come to her. She could see it in his gaze. Her father had gone ahead with her betrothal, so he must have truly thought Colin the right choice of husband for her. And if she didn't wed him, then who? Men would come, and she would be threatened because the men would want control of her home, and therefore, they would want her at any cost. She knew this. Her father had talked of it increasingly lately. How men would go to great lengths to wed her so that they would one day control the castle, which controlled the water passage into the Highlands. This land was strategic to making a Highland clan strong and prosperous, and therefore, she was a prize. Better to choose the man she would wed than have the choice forced upon her. Knowing this, she nodded at Colin, and a look of intense relief swept his face.

He came to her in a flash, pulled her into his embrace, and offered words of comfort. She didn't feel comforted, though. A dull ache invaded her head, and a deep coldness gripped her. "Thank ye," she finally replied, knowing it was appropriate, wishing she could have felt more, and untangled herself from his embrace. She felt a hundred gazes upon her, of her men and his, waiting for a clue of what was to come. Would their clans be joined or not? She should give word now, but something held her back. She had not a clue what or why. Instead, she took the final step toward her father and Beitris, who now knelt over him on the ground, weeping, and Maeve kneeled as well.

She slid her arm around Beitris's shoulder. Bee turned to her, eyes red but fierce. "He would nae have kept yer betrothal intact."

Maeve glanced at her father's still, gray form, put a hand on his chest, and recoiled at the coldness of his skin. She withdrew her hand and balled it into a fist. That's when she felt it, the tide of her emotions rising. It would not be long before she couldn't control it. Her heartbeat was escalating, shoving against her ribs, her eyelids, the skin that covered her bones and muscle. Her blood was thawing the ice that had been a temporary blessing. Her thoughts spun making her dizzy.

"But he did keep Maeve's betrothal to me," Colin said from behind her, even as he placed a hand on her shoulder and gave her a gentle squeeze. It was comforting and concerning at the same time. She knew what was coming the moment he opened his mouth to speak again. "Maeve, we should wed immediately so that ye and yer clan have the protection of mine."

"We only have it if ye wed her?" Beitris demanded in typical cheeky Bee fashion.

"Bee," Maeve said under her breath, even as her gaze was drawn back to her father. He was dead. *Dead.* She could not seem to quite wrap her mind around it.

"Of course, Maeve and the clan have the Fraser protection, but ye ken what I mean, woman."

"Beitris," Maeve said sharply to him without looking at

him. He'd always had a habit of treating Bee like his lesser, even though she'd told him plainly she thought of Bee like a mother.

"Aye, of course. Beitris," he replied, his tone mollifying not apologetic, or mayhap she was imagining it. She was agitated, after all. "Maeve, yer da wanted our union."

She didn't glance back at him. He was right. Her father had told Beitris he was going to the Fraser stronghold to break her union, but he had kept it. She was the reason he had gone. She was the reason he was dead. She would honor his wishes. She stood and faced the man who would be her husband. She didn't love him in the way she had hoped to love the man she would wed, but she respected him, and he was a good man. Yet, she could not make herself agree to wed him now. She needed time. "We'll talk of us tomorrow after I bury my father."

He looked like he was about to protest, but he nodded and held out his hand to her. "Come, Maeve. Ye should lie down. My men will carry yer da to the healer to prepare the body."

"I dunnae wish to lie down," she said. The notion of lying quietly and still for her grief to consume her was a horrifying thought. She glanced around, unsure what she wanted, and she realized it was no longer dark. The sky was a light-purple color with the sun of the new day that had broken through the darkness. Her da was dead yet the sun had still risen. Life would go on. It was horrific and unfair, and yet even she would go on. She stood here breathing even as her father lay there unable to take a breath. Her throat tightened so painfully she nearly whimpered. She had to be alone. She needed to get away. She wanted to ride until the ground beneath her fell away, until the horror of the morning disappeared. "I'm going to go ride."

"I'll come with ye," Colin immediately said.

"Nay." Images of her father and her were flashing in her mind. She had to be alone. She could see his protest written on his face. "I'll stay within the borders, and I'll take my dagger with me."

He frowned. "Nay, Maeve. I want ye in the castle where ye are safe."

His behavior was born out of caring, but the way he'd flat out forbade her, spiked her temper. "And I wish to ride. As we are nae wed, I'll do as I please."

Chapter Four

"I see her," Alasdair whispered. He wasn't sure why he'd whispered. They were far enough away from Maeve MacKenzie that it would have been impossible for her to hear him. Still, he did not want to take any chances. His clan's future depended on his getting his hands on Maeve without being seen. No one could come looking for her at his home before he'd managed to persuade her to wed him.

"Are ye certain ye did nae keep tracking this lass after ye discovered who she was?" Brodick asked from beside Alasdair as they crouched behind a tree. If memory served, Maeve would follow the trail straight to the end, taking a right at the bend where they were hidden, so she could make her way up the hill to the place where the forest was the thickest and held the best hunting.

"I did nae track her even once after I discovered who she was. I simply have a good memory and recall the direction the lass often took when I did track her years afore."

Brodick gave Alasdair a disbelieving look. "I've as good a memory as the next, and I could nae tell ye what color gown Brenna wore last night afore I took it off her."

"That's because ye're a simple creature," Alasdair responded, not taking his gaze off Maeve as she rode toward them. By the gods, she had grown even more beautiful since last he'd seen her. Likely, she'd grown treacherous, too, as her father was.

"Can ye tell me what color gown Anise wore last night?"

"I did nae take Anise's gown off her last night," Alasdair said, studying Maeve. She was wearing her hair longer than she had last he saw her. It flowed in fiery waves down her shoulders to graze her thighs and the horse she sat upon. She looked like a fae and despite his knowing who she was now, his body responded with the same wave of heat that had always consumed him when he saw her before.

"Whatever did ye talk to Anise about in the courtyard for so long after supper last night, then," Brodick asked, "if nae about making plans to rendezvous for a bedding?"

"Nae all conversations are about bedding, Brodick." He didn't know if it was the topic on hand or Maeve herself, but he suddenly had a vision of her straddling him with her flaming hair hanging down either side of her face as he entered her. He inhaled a long, steadying breath. Damned his lust. It was scrambling his thoughts of what he needed to do.

"So what were the two of ye talking of?" Brodick asked again.

Alasdair stole a quick glance at his friend. He frowned at the dagger Brodick clutched in his hand. "Put away yer dagger. She's one wee lass, and we're two grown men. If we need to use a dagger against her, there's a problem, dunnae ye think?"

"In my experience, wee lasses are the most lethal of all opponents, but if ye wish me to put away the dagger, I will."

"Sheathe it," Alasdair confirmed, turning back to watch Maeve. She'd stopped on the trail and looked lost in thought. Her bow-shaped mouth was turned down, and a look of sorrow had settled upon her face, making his chest tighten.

"I'll do as ye bid, but dunnae say I did nae warn ye."

"I'm duly warned," Alasdair replied. "When she gets to the turn, we'll jump up. Ye grab the horse's reins, and I'll grab her."

"Fine, but if ye ask me, she has a slippery look about her, like she takes after her wretched clansmen, who we've been unable to catch."

"She'll nae get away," Alasdair said as she started toward them again.

"Of course, she'll nae," Brodick replied, "because we'll nae let her."

Alasdair didn't like the grimness he heard in his friend's tone. He glared at Brodick. "Ye let me handle her. Dunnae interfere."

"Ye may need—"

"I will nae."

"Oh, aye? Is that how it is?"

"That's how it is," Alasdair said, his right temple starting to throb.

"Ye'll have to beg me to—"

"I'll nae," he said, ending the conversation by looking toward Maeve once more. She was close. Very close. His muscles tensed in preparation to jump up. He didn't relish scaring her. She was his enemy, but she was a lass. He also knew if they stood up and demanded she dismount, she never would, and he didn't want to train a weapon on her, either. That was no way to gain her trust, though grabbing her wasn't a particularly good way to start persuading her to wed him. Still, it seemed the lesser of the two evils.

When she was five paces away, he stole a look at

Brodick, who gave him a sharp nod of readiness. By the time Alasdair faced Maeve once more, she was at the turn, and he and Brodick jumped up at the same time.

"Ho there," he said by way of greeting, hoping to scare her as little as possible. Her attention fell to him, and her eyes went wide.

Brodick moved to grasp her horse's reins, but she surprised Alasdair and Brodick—at least based on the way he swore—when she yanked back on her horse and said, "Lucifer, kick!" Before Alasdair knew what was happening, the horse kicked up its front legs with a whinny. Brodick had to duck not to be kicked in the face, and Maeve gave a crack of her reins and the command, "Ride!" The horse jumped over Brodick and lurched past Alasdair. He lunged for Maeve and caught a handful of the material of her gown and held tight as the horse rode forward. She went flying off the back and into him, and they both fell hard to the ground with her on top of Alasdair.

"Help!" she screamed, hands punching and legs kicking, even as Alasdair tried to capture her wrists to still her. She was a damned hellcat, clawing at him, twisting and turning on his lap.

"We're nae going to hurt ye!" he growled, grabbing at her wrists again, even as she swiveled around, eyes glittering with anger, and punched him straight in the nose. As he was reaching to stop her from hitting him again, she kneed him in the groin, and pain exploded in his gut. She went to knee him again, and he caught her leg right before it connected with his throbbing groin.

"Help me! Help!" she screamed loudly enough to call the angels from Heaven.

He slapped his palm over her mouth, but with one hand on her mouth and the other clutching her right knee, that left the little hellion's other leg free. He saw her foot coming at his face just before she kicked him in his already aching nose. This time, bone crunched, and a string of expletives flowed from his lips as did blood from his nose. He instinctually reached for his nose, and she took the opportunity to scramble off his lap. He had the oddest urge to laugh as he pinched his nose and watched her gain her feet, huffing. Her skirts were bunched up, and before they fell back into place, he got a glimpse of slender, creamy thighs. She'd done more damage to his person than any male enemy he'd ever faced.

"How dare ye try to take me!" she shouted. It struck him that the lass was outraged and not scared. He didn't know why, but it pleased him to find that she was as brave as he'd remembered. She reached toward her right hip, and he tracked her movements to the leather strap where he assumed she normally kept a dagger, but it wasn't there. He swept his gaze over the ground and saw the glint of a silver blade in the sunlight by his left thigh at the same time she did.

"I wouldn't try it if I were ye," he said. Never mind that even if she could get the weapon before he could, which she most assuredly could not, Brodick was directly behind her and had tethered her horse to the tree beside him. He would never let her stab Alasdair. She seemed to have utterly forgotten Brodick's presence. And why wouldn't she have? Brodick hadn't done a thing to aid Alasdair in getting Maeve under control. Alasdair stole a quick look at his friend and found the man smirking at him with his right eyebrow cocked high, as if to ask, *Do ye need my aid yet?* Pride was a funny thing. It always seemed to rear its head when it hurt one the most.

Any more thinking on that matter was cut short by

Maeve stepping toward him quickly to go for the dagger. He scooped it up handily and waved it at her. "I told ye nae to try it. Ye ken I could throw this dagger at ye and wound ye strategically so that ye'd be much easier for me to ferret away."

"Ye're despicable, Alasdair MacRae!" she snapped. "Only a man without honor would come on this day to steal me for my—"

"Ye're a fine one to talk of honor," he ground out, realizing his mistake the minute the words left his mouth. He was meant to convince her he was taking her because he could not forget about her.

"What do ye mean by that?" she demanded.

Before he could formulate a response to fix the problem he'd caused himself, Brodick said, "Ye MacKenzies are a bunch of murderers, and yer da, as the leader, is the worst." Alasdair glared at Brodick, and Maeve flinched, confirming his suspicion that she'd forgotten Brodick's presence.

Her mouth slipped open, her face went white, and she clenched her fists by her side. Then a flush spread with impressive speed across her face, down her neck, and to her chest, which, he realized, was on full display. The laces at the front of her gown were undone. They must have loosened during her struggle with him.

"I hope I broke yer nose!" she bellowed, swung away from Alasdair, and pointed at Brodick. "I pray I get the chance to break yers, too!"

Always the lighthearted fool, Brodick flourished his hand in front of his chest while giving a mock bow as she dashed around him with a yearning look toward her horse. He wasn't worried about her getting away. He could easily catch up with her, but as he clambered to his feet, his head pounded from her surprisingly strong blows and his nose throbbed, making his temper spike.

"Ye might have lent a hand instead of opening yer big mouth," he snapped at Brodick, but his words were lost to the scream for help that Maeve let loose.

"God's blood, that woman is loud," he growled, racing after her now. His entire head throbbed each time his boots struck the ground, and just when she was almost within reach, she glanced behind her, eyes going wide, and ran even harder so that he had to do so as well. The throbbing in his head became more like a clap of thunder that consumed every part of his brain. By the time he reached her, he was in a foul mood. His fingers grazed the material of her gown, then she slipped out of his reach. He lunged for her, grasped her around the waist, and scooped her back against him and off her feet. Immediately, she began to scream, but he'd been more strategic this time. The arm he had encircled around her waist trapped her arms by her side so she could not hit him, but her screams would undoubtedly alert her clan's guards if he didn't quiet her. He didn't want to cover her mouth again, but he didn't see what choice he had. He laid his palm across her warm mouth, pressing gently, and brought his lips near her ear to speak. "If ye'll promise nae to scream again, I'll take my hand off yer mouth. Do ye promise?"

Little spurts of her hot breath hit his fingers as her chest moved up and down with the lingering effort of her run. As he stood holding her, he became acutely aware of how soft she was, the smallness of her waist, the heaviness of her breasts resting upon his arm, and how good she smelled, like fresh spring air with a hint of sweetness in it and a dash of zest. Her breath began to slow, and just as he decided he'd have to put a binding around her mouth long enough for them to travel out of earshot of her guards, she nodded.

He was no fool, though. Just because she was giving her agreement did not necessarily mean she intended to keep her word.

"If ye yell," he warned, "I'll put a gag on ye, and I'll nae take it off until we reach my home. That's a ride that will take us to the nooning meal." She nodded again, and he glanced toward her home and judged that he could risk it. He could get her quieted within a breath if she did scream.

"Dunnae do it," Brodick warned from behind Alasdair. He glanced over his shoulder to find his friend leading all three of their horses. He'd have to ride his with her horse tethered to his beast.

"She's given her word," Alasdair said, more for her benefit than true belief that she'd keep it.

"Ha. As if a MacKenzie's word is worth the spit used to form the sentence," Brodick sneered.

"Maeve," Alasdair said, instilling a warning in his tone. "I dunnae want to gag ye, but I will." She nodded again, and he slowly peeled his hand away, tensing and expecting her to go against her word. She sucked in a huge breath, and he brought his hand directly under her chin. She stiffened under his hold.

"Ye can remove yer smelly hand," she said. "I ken ye'll shut me up afore I can get a proper scream out, and I dunnae have a wish for a gag on my mouth."

"Wise choice," he said, swinging her up on his horse. She glared down at him, then he mounted the beast as well and settled himself behind her. Her back was ramrod straight, and she sat so far forward on the horse, he half expected Lore to protest the weight of her too close to his neck, but Lore merely sniffed his displeasure loudly.

As Brodick mounted his horse, Alasdair tethered Maeve's animal to his. When he twisted upon the horse to secure her beast, he felt her hand upon his thigh. He whipped back around, and her unwavering gaze met his. She smiled almost shyly, but from what he remembered of the lass, there was nothing shy about her, and her hand happened to be very close to her dagger, which he had sheathed. "I dunnae mind yer hand upon me one bit, Maeve. And I'm happy to invite ye to my bed tonight, but if ye think to grasp yer dagger, or any of my weapons, and use them upon me, I'll stop ye."

"Like ye did afore?" she said with a smirk.

He picked up her hand and moved it off him, though in God's truth, his body had immediately warmed at her touch. He'd not anticipated his desire for her to still be so strong after the years that had gone by, but that just worked better for his plan to woo her. "I was trying to take a care nae to hurt ye afore."

She snorted at that, and her gaze, stony with her anger, bore into him. "And now ye dunnae care if ye hurt me?"

"I did nae say that, but ye will be coming with us, and ye'll nae be stabbing me with my weapon or any other."

"Maybe nae this day," she said, her voice as hard as her gaze, "but ye best sleep with one eye open. I will get away from ye, and if ye think ye can force me to wed ye, ye're a bigger clot-heid than ye look to be. I'd sooner put a fire poker in my eye than wed the likes of ye."

"My temper is one thread away from breaking, Maeve. If I were ye, I'd turn around and nae speak another word unless ye have a great need."

"Or what? Ye're going to gag me?" Her eyebrows rose challengingly above her beautiful, glittering gaze.

"Aye, Maeve," he replied. He heard the harsh coldness of his own tone. This was not going well and was a terrible start to the plan. He supposed he should have expected it.

He was snatching her from her home, after all.

She stiffened and ever so slowly turned around, then she spoke again. "How did ye even ken about my da?"

Her admission to what her da had done surprised him. "When we found my da, he was clutching a piece of yer clan's plaid in his hand."

"What?" Confusion laced the one word. She raised her hands and pressed her fingertips to her temples. It struck him in that moment that she looked very vulnerable, and that she must feel great fear, but he could not turn back. She was a means to peace and a secure future for his clan. She was the payment for the debt her father had incurred by killing Alasdair's father.

She shook her head. "I…I dunnae understand. What do ye mean yer da was clutching a piece of my clan's plaid in his hand?"

Horns began to sound, and when he looked to her castle and to the rampart, torches began to blaze one by one across the castle and the bridge. "Search horns," he said.

"Nay." She shook her head. "Those are the horns for death."

"Whose death?" Brodick asked.

"My da's," she said, the two words coming out jerkily.

Her words froze him. Dead? Her da was dead?

"The gods have finally smiled upon us!" Brodick exclaimed. "We've snatched the new heiress to Eilean Donan Castle!"

Alasdair felt Maeve's hand upon the dagger sheathed at his thigh too late. By the time he reached to stop her, she was plunging it toward his shoulder. The blade cut through the skin easily and didn't stop until it met bone. Fiery pain ripped through his arm, and for a moment, the desire to shove her off the horse nearly overtook him. She must have seen the anger gripping him. She turned from him with a yelp and tried to jump off, but he yanked her hard against him with his good arm and clamped his thighs over hers until he swore he could feel the coursing of her blood through her body. She whimpered, so he eased up but not so much that she could move.

"Brodick," he said, the word hoarse because of the pain.

"Ye want me to take the wee wicked hellion?" Brodick asked, moving his horse beside Alasdair's.

"Nay. Pull out the dagger."

Brodick reached over and yanked the blade out before Alasdair had known he was going to. He wiped the crimson blade on his plaid while eyeing Maeve with a look that would have made most men shrink away. "I told ye she was a slippery one."

"Aye," he said, glancing down. Blood was already soaking through his plaid and dripping down his arm. Maeve MacKenzie was either going to be the death of him or his salvation. In this moment, he couldn't decide which, and there was no time to question his decision or form a new plan because horns began to blast again before he could contemplate it further.

"Maeve!" came a male's voice echoing through the woods. "Maeve, where are ye?"

The horns blasted again—once, twice, three times—and Alasdair felt Maeve's stomach suck in, and her chest rise with the deep breath she took to scream. Ignoring his pain, he smacked his palm over her mouth with one hand and used the reins with his other to urge his horse into a gallop.

Chapter Five

The way Alasdair MacRae's hand was clamped tightly over her mouth made panic edge Maeve's vision black, but no matter how she grunted and moaned, he did not loosen his grip. It was rather amazing that the Highlander was able to keep his hand firmly in place while riding them at breakneck speed away from her home. She tried to pry his fingers away, and every time she did, his thighs pressed harder against her. He was going to squeeze her to death.

Stabbing him had not been the wisest decision, but she'd panicked. He was clearly enraged, though he hardly had the right to be! He'd come on to her land and had snatched her, and for what purpose? Did he think to somehow hurt her father by taking her? The man clearly had not known her father was dead.

Just the thought brought grief crashing back over her. The weight of it made her sag, but she didn't fall forward a bit. She couldn't have moved even had she wanted to. Alasdair's thick forearm was positioned over her right breast so his hand could reach her mouth. She sucked in little gulps of air, her panic rising as they left her clan's land, and made their way toward the mountains. Her father was gone. He would not be coming to rescue her. She would never see him smile again, or laugh, or scowl. She'd never hear his tone go deep again, as it always had when he was giving her a warning, such as not to ride into the woods unaccompanied.

Why had she done that? She was a fool! No one would know where she was or who had taken her until, what? Until Alasdair made his demands? And what would he have demanded from her father had he still been alive? More sheep? More goats? Land in exchange for her life? Or to return her with her innocence intact? Her nostrils flared at the thought, even as she rejected the notion. Surely, the lad on the verge of manhood who had kissed her so gently years ago could not now be the sort of man who would ravish a woman against her will? It was one thing for a clan to be thieving, but it was quite another for a man to ill use a woman to get what he wanted. Fear gripped her, and she struggled against his hold again.

This time, he did remove his hand, and she gulped in a greedy breath in case he changed his mind and covered her mouth once more. "Why did ye take me?" she demanded as the horse slowed considerably. Maybe if she knew, she could reason with him, and he would return her to her home.

He didn't answer. Instead, he seemed to slump against her back, his chin coming to rest on her shoulder even as his thighs suddenly separated from hers, and the horse came to a near halt. The relief of suddenly being unconfined was instant.

"Alasdair?" his friend asked from behind them.

She chose to ignore the man. "Why did ye take me?" she demanded again, trying to shrug his chin off her shoulder. He groaned in response. Whatever was the man doing? "Did ye hear me?" she asked.

"Aye," he croaked in her ear. "I took ye because yer da murdered mine." And before she could even react to that, he fell sideways off the horse and landed in a heap on the ground. For one moment, she sat in stunned silence, and then she had a space of a heartbeat where she knew now was the time to flee. The other man, Brodick, was not paying her any mind. He was scrambling off his horse to aid Alasdair. She couldn't seem to move, to make herself go as she needed to. She was caught by fear, but not for herself, for Alasdair. The ridiculousness of worrying about a man who had taken her against her will was not lost on her, but she could not shake it, so when Brodick looked up at her, and said, "He's out. 'Tis the loss of blood, I'm certain."

Maeve winced as her gaze was drawn to Alasdair's arm, which she only just realized was covered in blood from the wound she'd given him. "Will he be all right?" she asked.

"If we get him to the healer in time, he should recover. If nae... Will ye aid me in getting him on my horse? I'll ride with him, and ye can bring the other two horses."

She bit her lip and stole a look over her shoulder back the way they had come. This was her chance to escape. Possibly, this was her only chance to do so. She could find her way back. It would take a bit of doing, but she could do so.

"If ye run, lass, I'll be forced to follow ye and leave him here," Brodick said, drawing her attention back to the man. His gaze, twin pools of appeal, took her by surprise. The man looked to be a hardened warrior with the scar on his face and the unfriendly look he'd worn since she'd had the misfortune of meeting him, but she could not deny the concern she saw now in his eyes, and she could not ignore it as much as it would behoove her to do so.

She swallowed, realizing aiding him would hurt her, but she'd not be able to live with herself if Alasdair died because she'd stabbed him. Sighing, she dismounted her horse and stood before Brodick. "What do ye need me to do?"

"Just hold him in place once I get him up and leaned against my horse. From there, I'll pull him up onto his belly."

She nodded and moved back as Brodick hoisted Alasdair up to his feet with a grunt. Alasdair's head lolled forward, and after Brodick stood him up and leaned him against the horse, he looked over his shoulder and motioned to her with a jerk of his head. She came forward, her breath hitching at the amount of blood coming from the wound in Alasdair's arm, which was now running down his leg. "I should nae have stabbed him," she whispered, her stomach roiling.

"Nay," Brodick replied, the word harsh, "ye should nae have." He turned his head ever so slightly so that her eyes met his, which were back to looking unfriendly. "He's the best man I ken. Now, slide yer arms around his waist and then lean forward to press yer chest against his back. It will be easier going for ye to hold him up if ye dunnae have all his weight. He's a solid man."

She could see that well enough by his broad shoulders, his well-muscled arms, and his long powerful legs. She did as Brodick bade, becoming acutely aware of how Alasdair felt and smelled the moment her arms settled around his toned stomach and her chest pressed against his hard back. The top of her head came just to his shoulder, and a swatch of his wavy dark hair tickled her nose where his head now rested sideways. She inhaled a deep breath and with it got the scents of smoky wood, earth, and horse, along with the faint tinge of blood.

"Do ye think ye have him if I release him?" Brodick asked.

She nodded, tensing in preparation. Brodick released

him, stepped back, and immediately, Alasdair's heavy weight settled on her, making her rock back on her heels and grit her teeth to keep him in place. Brodick was already mounting the horse, even as she was wondering if she could continue to hold Alasdair up. "Brodick!" she said, the word urgent.

"I ken!" he replied, leaning over the side of his horse toward her and Alasdair, and grabbing hold of Alasdair's shoulders. Brodick's gaze locked with hers. "I'm going to need ye to push him up as I pull him."

She nodded, and with a quick glance, she decided the best place to put her hands was on Alasdair's bottom. With no help for it, she set her palms against either of his firm cheeks, and she bent her knees to get under him and put her full weight into aiding Brodick, who was already tugging Alasdair upward with grunts of effort. Her arms were burning when Brodick announced, "I have him settled." Nodding, she gained her own horse, and as she did, Brodick added, "Dunnae forget, if ye flee, I will follow, and then he could die, and his blood would be on yer hands."

She glared at the man as she took hold of her reins. "Ye're the one running on with yer talk. I'll nae flee. Yet."

"I hope ye're a lass of yer word."

"I am," she replied, taking up her reins and following him as he set off at a gallop.

They reached the MacRae stronghold when the sun was full in the sky, but the day was still bitterly cold. Her bottom and head ached from the jarring ride, and when Brodick pulled up on the reins of his horse to slow it, relief swept through her. Ahead, she took in the castle that sat nestled on rolling hills with woods to the right and left and a lake in front of it. It looked to have once been a beautiful stronghold, but from what she could see, it needed a good many repairs.

The tower on the far right appeared to be crumbling, and one of the twin gatehouses was nothing more than a pile of stone, leaving the main entrance to the castle unsafe. The road to the castle was winding and littered with overgrowth, and at each guard tower they passed, she noted they were empty. "Where are the guards?" she inquired of Brodick.

"We dunnae have enough warriors to man all the towers. The raids from yer family and the Frasers took many of our men."

She frowned. "Raids? We only participated in one raid on yer lands, as far as I ken."

He jerked his head in her direction. "Then ye dunnae ken much. Yer clan and the Fraser clan raided our home thrice last year and once already this year."

"That's a lie!" she burst out as they drew close to the twin gatehouses where only one tower was manned. A man who looked to be near her age with bright-red hair came out of the tower, sword in hand. As his gaze fell to Alasdair, his eyes widened.

"Is he dead?"

Maeve frowned. The man sounded more curious than sad to her, but she was tired and was likely misjudging what she heard or mayhap she wasn't. Or mayhap Alasdair was not well liked by his men, except this friend Brodick. If he treated his men with the highhandedness with which the laird had treated her, she could understand if Alasdair's men did not care for him.

Brodick glowered at the man for a moment. "It's good

to see ye at yer post."

The man's face turned a shade of red that matched his hair, and he stood silent for a long moment before speaking again. "What happened?" he asked. Wisely, he did not ask again if Alasdair was dead. Brodick already looked ready to kill the man.

Brodick tilted his head toward her. "She stabbed him."

The man glanced toward her. "Who's this?"

"This is the MacKenzie's daughter," Brodick replied. It was impossible to miss the sneer in his tone when he said her father's name. "And this," Brodick said, waving toward the man, "is Darby."

A flush heated her from her head all the way to her toes. "My da was a good man!" she protested, the tears she still had not let come stinging her eyes.

Brodick's disbelieving sideways glance made ire sweep through her. He opened his mouth, shook his head, and then said, "Yer da killed my laird, so ye can understand why my opinion differs with yers."

She felt her fingers ball into fists by her sides. "I'm telling ye, my da would nae have given such an order."

"I dunnae have the time to argue with ye," he replied, moving the horse past the man, who stood there with a wary look upon his face. She stood by the man Darby as Brodick rode away from her, not pausing until he was halfway into the first courtyard. Only then did he seem to remember her. He turned back, frowned, and said, "What the devil are ye waiting for?"

She honestly didn't know. It occurred to her that she was squandering her last chance to flee before she was trapped behind the closed castle gate. Her heartbeat sped up as Brodick turned away from her once again. She had been dismissed by him as meek, and that was very good for her.

Whatever duty she'd had to aid Alasdair had been fulfilled.

She started to turn her horse away when Brodick's hard, deep voice cut through the silence. "Shoot her if she dunnae follow me, Darby."

Unease swept over the man's features, and he shot an almost hostile look toward Brodick, but Darby produced a bow and arrow and aimed it at her. "I'll nae take pleasure in shooting ye, but ye should ken I'm a true shot and have to do as ordered."

His words and expression gave her the sense Darby didn't like being ordered about, but she also got the distinct impression, with his arrow being pointed directly at her, that whether he liked it or not, he'd shoot her. She gritted her teeth and nudged her horse forward, along with Alasdair's horse, who was tethered to hers.

The outer courtyard had an elaborate stone fountain in the middle of it, and in the fountain, men appeared to be carved. She wanted to ask who the carved people were, but she knew now was not the time. It was notably empty in the courtyard, but laughter and the murmur of many voices came from behind two large wooden doors that she spied at the end of an arched stone passage. The doors had black iron across the front in multiple places, she assumed to make them harder to break through, and there was a small black iron plate at the top of the left door, which almost looked like a tiny window. "Tolly, open up," Brodick bellowed.

The black iron plate on the door abruptly slid open and a man's large, red, bulbous nose appeared in the door before an eye framed by a bushy black eyebrow did. "Who goes there?" the man asked, his voice jovial.

"Quit yer playing! Alasdair has been stabbed."

"Alasdair has been stabbed!" the man bellowed from the

other side of the wood door. This reaction of genuine concern was more like what she would have expected from Darby, so mayhap Alasdair was not disliked by all his men. Though, honestly, she couldn't fathom why she was even contemplating it. What care did she have if Alasdair's men liked him? None, that was what. As soon as she could, she would escape the brutish Highlander and his thieving clansmen.

The plate slammed shut, bars scraped, and the doors swung open with a creak. The inner courtyard was teeming with people, and they all seemed to have stopped in the middle of what they were doing. Warriors stood facing one another, swords in hand, some still raised for training, sweat glistening off them in the sunlight. Wash dangled from women's hands and looked as if they had been shaking the clothing out in the wind. Children had paused in obvious chase, and servants had stopped what they were doing, too. Some still had buckets balanced on hips and heads. An unnatural silence fell for a moment, and then a woman said from somewhere to Maeve's right, "Go and fetch Anise!"

A dull roar erupted, the crowd parted, and a tall, thin woman with peppered hair strode through the split with the blue silk skirts of her gown flaring out at the fast clip of her walk. Her bearing was proud and purposeful. Her head was held high, her shoulders were thrust back, and determination and fear etched her otherwise smooth face. She had Alasdair's eyes, or rather, he had her golden-brown ones rimmed with thick dark lashes and even darker eyebrows. Her gaze touched on Brodick, then Alasdair, and a whimper escaped her before her focus settled on Maeve. The fury in the woman's gaze set a chill in Maeve.

"Brodick, what happened?" the woman demanded, her tone authoritative.

Brodick shot Maeve a surprisingly apologetic look. "The MacKenzie lass stabbed him."

"Clyde," the woman bellowed, "take this woman to the block and rid her of her head."

Macve's throat instantly closed in fear.

"My lady, the MacKenzie lass's head needs to stay on her body," Brodick said, even as men came toward Maeve from the left and right.

"Whatever for?" the woman demanded, glaring at Maeve.

"For breathing," Maeve blurted, grasping at the first thing that had popped into her head. The incredulous look Brodick gave her made her cheeks burn. Foolish. That's what she sounded like—utterly foolish.

"I dunnae care if ye continue to breathe or nae," the woman said, her words laced with venom.

"Alasdair would forbid ye killing her," Brodick inserted to Maeve's relief, "and ye ken it. Besides that, she helped me to get him here when she could have fled."

Maeve's whole body went weak with gratitude for Brodick's attempt to aid her.

"Fine," the woman bit out, her attention moving to her son. "Take her to the dungeon!" she commanded, even as guards grabbed at Maeve to remove her from her horse. Men were now assisting Brodick in getting Alasdair down.

When a groan of pain came from Alasdair as they lowered him to the ground, the men who now had a hold of Maeve stilled, and their attention, as well as Maeve's, went to Alasdair. A collective gasp went up in the courtyard as Alasdair was settled in place. His unnaturally white pallor did not bode well for him, or for Maeve keeping her head. She bit her lip as fear pulsed through her for them both.

"Maeve," he groaned, and she blinked in surprise.

"Maeve," he repeated, and his eyelashes fluttered upward.

"Let her go," Brodick ordered the men holding her, and she jerked her arms out of their grasp at his command and came forward slowly, feeling all eyes upon her.

"Son," Alasdair's mother cried out and kneeled beside him.

"Maeve." Alasdair lifted his arm and moved his hand through the air as if to brush something or someone away.

She closed the distance between them and kneeled by Alasdair without asking permission. His mother looked up from him and shot her a withering glance.

"Maeve." His eyes were open but staring past her into another moment, likely already gone.

She couldn't say why, but the desire to soothe him overcame her. She set a gentle hand to his unhurt arm and leaned close. "I'm here. What is it?"

His head turned toward her, but his gaze was still unseeing. His mouth curved into an unconscious smile. "Ye have the softest lips, Maeve. Do ye ken that?"

Heat burned her cheeks, and she kept her gaze trained on him, acutely aware of his mother's stare upon her. "Do I?" she said, making her voice nearly a whisper.

"Like a warm, soft caress," he said as his lashes lowered once again. "I kinnae dislodge it from my memory. I tried, and I tried," he mumbled, then fell silent.

She rocked back on her heels, momentarily stunned by his words. She waited for what seemed like an eternity for him to say more. The silence was nearly deafening around her. His chest rose and fell in deep breaths, and she realized he had fallen back asleep. A sheen of sweat covered his forehead, and she set a hand to it, drawing it back at how hot he was.

"Move away from my son."

Maeve forced herself to look up to meet his mother's venomous gaze. The woman's eyes narrowed as she stared at Maeve, and her mouth twisted grimly. "Anise," she said, and suddenly, a strikingly beautiful woman kneeled beside Alasdair's mother. "Ye will save him."

It was not a question but a command. The woman nodded, her silky black hair falling to cover her face as she leaned forward to examine his wound. Maeve held her breath as the woman pressed her fingers gently into Alasdair's bloody arm, and he grumbled nonsensical words and tried to twist away from her, but the woman held his arm firmly in place. After a moment, she glanced up and her gaze met Maeve's. This woman was no friendlier than Alasdair's mother. She arched her black eyebrows upward as she assessed Maeve. "I assume ye are Maeve."

Maeve nodded.

"If he dies, I'll take yer head myself."

"Take her away," Alasdair's mother said with a flick of her wrist toward Maeve. She was jerked up by both arms, and then propelled around by a guard. She came face-to-face with Brodick for one moment.

"I'll see what I can do," he hurriedly said before she was dragged through a parted path of staring people and toward an open passageway, up a step, and around a corner to go down another long, narrow passageway. This one was damp and slippery underfoot and had a steady, frigid breeze blowing through it.

She was led through another stone door, down several steps, and into a vaulted room that extended beneath another passage. The room held one open, narrow space that could hardly be called a window but did let in light. Unfortunately, the wind blew in through the window, as well. The guard pushed her away with enough force that she staggered forward and only stopped herself from falling because there was a long stone bench in the cell that she set her hands on. "Ye'll nae get pity from me," he said, "or any other in this clan. We ken yer MacKenzie's daughter."

She stood up, wiping her stinging palms on her gown. It was clear the MacRaes hated her father, and if they thought he'd been raiding them constantly and had their laird murdered, she could understand why, but they were wrong. They had to be. She could not fathom that her father would have done such a thing.

"I dunnae need yer pity," she said, anger beating in her chest. "What I need is for ye, for someone, to listen. My da would nae have given an order to kill yer laird. He simply—"

"Save yer lies for someone who cares," the man said, then stomped toward the cell door and slammed it shut.

The room fell suddenly quiet except for the hiss and whistle of the wind through the opening and the dripping of water from somewhere in the room. Maeve's mouth started to water. By the gods, she was thirsty. She searched around the room until she found the source of water in a corner, dripping from the ceiling. She turned her head up, opened her mouth, and let the water fall in. It was cool and refreshing, but it also seemed to be the thing that was holding back a wail she did not know had been lodged in her throat.

A high keen of grief ripped out of her. She dropped to her knees as warm tears overflowed her eyes and tracked down her cheeks to drip off her chin. Her father was gone, and he was never coming back. She'd been ripped from her home, dragged on a harrowing horseback ride, confronted by people who hated her simply because of her clan, and thrown in a dungeon. And she had stabbed a man.

An image of Alasdair ashen, covered in blood, and

murmuring her name filled her head as she dug her nails into the cold dirt and squeezed her eyes shut. He had said he'd not been able to forget the kiss they'd shared those years ago. Had he meant that? Or was it some sort of ploy? She gave her head a little shake. She was confused. So confused. Why did she feel guilty for stabbing him? He had deserved it. Of course, he did seem to think her father had murdered his, but he was wrong, and she'd been protecting herself.

So why had she not fled? She should have fled. Her clan needed her. Her father's words were already coming to pass about the danger she'd face from men wanting to gain her hand to gain her castle when he was gone. She had to get out of this dungeon and this castle. She shoved up to her feet, dismissing the foolish memory of the kiss she'd gotten as a naive lass. She had not known who Alasdair MacRae really was. She'd imagined him to be honorable. She'd given him qualities she'd longed to find in a man to love her. He was dishonorable and a thief, and he'd taken her because he wanted misplaced vengeance, and it sent shivers through her to imagine how he intended to get it. And if he didn't recover, her odds were no better. Her head would be lopped off before his cold body was buried.

She didn't get more than two steps toward the closed door before the handle rattled and a key clanked. The door swung open, and a young woman with dark hair and bright green eyes stood there with an interested expression on her face. She stepped into the room and turned toward the door, and that's when Maeve saw Brodick. His attention settled on Maeve for a moment before he looked to the woman in front of him. "Yell when ye want me to let ye out."

"Ye," he said, now focusing on Maeve as he waved a

hand at her, "dunnae think to try and harm Lara."

"Brodick, I can take care of myself!" the woman protested, withdrawing a dagger from a sheath at her hip.

"I ken," he replied, and something suddenly soft in his gaze as he glanced at the woman made Maeve think he cared for her, but the look was gone almost instantly. "That one is slippery." Maeve supposed she was "that one." "I told yer brother and he did nae listen and look at him now."

It was a bit disconcerting to think she'd stabbed a man who was a brother, a son, a friend, but then he had snatched her. Honestly, she had not stabbed him purposely. It had been more of a reaction to the situation than thought out.

"I'll call ye if I need ye," the young woman Lara said with a tinge of exasperation in her voice. Brodick opened his mouth to speak, but she shut the door on him before he could. The boldness of the woman made Maeve smile, though she wiped it off her face as the woman turned to look at her.

She raised a dark eyebrow and leaned back against the door. "Ye should ken that my mother wanted us to hang ye or take yer head."

It was said in such a nonchalant way that a laugh of disbelief escaped Maeve. "So I gathered in the courtyard when she said as much. Do ye always speak of murder so matter-of-factly?"

"Nay," the woman replied, tilting her head in a way that made Maeve think the woman was assessing her. "For instance, when my da was found murdered, I did nae speak of it matter-of-factly, but in this instance, I ken my mother, and as much as she hates ye, she'd nae have ye killed, or at least nae unless my brother actually dies."

A wave of unexpected and unwanted concern for Alasdair washed over her, as well as the desire to ask why this woman, her brother, and apparently the entire MacRae clan thought Maeve's father had murdered their laird. She wanted to inquire about it, but she started with the more pressing question. "How is yer brother?" Maeve asked, moving to the stone bench.

Lara pushed off the wall and came to sit on the other end of the bench. "Anise says he will live."

Maeve thought of the beautiful woman in the courtyard and recalled Lady MacRae calling her Anise. "I'm relieved to hear he'll live."

"Aye?"

"Aye," Maeve said, surprised at the real relief she felt. Of course, it made sense. She did not want to take his life or any other. "I did nae mean to stab him."

Lara's eyebrows hitched higher, and amusement flickered in her eyes. "Are ye trying to tell me ye stabbed him on accident?"

A hot, unwanted flush singed Maeve's cheeks and traveled down her neck to her chest. "I mean, it was more of a reaction to him trying to snatch me."

Lara nodded. "I suppose I would have done the same." She gave a shrug and a small smile. "I told him it was a foolish plan."

"Exactly what was yer brother's plan?"

Lara's dark eyes held Maeve's for a long silent moment before Lara let out a sigh. "What did he tell ye?"

"That he took me because my da murdered yers, but I tell ye, my da would nae have done such a thing! He was honorable."

Lara made a derisive sound, but then a softer expression settled over her delicate features. "Brodick told us yer da passed. I'm sorry to hear it for ye, even though he was wicked."

"My da was nae wicked," Maeve insisted. She wanted to say more, to wipe the dubious expression off Lara's face, but Maeve had to swallow several times just to speak. Grief slid from her throat to her belly and settled there. She inhaled a shaky breath and said, "I dunnae how it came to be that yer da was clutching a piece of my clan's plaid in his hand when he died, but he would nae have ordered yer da murdered in cold blood. He was nae that sort of man."

Lara gazed at her for a long moment before speaking. "Ye were his daughter. Of course, ye wish to believe the best of him, but consider it from our viewpoint."

Maeve hesitated, wanting to refuse, but that would solve nothing, nor get her freed, so she nodded. "Tell me."

"My father was found at the foot of a cliff on the edge of our land that adjoins yers. It was made to look as if he fell, but at the top, my brother found traces of a struggle, and in my da's hand was a piece of plaid. He had to have grabbed at the plaid of the man who pushed him, it ripped, and he clutched a piece of it in his fist when he was pushed."

Maeve clenched her teeth as her stomach twisted at the thought of her father ordering the death of Laird MacRae. He wouldn't have. He was a peaceful man at heart. She stood, her mind turning, and strode back and forth as her thoughts tumbled. She could feel Lara MacRae's eyes upon her, tracking her. She finally stopped and met the woman's gaze. "I heard my father in talks with our council and the Fraser laird and council. My father insisted that they nae leave yer clan without any food for the winter when they raided ye this last time. My father was the reason they only took yer horses and sheep."

"Yer father lied to ye, Maeve. Yer clan and the Frasers took most of our horses, all our sheep, our goats, and set fire to our food storage on their last raid. We have been left with precious little. The men have had to go out nearly every day to hunt."

Maeve frowned. "That kinnae be. I saw my da when he came home from the raid, and he told me my clan helped release the horses, and then they provided a distraction while the Frasers released the sheep."

"I suppose the distraction yer father was referring to was the fire they set to our food storage."

Maeve's stomach twisted. Would her father have lied? Surely not?

"And they most certainly did nae leave any animals for us to survive with," Lara continued. "My brother Tavish was shot in the leg trying to stop men from releasing the sheep, and he vows the men were wearing yer clan's plaid. Tavish got an infection in his leg and the healer said he'd lose it, and then Alasdair came up with this plan."

Maeve pressed her fingertips to her now throbbing temples. "I'm sorry," she said, knowing how inadequate the words were for such a tragedy. She would have to speak to Colin about this when she returned home. He would know the truth of it because he had been there. "I dunnae ken what to say." Her voice was barely above a whisper. "But my father would nae have ordered yer father to be killed, and he told me his part, my clan's part, in the last raid was simply to release the horses and provide a distraction."

"Forget the raid for a moment," Lara said, waving a dismissive hand. "How do ye explain yer clan's plaid clutched in my da's hand?"

"I kinnae," Maeve said, shaken. "But yer clan started all this six years ago when they first raided us!" She remembered it clearly because it was only a sennight after the king had given her father Eilean Donan for services rendered.

"What are ye talking about?" Lara asked, giving her a

black, layered look. "Yer clan raided us first! 'Tis why we retaliated."

"One of us dunnae understand the truth," Maeve retorted in cold sarcasm.

"Aye," Lara replied, her face turning red. "And that is ye."

"Well, I ken one thing for certain, and that is that yer brother took me in revenge for something my family did nae do."

"So ye say, but we say different."

"Fine, we will agree to disagree for now. How exactly did yer brother mean to exact his revenge? What was the plan that ye disagreed with?"

The woman gave her a pointed look. "He did nae mean to exact revenge."

"I'm to believe ye? Ye are holding a dagger in yer hand, and ye have me locked in a cell."

"I kinnae let ye out of the cell because I dunnae trust ye nae to flee."

Maeve knew it was useless to claim otherwise, so she simply said, "Fair enough."

"But Brodick told me ye stayed and aided him with Alasdair, and ye did nae waste precious time making him chase ye, and for that, I set the dagger down." Maeve acknowledged Lara's action with an incline of her head. "Alasdair is an honorable man. He would nae hurt a woman in retaliation for a man's deeds. He meant to persuade ye to wed him so our clan would have an allegiance with yers and we would nae face starvation this winter. He wants peace."

Maeve took a quick, sharp, stunned breath. Wed her? He had intended to persuade her to wed him for peace?

"I kinnae wed him," she said. But she could *if* she wanted to. The day she'd met him years before came immediately to mind, along with the emotions he had stirred in her when he'd kissed her. Those emotions had lingered, and she had fantasized that he was different from his clanspeople, who had raided hers not long before. Her silly lass's mind had fancied him an honorable lad who would treat her as an equal all because he had allowed her to kill the boar in the woods, but eventually, when she had grown older, she had realized he had undoubtedly only allowed her to kill the boar to get the kiss from her. That was calculating, not honorable, and so she had finally laid her fantasy of him to rest. She had put aside her hope to wed for love, and beyond that, her da had clearly wanted her to wed Colin. He had not broken her betrothal, even to obtain his own happiness. She could not go against what he had wanted for a man she did not know and did not love, and who she honestly had no notion of whether he was telling her the truth or not. But she could offer something else. "I will speak to Colin, and I will elicit a promise from him afore I wed him that there will be peace with yer clan, but yer brother must promise it, too. He must give his word."

Lara stood up slowly and paced back and forth for a moment. "I dunnae think that will be accepted. My brother's word is good, but a Fraser's—"

"Colin's is," Maeve said. She may not love him, but she knew he was honorable.

Lara bit her lip. "I'll speak to my brother when he awakens."

When the woman turned toward the cell door, Maeve realized Lara had forgotten about her dagger, and Maeve quickly slid it under the skirt of her gown. Lara turned back right as Maeve was setting her hand in her lap. When Lara's brows dipped with a look of concentration, Maeve was certain Lara was about to recall the forgotten dagger. She blurted the first thing that came to mind in hopes of distracting her. "What if yer brother will nae accept my offer? What then?"

Lara's frown deepened. "He will likely try to persuade ye to wed him."

"I dunnae even ken yer brother," Maeve sputtered.

"Do ye love another?" Lara demanded.

"Well, nay, but—"

"Then get to ken him. Only then can ye decide if ye wish to wed him or nae."

When the cell door slammed shut behind Lara and the lock clicked into place, Maeve slid the dagger out from under her skirt and glanced at it. She grinned to herself. She'd not be around long enough to learn Alasdair MacRae. She stood up and walked to the cell door, immensely glad she had watched her da teach a group of men how to get out of a locked cell if they had anything sharp on them. Brodick had spoken the truth about one thing: she was a slippery one.

Chapter Six

*A*lasdair awoke with a start from the reoccurring dream he had about the day he'd found his father dead. His da's face, slack in death, eyes wide open, stayed with him until he blinked his own eyes open and squinted at the bright sunlight. His next thought was of that hellion Maeve MacKenzie. She'd stabbed him! A sense of urgency filled him, and he knew it had something to do with her, but he was having trouble figuring out why. It felt like he was trudging through thick mud to organize his thoughts, but it hit him at once. If he was in his bedchamber, where the devil was that nuisance of a lass? He started to sit up when a voice split the silence of his room.

"Finally!"

He turned his head to locate his sister. She stopped in the entrance to his bedchamber. "I'm so glad ye're finally awake. I need to speak to ye." He jerked upward and was scrambling off his bed even as Lara was taking a deep breath to launch into whatever it was she wanted to speak to him about. His sister could be the most long-winded person he knew, and he did not have the time or patience for it at the moment.

"How did I get in here?" he demanded, bending down to scoop his plaid off the ground with his right hand. He clenched his teeth at the pain that shot down the length of his right arm. Glancing down, he took in the bandage that was wrapped around his arm. "How long have I been asleep?"

"Since yesterday after ye arrived," Lara answered, positioning herself in the middle of his doorway.

He eyed her for a moment. Was she attempting to keep him in his bedchamber? She did have a certain glint in her eyes. The one she got when she had decided not to be deterred. Lara could be like a dog with a bone when the mood overcame her. He glanced around for his weapons, saw them piled in the chair in the corner of his bedchamber, and closed the distance to them in a flash. He had them all sheathed before he'd taken three full breaths. When he turned back to Lara, Brodick was standing beside her, and they both had their arms crossed over their chests.

"I was just coming to check on ye," Brodick said.

"Well, as ye can see," Alasdair replied, walking to the door and scowling when neither of them moved, "I'm fine."

"Anise said when ye awoke ye should take it slow to ensure ye are nae dizzy from the blood loss."

"I've a clan to run and a lass to persuade to wed me. I'm nae dizzy."

"I told ye she was a slippery one," Brodick said.

"Aye, ye did," Alasdair responded, giving his friend a pointed look. "Do ye mind removing yer arse from my doorway?"

"Nae at all," Brodick replied with a grin, "but first I want to say something on the lass's behalf."

Alasdair stared slack jawed at Brodick for a moment. "Ye're speaking on behalf of Maeve MacKenzie? Did ye nae just say she's slippery, which implies ye dunnae like or trust her?"

Brodick nodded. "I dunnae trust her. She's a MacKenzie, after all, but beyond that, I dunnae have anything personal against her."

"Ye seem to have forgotten she stabbed me," Alasdair bit out.

"Ye did snatch her after all," Lara said sweetly.

Brodick nodded. "Aye, ye did."

Alasdair felt his brows dip together. "What the devil is going on here?"

Brodick shrugged. "She showed me a thread of honor, so I feel obligated to pass it along."

"Explain," Alasdair replied, his impatience mounting.

"Someone awoke in a foul mood," Brodick said.

"Aye," Lara added, "ye're acting like a hornet."

"I was stabbed!" Alasdair said through gritted teeth. He locked his gaze on Brodick. "Exactly how did Maeve MacKenzie show ye honor?" He was having a hard time feeling the least bit of generosity toward Maeve.

"When ye fell off yer horse, she did nae flee. She could have, and I would have had to give chase, which would have meant squandering important time to get ye here and to Anise, but I told the lass as much, and nae only did she nae flee but she aided me in getting ye on the horse so I could ferret ye back home."

The revelation gave Alasdair pause, but then he waved his momentary loss of sound judgment away. "She stabbed me, plain and simple."

"Ah, Alasdair, my boy," Father Bernard said, as he suddenly appeared behind Brodick and slapped a big, meaty palm on Brodick's shoulder. Father Bernard had been the clan priest since before Alasdair had been born, and he always seemed to appear out of thin air. Alasdair never could understand why Da had put the man on the clan council. He drank too much mead, and he frequently fell asleep at the most inopportune times—like in the middle of a council meeting he should be paying attention to—but his da had adamantly sworn the man was astute and had often come up with solutions to problems no one else could think of. Alasdair had not once himself seen an example of this, and the one time he'd asked his da to provide some examples, his da had told him to give people grace and to simply watch, and eventually he would see.

"Father Bernard, what can I do for ye?"

"'Tis what I can do for ye that brings me here," the man replied as he produced a mug from behind his back, took a big sip, and let out a large burp.

Alasdair's patience was dangerously close to expiring. "Father, we're in the middle of an important conversation. Come back," he said, more as an order than a request, and though the man didn't move to do as Alasdair had directed, Alasdair turned his attention back to Brodick. "I am nae of the mindset to trust Maeve MacKenzie or wed her, but I dunnae have a choice about the second one. The problem is," he said, shoving a hand through his hair as his frustration started to mount, "I think I may have underestimated how difficult it will be to get her to consent to wed me."

Lara snorted. "I told ye yer plan was daft."

"Ye actually agreed to my plan," he said, glaring at his sister.

She pursed her lips at him. "*After* I told ye it was daft."

"I dunnae have time to argue with ye," he snapped. "I'm thinking the best course of action is for me to make the lass think I'm besotted by her, and—"

"That may actually be a problem," Lara said, taking a step backward as a guilty look settled upon her face.

"Lara, ye did nae meddle, did ye?" There weren't enough fingers and toes in this room to cover all the times Lara had meddled and made matters worse.

"*Meddle* is such a nasty word," Lara replied. "I went on a mission to aid ye—aid us."

"God's blood," he moaned. "What did ye do?"

"Brodick did it, too!" she cried, pointing at Brodick whose jaw slipped momentarily open before he clamped it shut and pointed back at her. For being a hardened warrior, Lara seemed to have a knack for making the man speechless.

"She bribed me!" Brodick finally burst out. "I did nae have a choice."

Alasdair's nostrils flared, as did his temper. "I dunnae care who made whom do what," he growled. Those two had been getting into trouble together since his sister was old enough to keep up with Brodick, and it was often hard to tell who had led whom in the misadventure. "Tell me what ye have done, Lara."

"Well," Lara replied, nibbling on her lip for a moment and then casting a glance at Brodick.

Brodick threw up his hands. "Dunnae look at me. I was nae in the cell with ye. I—"

"The cell?" Alasdair asked, almost afraid to hear what this was about.

"Mama ordered Maeve locked in the dungeon."

"And ye allowed it?" Alasdair demanded, looking between Lara and Brodick.

"Have ye ever tried to stop yer mama when she's set her mind to something?" Brodick asked. Before Alasdair could answer that question, Brodick said, "she's grieving Tavish's toe still, too. She's all worked up over it."

Alasdair frowned in confusion. He knew he'd been sick, but Brodick's statement made no sense. "Ye mean Tavish's leg? The one he lost?"

"'Twas a miracle," Father Bernard boomed, reminding

Alasdair the man was even still there.

"What was?" Alasdair demanded, starting to feel irritable with the conversation.

"Anise did nae have to take his leg. She only had to take a big toe," Father Bernard pronounced.

"A big toe. Toe, did ye say? A toe?" Alasdair could hardly believe his ears.

"Aye," Lara said, "but ye would have snatched Maeve anyway, aye?"

Would he have? Believing his brother was losing a leg because he'd been shot had propelled Alasdair to go forward with the plan he'd thought of, but even without believing Tavish was going to lose his leg, Alasdair would have gone forward with his plan. Maeve's family was responsible for the dire situation his clan now faced and she was the only solution he could see. "Aye," he said, not feeling good about the answer. "I would have. Wedding her is our best hope for peace, men, and nae to starve this winter. So what did ye do, Lara?"

"I told Maeve the truth." Lara took another step away from him. Smart lass. Alasdair had the urge to ring his sister's neck.

"Why did ye go and do that?"

Lara pointed at Father Bernard. "He told me I should come up with another plan because yer fool plan would nae ever work. He said every MacKenzie he'd ever come across was stubborn as the day is long and the one look he'd gotten at Maeve told him she'd rip off her own fingernails afore she'd wed ye."

Father Bernard frowned as Alasdair glared at him. "When the devil did I tell ye that?" the priest bellowed at Lara.

"Last night," she said sweetly. "Ye dunnae remember? I

spoke with ye after supper when Mama would nae allow the servants to take a tray of food to Maeve."

"Maeve has nae been given food?" The information infuriated Alasdair. Never, in his plan, had he intended to starve the lass, enemy or not.

Father Bernard waved a hand. "I saw to it right afore I came to see ye. I sent a servant girl to take her a tray. She did nae want to go because of Lady MacRae's order, but I assured the girl she'd go to hell if the MacKenzie lass died of starvation."

"Ye're a wily old devil," Brodick commented, grinning.

Father Bernard looked rather pleased with himself. "Thank ye." He glanced around at Brodick, Lara, and Alasdair as the man's cheeks reddened. "I do believe I must have been overserved last night," he said, clearing his throat. "I dunnae exactly recall telling Lara to come up with another plan. But if I did—"

"Ye did!" Lara said and stomped her foot.

"If I did," the priest said, twisting his mouth into a funny pinched state before releasing it, "I'm certain I meant for ye to get the approval of yer brother—yer laird." Alasdair suddenly saw what his father had meant about Father Bernard being coming up with solutions to problems no one else had thought of. The priest was quietly cunning.

"Ye did nae say that," Lara grumbled.

"Exactly what did ye say to Maeve?" Alasdair asked his sister.

Lara sucked her lower lip in and stared at him with a sullen look for a moment before releasing it with a pop. "I told her ye meant to persuade her to wed ye so our clan would have an alliance with hers. I told her ye wanted peace."

Alasdair's right eye began to twitch. "What did she say?"

"She said she could nae wed ye because she dunnae even ken ye, and I told her she should get to ken ye."

Lara stood there silently, which made him want to bellow at her. She also had the exasperating habit of not finishing her stories. "And?" he demanded, the word clipped.

Lara narrowed her eyes. "And she said she did nae think so, but she'd ensure Colin Fraser gave his word that there would be peace between our clans. So ye see," Lara said, grinning, "I did ye a favor by going to her."

"I'd like ye to note here," Brodick said, "That I told Lara it was nae a good idea."

"Ye did nae!" she cried out.

"I seem to clearly remember saying this plan was about as clot-heided as yer brother's."

"Ye did nae ever say that," Lara snapped.

The mutinous expression she wore was the final cut to the strings of Alasdair's temper. "Lara," he bellowed now, "the last thing I can allow is for her to wed Colin Fraser. The Frasers have proven repeatedly that they are nae honorable, and of course she would say she'll elicit a vow from Fraser for peace! She'd say anything for me to let her go! Ye've nae aided me at all. Ye have made things worse!"

Lara glared at him. "I was trying to help!"

"Well, ye did nae! Now what am I to do? She'll nae ever consent to wed me."

"She would if she did nae ken that was what she was consenting to," Father Bernard said.

"What?" Alasdair looked to the priest.

"'Tis why I came to see ye," Father Bernard replied. "Yer mama told me of yer plan, and I kenned right away it would nae work."

Alasdair wasn't certain if he was offended or curious to

hear what the priest had to say, and since being offended would not aid him at all, curiosity won out. "Why do ye nae simply tell me exactly how I'm to get an astute lass to consent to wed me without realizing that's what she'd be doing. And then even if that did work, what after that?"

"All she has to say is 'aye' and 'I do,' and give me her name and yer name. 'Tis nae hard." Father Bernard shrugged. "The hardest part is getting the binding strip wrapped around both yer hands, but ye leave that to me." He winked. "I'll think o' something."

"Father Bernard, ye are a surprising man," Alasdair said.

The priest looked almost as if he was getting misty eyes. "Yer da used to say that."

Alasdair had a flash of memory of his da and Father Bernard sitting in the great hall all alone in front of the fire before many a council meeting. Had they been plotting? Alasdair suspected they had.

"Father," Lara said, "'tis it nae a sin to trick the lass into wedding my brother?"

"What would be a sin is to let the lass wed a Fraser," Father Bernard pronounced.

"She thinks Colin Fraser honorable," Lara said.

"She's misinformed," Alasdair, Brodick, and Father Bernard said at the same time.

"Fine, fine," Lara replied, "but what of redemption?"

"Lara, are ye on my side or nae?" Alasdair demanded.

"Of course I'm on yer side. I'm merely asking a few questions that she may eventually ask."

"Maeve MacKenzie has been betrothed to Colin Fraser for five years now," Father Bernard said. "If she loved the man, she would have already wed him. I happen to ken her da wanted her to do so for the alliance, or at least he did half a year ago. So, kenning all this, I'd say it's safe, if we're considering serving God's will, to accept that it is nae Maeve's lot in life to be the light to guide Colin Fraser away from the dark. I think God has other plans for her."

Alasdair stared at Father Bernard in shocked amazement. It took him a moment to decide exactly what he wanted to ask. "How do ye ken how long Maeve has been betrothed to Colin Fraser?"

Father Bernard blushed, which was a sight, given the man always had a rosy appearance anyway due to his fondness for mead and wine. "My cousin Beitris MacKenzie used to be Maeve's nanny." He shrugged. "She's head of the kitchens now. We exchange missives every now and again."

"Ye kinnae tell her Maeve is here," Alasdair said.

The priest scowled at him. "I'm nae a clot-heid, Alasdair."

"Nay, of course nae," Alasdair replied. Father Bernard was a man of many unexpected layers. "How did yer cousin come to be a MacKenzie, and why did ye nae ever say as much?"

"She wed into the clan, but her husband died nearly right after they were wed, right around the same time Maeve MacKenzie was born. After the lass's mother passed, Beitris was appointed her nanny. She's fiercely loyal to the MacKenzie, so there was nae any point mentioning she was my cousin because she would nae have been willing to aid us with them."

Wedding Maeve was supposed to be simply to aid his clan, yet hearing she lost her mother as well as her father stirred that protective feeling he'd had before, which was laughable considering she'd stabbed him.

"What's so amusing?" Brodick asked.

Alasdair blinked. He'd not even realized he'd laughed aloud. "Nae anything ye'd understand," he replied because he didn't want to admit he'd been thinking about Maeve and he didn't quite understand what was happening with him and his thoughts toward her. It was as if hearing these few pieces of information on her history softened him toward her and reminded him he had once truly been intrigued by her.

"When do ye want to try to perform the ceremony?" Alasdair asked the priest.

The man grinned at him and produced the traditional white MacRae marriage binding from his robe. "I'd say the sooner the better, aye?"

"Aye," Alasdair agreed. "Once Maeve and I are wed, we can ride to her home to let it be kenned that I'm their new laird."

"Ye ken it will nae be as easy as that," Brodick said.

"I ken," Alasdair replied.

Father Bernard swiped a hand across his face. "It seems to me it would be best if ye could win the lass over after ye wed her so she will give ye her full support in taking control of her clan. It will make it much easier to gain her council's support if they ken she is in full favor of it. Though the castle will be hers as heir, gaining her favor would go far in avoiding possible war."

"Ye want me to woo her, in truth? The enemy?"

Father Bernard put a hand on Alasdair's shoulder. "I want ye to do what ye must for the clan. I did nae say ye have to develop a tendre for the lass, but I saw her in the courtyard. She's lovely. Wooing her should nae be such a hardship, and once ye have control of Eilean Donan and the MacKenzie men, well, then ye can decide how ye wish to proceed with her."

"I dunnae," he said tersely. "She's proven so far to be a MacKenzie through and through."

"Dunnae forget she aided me to get ye here," Brodick added, to which Alasdair nodded.

"Maeve believes our clan was the one to start the conflict with hers," Lara said.

"Why do ye think that?" Alasdair asked.

"Because she told me so. She said that we were the ones to strike first, which was why her da joined the Fraser clan in raiding us."

"That's a lie, and ye ken it," Alasdair snapped.

"I ken it," Lara replied, "but she dunnae. She believes it. Likely her da told her the lie."

"Aye," Alasdair agreed, scrubbing a hand across his face. "Shall we go let my future wife out of her cell so she can be wed?"

"Aye," Father Bernard said with a wink.

"I'm coming, as well," Lara said.

"I'll nae be left behind," Brodick added.

"Should we fetch Mama?" Lara asked.

Alasdair shook his head. "If I'm to win over Maeve until I have control of her clan, it may be wise to keep her and Mama apart given Mama despises all MacKenzies."

"Good point," Lara said.

"Aye," Brodick added, "and she did try to have Maeve beheaded," he added casually, as Lara opened Alasdair's bedchamber door.

"What?" Alasdair bellowed. "Why did ye nae start with that fact?"

Lara and Brodick shrugged in unison, glanced at each other, and Alasdair could have sworn it was like a secret, unsent message passed between them. But that could not be. The effects of his fever had to still be lingering and muddling his thoughts. "So it's decided," Lara said. "We'll keep Mama away from her." On that last word the door swung all the way open, and on the other side of the threshold stood their mother.

She narrowed her gaze upon them as if they were still children. "Ye'll keep me away from whom?"

Alasdair, Lara, and Brodick all said a different lass's name, but Father Bernard said, "The MacKenzie lass."

When Alasdair shot him a glare, he said, "Sorry, Alasdair, but as a man of God, I kinnae tell a lie."

"That did nae ever stop ye afore," Alasdair snapped.

"I dunnae why ye were trying to keep me away from that woman, but ye need nae bother."

"Mama, Maeve better still have her head," Alasdair bit out, joking, but his mother's indifferent look made his chest go tight. "Mama, please tell me ye did nae do something rash."

"Nae a thing," she retorted. "Maeve MacKenzie is gone. I went to speak with her a moment ago to tell her she'd nae ever be welcome here truly, even if she was yer wife, and she was nae there. The cell door was open. The guard said he'd gone to relieve himself, and when he came back, he found the door that way. Seems she picked the lock."

"God's blood!" Alasdair thundered. "We have to get to her afore she gets home!"

Chapter Seven

*M*aeve could hardly believe how easy it had been to get out of the cell and even the castle. Then again, she thought as she moved silently through the empty shadowy courtyard, she could believe it. She had not passed a single guard—not one. There had not even been a guard stationed outside her cell. She'd been prepared to have to sneak or fight, but there had been no need. And it had been the same throughout the castle. Her father would have had a fit if their castle had been guarded so poorly. But the MacKenzies had the necessary warriors to keep their castle secure and their prisoners where they were supposed to be. It seemed at least part of what Brodick MacRae had told her was the truth: the MacRaes were indeed in desperate need of men. This castle would be easy to take in its current state.

Maeve moved from shadow to shadow, staying close to the walls, but there didn't appear to be a need to worry. The outer and inner courtyards were bereft of people. It would not have been totally surprising to find no one here but the guards, as she had heard the call for supper and assumed all the clanspeople were in the great hall, but to have no guards in the inner courtyard was foolish. She moved easily out of the inner courtyard and through the doors to the outer courtyard, and she looked up ahead to the one good gatehouse and the one crumbling one. Two torches burned bright in holders on either side of the still standing gatehouse, and she could see it was manned.

She quickly assessed the situation and decided her best hope for getting by the guard was to create a distraction to his right and then slip past him on the left. She bit her lip, thinking. It had taken a half day to get here from her home, which meant on foot it would likely take her an entire day, which meant she would be spending the night in the woods—alone. She didn't relish the thought, but trying to find the stables and take her horse back was not an option. Even if she could manage to get her destrier back, she'd be much easier to spot leaving the castle on horseback than slipping away on foot. And though, currently, the only guard around to come after her would be the one in the tower, she imagined all it would take was a blow on a horn for him to summon other MacRae men, including Alasdair. Something about the man—perhaps it was the hard glint in his eye or the way he'd boldly come to her land and snatched her—told her once he was on her trail, he'd not be easy to lose, and if he caught her again, escaping would not be nearly so easy.

She bent down to gather a handful of rocks to throw. Of course, Alasdair could well be abed still from the wound she'd given him. A rush of guilt filled her, but she dismissed it. She refused to feel another moment of guilt over defending herself from being taken against her will. Lara MacRae's claim that it had been Maeve's clan to start the feud between their families came to her unbidden and somewhat unwanted. That could not be true, and yet, some clan had indeed invaded this castle and left the MacRaes in desperate need of coin and men. And if Lara was telling the truth about her father being found pushed off a cliff with a piece of the MacKenzie plaid clutched in his hands, who was responsible, really, for that? Certainly not Maeve's father.

Now that Maeve's thoughts were turning, she could not stop them. Questions pelted her mind one after another like what of Lara's claim that Alasdair took Maeve to wed her for peace? Likely lies to get Maeve to wed him so he could simply take her land, and yet, the smallest sliver of doubt was in her gut. Maeve swallowed as her thoughts tumbled, and she shifted from foot to foot with the weight of the anxiousness settling on her shoulders. It was entirely too bad being anxious did not keep one warm. There were decisions to be made, such as whether to demand Colin give her his vow to keep peace with the MacRaes in order for her to consent to wed him, or whether she should lead an army herself on an attack against the MacRaes for daring to take her. Now was not the time to make such decisions. She needed to escape before decisions were made for her and not by her.

She took all but two of the rocks in her hand and slung them as hard as she could at the right side of the guard tower, and then she prepared to run.

"Ho!" came a voice from within the tower, and then the door was slung open and Darby appeared. He went to the right side of the tower, as she had hoped he would, and then she slung the last two rocks toward the woods and prayed he would investigate. For a long moment, he stared into the woods but did not make a move to go to them, and she feared he'd not do so, but then he swore and stomped off toward the thick woods. She stared narrow-eyed after him. If she ran this castle, the first thing she'd do was release that man from his duties. He clearly did not care whether he performed them well or not. She watched until he disappeared, and then she ran past the guard tower and down the long bridge that went from the castle, across the water, and to the mainland.

From either side of the bridge, the swish of water rolling on itself filled the air and the fresh smell of the loch water rose to tickle her nose. She should have tried to steal a birlinn. It would have gotten her home much faster, but no, if they had guards in their guard tower, she would have been far too easy to spot. She ran down the length of the bridge and stopped at the foot of it, trying to recall which way they had come from. She was almost certain it had been from the right.

She followed the path to the right into the woods, shoving stray branches out of her way as she went. Her heart thundered in her ears, and at any moment she expected someone to stop her by grabbing her from behind. She ran as fast as she could over land that was gnarled with vines and holes where rain had worn away the ground. Twice she fell into a hole, going down once on her knee so hard that she cried out. The next time her foot slipped into a hole, her ankle twisted sharply to the right, sending searing pain along her foot and up the length of her leg.

Her first attempt to stand back up caused her eyes to flood with tears and made her release a hiss, but she pushed through, gritting her teeth, and tried again. If she stayed here, she had no doubt she'd be wed to Alasdair MacRae by the morning if she could not resist whatever torture they devised to force her to agree to the match. She tentatively set her foot down once more and pressed, crying out at the searing pain that shot through her foot once again.

She sat with a thud on the ground, drew up her uninjured leg, and rested her head against her forearms. Her nostrils flared as she breathed in and out, unable to concentrate with her fast breaths and rapid heartbeat. She forced her breaths to slow down, her nostrils flaring with her effort. After a short while, her heart returned to a somewhat normal rhythm, the speed of her breathing decreased, and she could think in a reasonably logical manner.

The healer at her castle had wrapped such wounds on warriors when they needed to train but complained of pain in an ankle or foot. With that in mind, she straightened herself up and gathered the edge of her gown in her hands, glad to find it ripped at one spot, and she gave a mighty tug. The material tore, and after a moment of effort, she had a complete strip removed from the front edge of her gown. She wrapped it around her ankle, and though her skin pulsed underneath the material, when she put weight upon her right foot with care, the pain wasn't nearly as bad as it had been.

It took some grunting and several tries to hoist herself out of the hole, and when she finally was standing on level ground again, dampness covered her brow, underneath her arms, and down her back. She trembled with the cold of her own sweat and the way it made her gown cling to her, but that was a minor problem. The start back toward home was slow going at first, every step making her ankle throb more, but after a while, an unexpected numbness took hold of her ankle so that she almost couldn't even feel the pain.

She followed the path around thick brush and up a rocky incline, gripping sharp ledges that cut into her palms as she went. She hadn't realized just how treacherous the terrain was on the way here, as she now understood that the horse had taken most of the punishment of the grueling journey, despite Maeve having thought she had. Her bottom certainly had ached, but the biggest ache she had now that her ankle was numb was in her gut. She'd not eaten anything since she'd been snatched two days ago. When her stomach gave an impatient growl, her regret over being so stubborn as to not eat the food the MacRae guard had offered her was so powerful she whimpered with it. As soon as she got home, before she even had a proper conversation, she was going to eat a mince pie and a trencher of bread sopped in that warm rich sauce that Beitris made.

Birds suddenly rustled from trees overhead, flying out of the branches in loud squawks to fill the night sky. Worry exploded and nearly choked her. Birds were smart. They always took flight before danger, which meant danger was near. She pushed herself harder, racing almost blindly up the path, or at least she thought she was still on the path. It was nearly impossible to tell in the dark. The light from the moon had been swallowed by the trees overhead, and as the limbs she pushed out of the way got thicker, her certainty that she'd accidentally ventured off the path grew. She shoved a branch out of the way, only to have part of it fly back before she'd gotten past, and it had left a stinging scrape across her right cheek. She brought her fingers up to her cheek as she ran, and the warm stickiness of blood met her fingertips.

But she could not slow. There was a growing sense of being followed punctuated by more birds taking flight out of the trees, and when she slowed to jump over a log, she was still long enough that vibrations from the ground seeped through her tattered, thin slippers. She recognized those vibrations—horses, many of them, and there was no doubt in her mind it was—

"Maeve MacKenzie!" Alasdair MacRae boomed out, obliterating any slight hope she might have held.

She let out a yelp, slapped a palm over her mouth to stop herself from doing so again, looked wildly around the darkness, and with no help for it, plunged ahead. She didn't bother to shove the branches out of the way. Twigs crunched underfoot as she raced ahead, her breath coming in gasps and a pinch taking hold of her side. She stumbled over vines, landed knees first against the nearly frozen ground, and grunted with the force of the hit. Pain vibrated into her bones, making her clench her teeth. Cold seeped into her palms as well as strong vibrations. Her pursuers were closer. She gained her feet just as Alasdair called out to her again.

"I dunnae mean ye harm, Maeve, but harm will come to ye in these woods. Stop where ye are."

She bolted forward with a cry, as an odd gust of wind hit her face, but there was no time to ponder it. She plowed through the thick vines before her, cried out when one caught her hair and ripped some out with her forward motion, and then confusion hit. As the overgrowth disappeared, the moon filled the space, and she stepped forward onto nothing. A scream ripped from her throat as she fell off a ledge.

Chapter Eight

*H*er frightened scream came as he gave the order to dismount to climb the path to Devil's Cliff. "God's blood," he swore. He hit the ground with a thud and didn't pause. He was climbing, hand over foot, even as he bellowed for his men to follow. Brodick didn't have to be told twice. His friend matched his pace as they raced up through the woods to the ledge.

"Do ye think she fell?" Brodick asked, his words coming out in little jerks.

"Aye," Alasdair replied, grimness almost lodging the word in his throat. If Maeve met her death this night because he had taken her, he would never forgive himself. His aim had been peace, not to kill the lass. And though he wasn't particularly pleased with her currently—and the idea of being chained to her for life, no matter how bonny she was, didn't appeal, given what her clan had done to his—he had not meant her harm.

He set a dizzying pace to the top, shoving through the branches that barred the path to the very short clearing that appeared right before Devil's Cliff. It was called this for good reason. Many had met their death here, not knowing the land and not suspecting a steep cliff hidden by the thick woods.

"Help!"

Her voice washed over him, and the relief that flooded

his veins made him momentarily weak kneed and that made him frown.

"Help!" she cried again.

He ran to the ledge, looked down, and located the shadow of her frame to his right. He could hardly believe his eyes. She was dangling there in mid-air. What the devil was she holding on to? "Dunnae let go!" he commanded as he fell to his belly directly in front of her.

"Do ye honestly think ye need to tell me nae to let go?" she said just as he reached over and grasped her around both her wrists.

"I dunnae ken what I need to tell ye, woman," he bit out, searching for a place to brace himself so he could haul her up. He found none, cursing, and then felt two hands clamp down on the back of his calves.

"Go on and haul her up," Brodick said, pushing down hard on Alasdair.

Alasdair pulled hard, his biceps burning as he inched her up until her head was in view and then her face. He couldn't quite see her expression given the poor light and her hair hanging in her face, but a string of unladylike curses poured from her lips. He gave her another tug, and then she was fairly scrambling over him, using his body to get all the way on land. He didn't mind. He knew she was frightened half out of her wits, and the knowledge was confirmed when she collapsed onto her back and lay there panting.

"I almost died," she whispered, and the tremble in her voice did something odd to him. His stomach clenched at her words. She was right, and he was suddenly livid with her. He didn't give a damn whether it was unreasonable or not.

"Ye did almost die, ye foolish lass. Why did ye think ye could run blindly through dark woods that are unknown to ye?"

"I dunnae," she retorted, her words dripping with sarcasm. "Mayhap I felt I did nae have a choice since ye kidnapped me, and yer mother tried to have me beheaded!"

She had a point, but he'd eat dirt before admitting it. "If ye'd nae stabbed me, she would nae have tried to have ye beheaded," he retorted, not caring that the statement was ridiculous. He could not seem to think past the fact that Maeve had almost died, and it was making logic hard to grasp. He gritted his teeth and came to his knees as his men started to pour onto the ledge from their climb.

"If ye had nae kidnapped me, ye stubborn, highhanded Highlander, I would nae have needed to stab ye!" she bellowed just as Father Bernard appeared on the ledge.

"Maeve MacKenzie!" he cried out. "Are ye okay? I'm the priest of the MacRae clan," he said, his voice both soothing and authoritative. Alasdair's lips parted as he stared at the priest. The man was like one of those wood insects that changed color to match their surroundings.

"A priest!" she exclaimed and clambered into a sitting position. "Did ye ken I was taken against my will?"

"Aye, lass," Father MacRae said, kneeling beside her. "I'm here to help ye. Alasdair asked me to come on the search for ye, to aid him."

"Oh, thank the gods," she cried out, then unexpectedly leaned over and threw her arms around Alasdair. He stilled with surprise, and then instant desire smacked him full on. She was all softness and silky skinned, and she smelled like sin to come—sweet, tangy, and spicy. "Ye came to yer senses!" she said. Her head was turned just enough toward Alasdair's neck that when she spoke, her warm breath wafted over his skin like a caress, and he had the ill-timed wish to see if her lips were as warm and sweet as he remembered.

"Are ye hurt anywhere?" Father Bernard asked.

Maeve pulled away from Alasdair, and the loss he felt unnerved him. "My hands are scratched up, and my cheek, and I twisted my ankle, I do believe."

"Laird, see to her hands," Father Bernard ordered and shoved the binding strip at Alasdair.

Alasdair almost laughed aloud. This man was crafty. Alasdair intended to seek his counsel a great deal more from this day forward. He took the strip and carefully wrapped it around both their hands, Brodick bending beside him, and finishing the awkward deed for him.

"This is nae necessary," Maeve sputtered. "I dunnae think my hands are that scathed."

Alasdair ran his thumb on her inner palm and could not stop the smile that tugged up the corners of his mouth at the soft hiss that escaped her. His touch affected her. It shouldn't matter at all to him, but he found it did. He always had carried too much pride inside him.

"Let the laird atone for the injuries he caused," Father Bernard said. "Aye, Maude."

"It's Maeve," she replied. "Maeve MacKenzie."

"I was just testing ye," he said with a chuckle. "Sometimes a great scare can make a person forget things. Do ye recall who this is?" Father Bernard asked, pointing at Alasdair.

"Of course," she scoffed. "That's the devil."

Brodick burst out laughing, as did several of Alasdair's men. Alasdair cleared his throat. "Poor wee, feeble-minded lass," he said, making his voice purposely provoking. If he judged Maeve correctly all those years ago, she would not take kindly to being thought weak, and she'd likely do all she could to prove him wrong. "She kinnae recall my name, but 'tis to be expected. Women are such weak creatures."

"Ye are an offensive creature," she bit out. "I recall who ye are perfectly, Alasdair MacRae."

His name was a curse on her lips, but all the same, he found himself grinning.

"Ah, good. Good, lass," Father Bernard said. "So ye ken him still?"

"Of course I ken him."

"And ye want him to take ye home?"

"Aye. I want him to take me—"

"Excellent!" Father Bernard interrupted. "Ye want him to take ye, so he shall, with God as the witness."

"Ye are a strange man," she muttered.

"Ye recall yer name, dunnae ye, Laird?"

"Of course he recalls his name," Maeve bellowed.

"She's right," Alasdair replied. "I was nae injured, this time, Father. The hellion did nae have a dagger upon her." His men snickered, and she glowered at him.

"If ye'd be so kind as to prove yer mind is sound afore we travel," Father Bernard said, his tone as smooth as silk.

Maeve leaned toward Alasdair and whispered, "Yer priest is touched in the head."

"Aye," he whispered back, hoping she did not detect the amusement he was struggling to contain. "Best to indulge him so he'll leave us be." When she nodded, Alasdair said, "I'm Alasdair MacRae, and afore ye ask, this is Maeve MacKenzie."

"She wants ye," Father Bernard said. "Do ye want her?"

"Father," Maeve started to say, but Alasdair interrupted.

"Aye, Father," he replied, giving Maeve's hands, which were cupped between his, a little squeeze. Partly it was to calm her and make her think he was simply indulging the priest, and partly, he realized with shock, he wanted to soothe her. She would be his wife, and whether he had wanted that or not, the impact of it was hitting him. Whether he thought her his enemy or not, she would be his wife, and that meant he would protect her with everything within him, down to his last breath. "I want her." And the way his body hardened at the thought made it seem more truth than lie.

"Excellent," the priest cried out. "'Tis done!" A cheer went up all around them from his men.

"What's done?" Maeve asked, and the confusion in her voice touched on his protective instinct again.

"Maeve," Alasdair said, wishing wholeheartedly that they were alone now. He had said he would not care one bit about her feelings. He had said he would put her aside, treat her as his enemy, but he couldn't do that. He wanted to judge her on her own merit and not the actions of her clan. "There's nae an easy way to tell ye this, lass."

"Just spit it out."

"Ye're my wife now."

Chapter Nine

*I*nstinct took over, but what a poor instinct it was. She tried to bolt from Alasdair, but in her haste and disbelief, she forgot they were bound hand to hand. She jerked back so hard that she pulled him on top of her. She lay trapped under his hard, hot body with the cold ground pressing into her back, and her ears ringing from the hit her head took when it met the dirt.

"We kinnae be wed!" But as her mind raced through what had just occurred, disbelief gripped her. She'd given her name, and his, and that wily priest had twisted her words and gotten her to say she wanted Alasdair. "Ye!" she seethed. "Ye tricked me."

"Aye, lass, and I'm sorry, but there was nae another way. I could tell ye were nae going to wed me of yer own accord."

"Get off me!" she bellowed.

"Brodick," he bit out. The one order was all that was needed. Alasdair's man was beside them, even as Alasdair rolled onto his side and took her with him onto hers. For one breath, all she was aware of, all that it was possible to be aware of, was him. The length of their bodies were pressed against each other with their hands bound between them. She could feel that he was made of corded muscle from his head to his toes, and his undeniable strength stirred something in her she didn't care to think about in this moment. She hated him, yet she had the flash of a memory of him letting her kill the Black Boar.

He was her enemy, yet they had never done anything to each other specifically. It was more accurate to say their families were enemies. She didn't know him well enough to know if she hated him truly or if she should truly consider him her enemy. They had once stood in the woods, naive of who the other was, and made a connection that had filled her with hope, made her dream, and stayed with her for quite a long time. Even as all these thoughts poured through her head, Brodick worked to unbind them. The bindings grew loose, and then Brodick slid them away.

She drew her hands back to her and pressed up into a sitting position to bring her knees to her chest. She laid her forehead against her knees and sniffed. She was tired, and hungry, and in pain, and now she was wed. He had taken her against her will, and now he had tricked her into wedding him. "Why?" she croaked, tears filling her eyes and making her throat ache.

"Leave us," he commanded. She did not look up. She did not want his men to see her at her weakest. She did not want him to, either.

Silence stretched, and she decided he was not going to deign to answer her, but then he inhaled a long breath and said, "I ken ye will likely nae believe me, but for peace. I need our clans to be at peace. I need an ally against the Frasers."

"They would nae be yer enemy, nor would we, if ye would quit raiding our land."

"We only raided yer land and theirs because ye both raided ours first."

"That's a lie," she said, misery making her head ache.

"Nay, Maeve. What ye believe is a lie. Ye have nae been

given the truth. I vow it to ye."

She jerked her head up and turned to glare at him, wishing he could get the full effect of her anger, but she knew he couldn't because she could not fully make out his expression. "I'm supposed to take yer word?" she spat.

"Nay. Nae yet. But I hope eventually."

"Hope is for fools," she muttered, biting her lip at having said a sentence that might have revealed too much of what she held hidden inside.

"Hope is for the brave, Maeve."

She didn't like that he sounded sincere. She didn't like that he sounded truly regretful. She didn't like that it felt as if her anger was cooling a smidgen. She wanted to burn with it. She wanted it to make her sweat. She'd been used! She wanted to blast him with the heat of her ire. He had taken her choice away from her. Though, in all honesty, she had not wanted to wed Colin, either. She would have, though, out of a sense of duty to her father and what he had wanted for her. What he had been willing to give up for her.

"Who told ye that clot-heided lie?" she asked, refusing to give, refusing to meet him even a slither.

"My da." The words were quiet and filled with emotion she could not deny, but she wanted to. God above knew she wanted to.

She pressed her lips together on responding. She might feel the slightest something for him. It was, in all likelihood, pity at the lengths to which desperation had driven him, and well, the smallest, tiniest bit of memory of the yearning he had once awoken in her. But in this moment, she hated him for that as well. "My da always said only the bravest of souls had hope... I'm sorry about yer mama, Maeve."

She frowned as the old, familiar knot lodged simultaneously in her throat and gut. "What do ye ken about my mama?" Each word was punctuated with all the unfriendliness she could muster.

"I ken she died when ye were a wee one." Maeve swallowed at his words, but the knot in her throat refused to move. "I can only imagine the loss ye must feel from it."

"Ye dunnae ken a thing about the loss I feel."

"Nae fully, but I can relate to what it's like to lose a parent. Losing my da was verra hard."

"I'm sorry," she said. She reached out and set her hand on his forearm. His muscles twitched under her fingertips. Her eyes widened. She had no idea why she had done that except, enemies or not, in this moment they were two human beings bound by the shared experience of grief. No one walked through life without losing someone, but to hear sorrow in his voice that seemed to match hers made her feel less alone than she had in a long time.

When he put his large hand over hers, her breath hitched. "I will do my best for ye, Maeve."

"And what do ye ask in return? Dunnae tell me there was nae any part of ye that wanted revenge when ye think my father had yers murdered."

He sighed. "I'll nae tell ye that. It was a part of my plan in a sense. I thought to wed ye, get peace, and take control of yer clan so that I would gain the necessary warriors I need to keep my clan safe, and then live as I please without being concerned about ye."

"And now?" she asked, weariness pressing so hard on her that she yawned and closed her eyes for a moment.

"I kinnae explain it, but when I realized ye were about to become my wife, I kenned I would do everything I could to protect ye, and that includes treating ye with respect and as a true wife."

"Honeyed words to gain my cooperation, I suspect."

"I told ye long ago, Maeve, I dunnae need to use honeyed words to get a lass."

Her mouth slipped open that he remembered a bit of their conversation from the years before. She cleared her throat, refusing to be swayed so easily. "I'm nae a fool. Though, being duped into wedding ye so easily would say otherwise," she admitted with a laugh.

"Dunnae be too hard on yerself, lass. Ye were up against a formidable opponent."

"Ye think verra highly of yerself."

A rich, deep laugh came from him that tightened her belly and made her scowl at her reaction.

"I'm nae speaking of me," he said. "I'm talking about Father Bernard."

"Are ye trying to tell me this was Father Bernard's plan?"

"I'm nae *trying* to tell ye anything. I just did."

"I'll nae be confessing my sins to that man," she muttered, and as soon as the words left her mouth, she was struck with a memory that made her gasp.

"What is it?" Alasdair asked.

She couldn't tell him. It was the thing that would save her until she could escape. She recalled clearly Beitris talking about one of the king's foolish daughters who had thought to wed her appointed protector—a commoner. By the time the king's men had found them, they'd not consummated the marriage yet, so the marriage could be undone. It seemed the crafty Father Bernard had not thought of everything, and neither had Alasdair. A shiver of excitement coursed through her.

"Come," Alasdair said, standing and then holding his hand out to her. "I imagine ye're starving and in need of a bath and sleep."

Everything he said was true, but she could not allow herself to forget that he was her enemy. Or at least he was, of a sort. She wanted a choice in whom she wed, and she chose Colin for her da, since she knew she still could. All she had to do now was escape and then get the marriage dissolved by her priest. She bit her lip. What if Alasdair thought to make her his truly tonight? She had to do something to prevent that, but what? She needed to stall.

"Please, Maeve. I vow nae to hurt ye."

He had just unwittingly given her the perfect idea. She took his hand, and an odd warmth filled her as his fingers curled around hers. His hand was much larger, his fingers longer and wider as was his palm. She could feel the strength in his grip as he pulled her to her feet, and the minute she put weight on her right ankle, the pain came back like a clap of thunder. She cried out as it shook her entire body. She didn't have time to even pull her foot up before Alasdair had scooped her off her feet and against his chest.

"Yer ankle's bad, aye?"

"Aye," she admitted, not too proud in this moment to do so. Even if she wanted to try to escape again tonight, she couldn't walk, and now she knew that she needed to be extremely careful traveling through this land. "Alasdair," she said, "I'd like to ask something of ye—a gesture of goodwill to begin our marriage." She could be just as crafty as that priest and Alasdair.

"What would ye like to ask of me?"

The concern in his voice sounded so genuine that a small twinge of guilt went through her for the deception she was about to perpetrate, but it was not so strong as to make her change her mind. "I'd like to ask ye to give me a little time to get to ken ye afore we lie together." She was glad it had gotten even darker out. Her cheeks were on fire with the request she'd just voiced.

"Aye, Maeve. I'd like to get to ken ye better first, too."

"Ye would?" She couldn't help but be surprised by his admission. It wasn't that she thought all men were rutting beasts, but she'd heard the women in the kitchens talk about how men could not control themselves when they were truly attracted to a woman. Did that mean he didn't find her attractive anymore? The thought should be of no concern, but it was, despite her knowing if he didn't find her comely, it would be that much easier to keep their marriage in a state that could be dissolved.

"Aye, of course. I'm nae a barbarian, after all."

Chapter Ten

"Is yer wife snoring?" Brodick asked, pulling his horse up alongside Alasdair.

"Aye," Alasdair said, surprised he found it endearing. Everything about the way he had been reacting to Maeve since they were wed had been odd and not like him. He never thought things about women were endearing, except, well, that wasn't quite true, he realized. He had thought the way Maeve had bantered with him years before in the woods had been endearing, and her desire to hunt the Black Boar and her bravery in doing so had endeared her to him until he had discovered she was a MacKenzie.

"How long has she been asleep?" Brodick asked.

"Since nearly right after I put her on my horse and settled her between my thighs," Alasdair replied, unable to stop the memory of her soft bottom pressed firmly against him, nor could he stop his body's reaction to the memory. He was hard instantly.

"That's nae going to make for a verra exciting wedding night if she's asleep," Brodick said. "I suppose ye can wake her when we get to the castle, though."

"I'll be taking her to Anise to see about her injuries."

"And then ye'll have the bedding? The clan will wish to witness it."

"There will nac be a public bedding."

"Ye mean tonight?"

"I mean ever. I have nae ever liked that tradition, and as laird, I dunnae have to adhere to it if I dunnae wish."

"True. If proof is needed that ye did lay with her, Anise can examine her, and Athelston, as head of council, can be in the room to witness it."

His reaction to thinking of Athelston seeing Maeve in a compromising position was physical. His hands curled into fists, which caused Maeve to moan in her sleep because his right hand had been splayed on her belly. He resettled his hand there, aware instantly that he was sinfully pleased with how it calmed her immediately. "I'll nae have another man looking at my wife without her clothes on, poking her, prodding her, touching her. Nay."

"Ye're awfully possessive for a man who wed a woman to gain her lands and clan."

"What's mine is mine," he replied. In truth, the answer didn't sit well with him, yet he wasn't certain why. They rode in silence through the woods for a bit, his men and Father Bernard well enough ahead of them that the only noises in the woods were the night creatures and Maeve's soft snoring.

Brodick suddenly cleared his throat, and Alasdair barely held in his sigh. His friend was not one to let things go. It was a benefit at times and a detriment at others. "Ye ken there may come a time when Fraser demands proof that the marriage is good and true, and the king may well agree with Fraser that ye need to give it. I dislike politics as much as ye, but the king's right hand is a Fraser, and Robert bends the king's ear. Ye ken it as well as I do."

"Aye," Alasdair said, a sense of grimness gripping him. "I do. I have nae forgotten it was Robert who judged his clan could nae possibly have started the skirmishes with ours first."

"So what will ye do if that time comes?"

"I'd hope by then Maeve would have my bairn in her belly, but if nae, mayhap they'd take Maeve's word."

A derisive noise came from Brodick. "Ye honestly think that woman is going to speak up for ye?"

"Nae now," he said, thinking on the cunningness his wife had shown with her little act of claiming she wanted to become familiar with him before they made their marriage good and true. He'd heard the lie in her voice, which had pitched particularly high. He'd gone along with her attempt to deceive him because, in truth, he did not want to force her to his bed. That was not something he would ever do, no matter what was at stake. He'd realized when Father Bernard had come up with the plan that the marriage would need to be made true or she could plead to have it dissolved, but it had not occurred to him that Maeve would realize it as well.

It should have, though. She seemed uncommonly smart. Mayhap, one day, she could join him on the council as his mother had done with his da. Alasdair had always thought it was one of the reasons their marriage had been so happy and strong. They had listened to each other's opinions.

"So are ye going to woo yer wife? Is that what ye are saying?"

"I'm saying I'm nae concerned about it now," he snapped, not wishing to discuss a topic that involved feelings he hadn't sorted out. "My concern this night is for her injuries and comfort." And they'd be arriving at the stronghold soon. He could see the outline of the castle in the distance now because the moon shone down upon it.

"Are ye really going to have yer former mistress tend to yer new wife?" Brodick asked, his tone incredulous.

"Aye, that is her job as healer."

"She'll nae be pleased."

"Why should she care? I told her plainly we could nae wed when we started our liaison. She kenned I had to wed for land, men, and coin."

"If ye say so, but my experience has been different," Brodick replied. "What of after? Tomorrow? The next day? What do ye wish me to tell the men? Ye'll need to address the council and clan, too. Ye ken most will nae be pleased ye wed her, even if it will save us."

"I ken," Alasdair replied and scrubbed a hand over his face. "They will eventually accept her, and if nae, I'll command it."

Brodick snorted at that. "This will be amusing to watch. But mayhap she'll win them over with niceness."

It was Alasdair's turn to snort. "I'd nae hold yer breath on that hope. She's already plotting to escape me." Alasdair quickly told Brodick of Maeve's plea to become familiar with him before they lie together.

"Why did ye agree to that?" Brodick asked.

Alasdair brought his horse to a stop at the guard tower and motioned for Darby to come forth. This was the second grievous guarding error Darby had made in the last fortnight. Alasdair had not had time to speak with the man before going after Maeve, nor had there been a chance since returning, but it could not be put off a moment longer. The man had allowed Maeve to slip by him and away from the castle, and Alasdair wanted to know what the devil Darby had been doing.

"Alasdair?" Brodick prodded. "Why did ye agree to delaying the bedding?"

"Because I dunnae wish to bed my wife when she's nae ready."

"Women are funny creatures, aye?" Brodick said. "I kinnae understand why they think as they do."

"I was nae aware ye gave a moment's passing thought to why women think as they do," Alasdair said, watching Darby walk slowly toward them. The man's hesitant steps told Alasdair the guard knew well his mistake.

"A moment's," Brodick said, his answer sounding oddly evasive. "It was afore that if a woman was bonny and willing, I did nae care if I kenned her life beyond that."

"Afore?" Alasdair asked, intrigued. "Is there someone—"

"Nay," Brodick interrupted, but it was quick and curious. Still, Alasdair didn't question him. If there was a lass that Brodick had fallen for, he clearly did not have the desire to reveal it yet.

"Laird," Darby said, meeting Alasdair's gaze. "I'm sorry. I dunnae ken how she got past me."

Alasdair inhaled a long breath and held it for a moment, thinking exactly what he wanted to say. He needed to convey to Darby that he'd be demoted if he made another mistake, but he also felt responsibility as laird to aid the man. "What were ye doing when she slipped by ye?"

"I heard a sound in the woods, and I went to investigate it."

Alasdair nodded. "She used a verra simple tactic on ye to draw ye away from the guard tower, Darby. Ye should ken better than that. Let the enemy show their face, come to ye, and then ye defend."

"Aye, Laird. I recall my training from Athelston."

"Well, either ye were nae listening and heeding well or Athelston did nae train ye well. Which is it?"

A long, taut silence ensued, and Darby shifted from foot to foot, revealing his edginess. Alasdair understood the man's discomfort. He'd been put in a position to either face his shortcomings or reveal his superior's. Alasdair didn't believe for a moment that Athelston had failed to properly train the man. He'd seen his cousin teach enough warriors to know he was a good trainer.

"Athelston trained me well," the man said, but his tone was begrudging. "It's my own deficiencies. I suppose nae being worthy runs in my family."

The reference to the man's father surprised Alasdair. "Are ye trying to gain my pity?" he bluntly asked.

"Nay." The response was so fast and sharp that Alasdair believed it to be true.

"Then what?" Alasdair demanded.

Darby tugged a hand through his hair. "The men say ye put me as head of gate guard out of pity. I'm the only head of guard ye did nae personally train, and they say it's because ye thought less of me because of my da."

Alasdair glanced to Brodick, who confirmed it with a subtle nod. Alasdair let out a sigh. "I may have felt partly sorry for ye, but I dunnae think less of ye because of yer da. His mistakes are nae yer mistakes. I did nae personally train ye because I have been spread too thin," Alasdair admitted, "and that is my mistake. But I'm going to correct it."

"Truly?" Darby asked.

Alasdair heard the excitement in the man's tone. "Aye. Meet me by the water's edge tomorrow morning."

"Aye, Laird," Darby rushed out, showing his enthusiasm.

"When we're done training together, if Maeve, or anyone else, gets by ye again, ye and I will have a problem, ye ken?"

"Aye, Laird, I ken."

Alasdair gave his horse a nudge toward the castle with Brodick beside him. "I could have trained Darby tomorrow," Brodick said.

"Aye, I ken, but it needs to be me, and I've another duty for ye."

"What?"

"I want ye to gather two dozen of our best warriors, so ye will need to ferret out who that is exactly."

"What for?"

"To ready the castle for attack. I've nary a doubt that Colin Fraser will come here looking for Maeve. We'll be outmanned if we have nae brought any MacKenzie warriors into our ranks when it occurs, so we'll need to be crafty about how to ensure the stronghold dunnae fall to the Frasers if they will nae accept that Maeve is nae here."

"Mayhap the lass will fall to yer charms quickly," Brodick said.

The appeal of Maeve falling to his charms was surprisingly strong, and in that moment it had nothing to do with the advantage it would give him over the Frasers and everything to do with the lovely lass who was asleep in his arms. She shifted then, her head pressing more firmly under his chin, her bottom rubbing against his staff, and her heavy breasts moving against his arm. White-hot desire coursed through his veins, and he had to clench his teeth on hissing with the impact of the fresh yearning for her.

He tilted his head down as she whimpered a bit and pressed a gentle kiss to the top of her silky hair. He blinked afterward, surprised at himself. He couldn't even say what had made him do that, except there was tenderness stirring within him for the lass. He hoped it wouldn't be the thing to do him in.

They reached the castle shortly after, and he dismounted, bringing a groggy Maeve with him. She awoke in his arms, and when she turned her face up to him, with all the torches in the courtyard illuminating it, he saw her many injuries. She had a nasty cut on her right cheek that was caked with blood, and her gown was torn and filthy with ruby stains on the arms where she'd been injured and the blood had soaked through. Her lip was busted, likely from the fall over the ledge, and when she raised a hand to smooth her tangled hair, he saw her raw palm.

He caught it, turned it over, and grunted with displeasure. Then he bent his head and pressed a gentle kiss to the inside of her right palm and then the left. He felt Brodick's stare upon him, but he didn't care. Maeve's gaze burned into him as well. Raising his head, he met her eyes.

"Why did ye do that?" she asked, her voice and expression suspicious.

"Because I caused this." He gently touched a finger to each of her hands.

"Ye did? I'm the one who ran in the dark like a fool."

"Aye, but ye ran because I took ye. I vow to ye, Maeve, if there had been any other way to achieve peace and save my clan, I would have taken it."

"Ye could have come to declare yer intentions first," she said, her voice dry. "Ye could have asked to court me."

"Would ye have allowed me to do so?"

"Nay," she said, matter-of-fact. "Ye are my enemy."

"Ye mean I *was* yer enemy. Now I'm yer husband."

"Oh aye," she replied. "Wedding me by trickery changed my mind completely."

"Nay, I dunnae imagine it did, but I will do my best to change yer mind by being a good husband."

"Pretty words from a deceptive mouth."

"Much the same could be said of ye, lass."

"Alasdair!" came Anise's cry from across the courtyard. She was racing toward him even as he set Maeve down and motioned to Brodick. He did not want Anise to say anything that might make matters worse with Maeve, but she fairly shoved Maeve at Brodick in his haste to try to avert the storm and flung herself in his arms. "Tell me it's nae true!" she cried out. "Tell me ye did nae really go through with it and sacrifice yerself for us by wedding the MacKenzie lass."

"'Tis true," Maeve said from Brodick's hold. "So I'll kindly ask ye to disentangle yerself from my husband."

Chapter Eleven

Maeve could not even believe she'd said that. What had come over her? She should have been glad that the woman wanted Alasdair. It would keep his lust turned from her, and yet, she was not glad. She was… She was… She examined the emotion for a moment and bit the inside of her cheek in surprise as she felt her eyes widen. She was jealous! Clearly, her ordeal—being snatched, her hunger, her weariness, and nearly dying—had made her daft, and suddenly, she did feel particularly unwell. The ground seemed to shift underfoot, black appearing at the edges of her vision and bright specks dancing before her.

"I dunnae feel verra well," she mumbled as heat washed over her. The world felt as if it were sliding away, and the picture before her went dark.

Maeve awoke in confusion to Alasdair standing over her alongside the woman who had flung herself in Alasdair's arms.

"There," the woman said, pointing at Maeve. "I told ye she would be fine. Go on with ye now and let me examine her."

"Maeve," Alasdair said, leaning over her. The concern in his gaze and voice filled Maeve with a warmth she didn't welcome. She didn't want anything the man did to please her. It made things confusing. She clearly was still beset with daftness. Likely, it wouldn't disappear until she had sleep and food. "Anise is the castle healer."

"Is she now?" Maeve's voice came out in a croak. By the gods, she was thirsty. Alasdair immediately left her side, and the woman Anise stared down at Maeve. It was more likely this woman would try to poison her than heal her. It was obvious she had an active dislike for Maeve. Maeve sat up, not wishing to be lying down next to this woman.

Alasdair came back to her and held out a goblet. "Drink this. I imagine ye're thirsty."

"I am," she said, taking the goblet and not hesitating to take a gulp. It hit her mouth with a burst of strong, smoky flavors, along with honey and something that tasted of oats. She swallowed the liquid down, her eyes watering. The drink created a fiery path from her throat to her belly, making her cough. Alasdair immediately moved to her side and patted her gently on the back while Anise shot daggers through her. Maeve should have moved his arm off her when he slid it around her shoulder, but her petty side got the best of her. The woman had basically said wedding Maeve was a sacrifice for Alasdair, and that did not sit well with her.

"Drink it slow, aye. I doubt ye're used to anything this stout," Alasdair said.

"Whatever is it?" She brought the goblet up to her nose to smell the strong aromas. Her mouth immediately started to water in memory. Though the drink was indeed strong, it was delicious.

"'Tis Atholl Brose," Alasdair said. "My granda invented it.

"What's it made from?" Maeve asked, taking a very small sip this time. Again, flavors burst, but now, she swallowed without coughing, and a pleasant warmth seeped into her entire body. She sighed.

"Whiskey, oat, and honey."

Maeve nodded and took another sip, but this one was a bit bigger. Not only did she feel warm but she felt so happy that she giggled.

"Maeve," Alasdair said, plucking the goblet from her hands.

"Ho!" she cried out and reached for the goblet, but Alasdair walked it back over to the table where he'd poured it and set it down before turning back to her. She was struck at that moment with just how handsome he was. There was an inherent strength in the chiseled lines of his jaw and cheekbones, and his thick, dark locks gleamed in the light of the torches, lending a sort of wildness to him that offset the perfection of his face. Her gaze fell to his mouth, and she could feel the warmth and pressure of it from memory. That memory made her heart pound in an erratic rhythm and sent a dizzying current racing through her.

"Ye've a mouth for kissing," Maeve said and then hiccupped before heat singed her cheeks. She could not seem to keep her thoughts silent today.

Anise made a derisive sound, and Maeve would have loved to look away from Alasdair after saying such an embarrassing thing, but she did not want to appear weak. A slow, sensual smile pulled at his lips and made her blood leap from her heart and rush to her nether region. The feeling was so strong, so deliciously wicked that she could not contain her gasp, and the knowing look that lit his face made her certain he realized exactly what she was feeling.

His gaze slid over her like a caress before he said, "I'm going to go fetch ye some food." Before she could murmur her appreciation, he turned to Anise. "Dunnae allow her to drink more. She needs to eat first, aye."

"Aye," the woman replied. Alasdair headed toward the

door, his strides long, sure, and powerful, and Maeve darted her gaze between him and the woman, who stared at Alasdair with such open longing that Maeve felt momentarily sorry for Anise. She obviously had feelings for him.

"I'm sorry," Maeve said, stopping herself from saying more, from revealing to the woman that she need not worry that she had lost Alasdair to Maeve because Maeve had no intention of keeping him. But Maeve certainly didn't need to reveal her plan to leave.

"I dunnae need yer pity," Anise said, her words dripping with malice and obliterating the pity Maeve had felt moments before. "It's ye who is pitiful, nae me. Alasdair wed ye for what ye could bring him, nae for ye. He dunnae love ye. He dunnae even desire ye, and he will nae ever. He desires me. He loves me, and he always will. Ye are his wife in name, but I'm the wife of his heart. He wanted ye for yer stronghold, but he wants me for me."

Pride was a dangerous thing. Maeve knew it. Her da had told her so at least a hundred times. He's always said pride destroyed a person more times than any weapon. Yet even knowing all this, her pride had been sliced good by Anise's barbed tongue, and the woman had struck at one of Maeve's secret fears: she'd only ever be wanted for Eilean Donan and not for herself. She'd been fighting this irrational fear since the day her da had inherited it, and to have this woman seem to know instinctively what to say to hurt Maeve, and to see in Anise's triumphant gaze that she believed it, made Maeve's blood boil and sent her good sense skittering.

It was in that exact moment that Alasdair reappeared with a trencher in hand. He smiled as he came in the room and held up the trencher. "Lara was bringing a tray of food for ye, Maeve. We met up on the stairwell..." His words faded as his gaze darted between them, then his smile faded, too. "What's afoot?" he demanded as he walked to the bed she was sitting on, and an irritated expression settled on his face. He glanced between Anise and Maeve and arched his eyebrows expectantly. "Well?"

"Nae a thing," Anise said, throwing a quick daring look at Maeve. One that said, *Go ahead. Tell him. It will nae change the truth of the matter that I'm the one he wants.* And as if the woman could hear Maeve's inner thoughts, she tossed her hair over her shoulder and batted her eyelashes at Maeve's husband. Never mind that he was a husband she did not want and didn't intend to keep. He was currently hers, and by the gods she wanted to make him want her for her, if only for a moment, and definitely in front of this conceited woman. Maeve's blood grew so hot it scorched her veins as it flowed through them.

"Everything is well, Husband," she practically purred. Alasdair's eyes widened with obvious shock, and who could blame him? She sounded like a fool, and her attitude was as changeable as the wind. Still, her pride beat like a drum through her, and the rhythm demanded she prove her desirability. "I was just remembering the kiss we shared long ago in the woods, and I relayed the story to Anise." The woman's suddenly slack jaw was the most splendid display of shock Maeve had ever seen. It made her want to crow like a rooster. "Do ye remember the kiss?" She knew he did. He'd said as much in the courtyard the day they'd arrived here.

"Aye," he said, and she did not miss the huskiness of his tone. It kindled a fire in her.

"Ye did nae kiss me after we wed, ye ken?" She could hardly believe what she was doing. Daft did not adequately describe her current state. She feared she had run temporarily mad, but it was exhilarating!

He closed the distance between them in three lazy, long steps, not even glancing at Anise as he passed her. His gaze was riveted on Maeve's face. When he got to the side of her bed, he leaned down, and with the nearness of him, the heat rolling off his body, the way his arm muscles bulged when he placed his hands on her bed to brace himself before leaning so close, his presence nearly overwhelmed her, and she saw for the first time the streaks of hazel interspersed with the gold and brown of his eyes. Her body tightened at her core, her breasts grew tingly, and an ache sprang up at her core. The instinctive response was so powerful that she gasped.

His smile was that of a man who was only too aware of his effect on women, and the look he gave her—hot, lustful, longing—was an invitation to sin. "Do ye wish me to kiss ye to seal our vows?"

At the base of her throat, her pulse beat and swelled as though her heart had left its usual place, and she nodded, fully aware that what had started with anger, with a wish to prove her desire, had morphed into a need for his lips on hers once more, to see if it was everything she remembered or if her young mind had conjured an impossible, unrepeatable fantasy.

A triumphant glint appeared in his eyes before his large hand brushed against her cheek. The graze of his hot skin against hers made her shiver, and when he slid his fingers into her hair, her flesh prickled deliciously at his touch.

"Please leave us," he said, not taking his gaze from her, and for a moment, Maeve could not think who he was commanding, but then Anise was moving toward the door. She opened it, cast a parting, vexed look over her shoulder, and disappeared from Maeve's view as the door closed behind her. Alasdair stared at Maeve for a moment as the golden brown of his eyes darkened to a smoldering invitation to pleasure. "I dunnae ken what occurred between ye and Anise, but I recognize a lass intent on proving herself to another." That he'd seen through her so clearly shocked her to her core and made her stiffen in embarrassment. She opened her mouth mayhap to defend herself, mayhap to deny it, but she honestly wasn't certain which. And she'd never know, because he placed a gentle finger against her lips, a wolfish smile gracing his own. "Ken this, Wife. Ye dunnae need to prove yer worth to anyone, and ken this as well: when ye look as ye do, and ye invite a man to taste ye, there's nae any turning back."

His finger left her mouth, but before she could even order her thoughts to string some coherent ones together, his lips brushed hers. After a brief moment, his tongue darted out to trace her upper and lower lip and steal whatever senses she had left. The caress of his lips to her mouth once more took the fire from kindling to roaring. She moaned, wanting more of his lips, wanting him to kiss her harder, more thoroughly, and in a way that allowed her to see if he tasted as she remembered.

A growl came from him before his mouth claimed hers, the bed dipped beneath his weight, and he crushed her to him. Passion rose so swiftly, there wasn't even a choice of whether to give herself to it or not. She was helpless in his arms as his mouth covered hers hungrily, with his persuasive lips, then tongue asking her to open her mouth and then demanding it. She whimpered with the ache between her thighs going to a near unbearable need, and she opened her mouth to his.

His tongue entwined with hers, touching, circling, teasing before retreating for soft tugs on her lips with his own, and returning once more to do it all again. Spirals of ecstasy went through her, and she returned his kisses with an eagerness, a wantonness that she had not known dwelled within her. Her hands slid up his strong forearms, over the hard, knotted muscles of his biceps, grazing his broad shoulders to skim over the soft stubble covering his jaw and to slide over his sharp cheekbones and into his thick hair. Every touch was heaven. *He* was heaven.

She settled her hands in his hair and tugged him closer, eliciting a grunt from him. His hands came to her chin, and he broke the kiss to tilt her head back and kiss his way from under her chin to the pulsing hollow at the base of her throat. Desperate need burst within her as his firm mouth promised Heaven and demanded a response.

She curled her nails into the back of his skull while his lips seared a path of pleasure over her collarbone and down her chest. He released one hand from her chin to slip a finger under the upper edge of her bodice. Confusion touched her for a moment, but when he tugged her bodice down to expose her right breast and his tongue circled her nipple, she nearly came off the bed with wanting. She cried out, pressing her body up toward his and was rewarded by his sucking her nipple into the warm recesses of his mouth in the most glorious fashion she'd ever known. She heard herself panting, felt herself squirming, and then a knock came at the door, and it was like a pail of freezing loch water had been thrown on her. She gasped and reached for her bodice, but he was already pulling it up.

The desire that swam in his gaze made her feel heady with a power unlike any she had ever known.

"Alasdair, may I come in?"

He did not acknowledge whoever it was at the bedchamber door with even a flicker of his gaze. His attention was riveted on Maeve. "Ye're mine," he said, his tone hard and possessive. "And that was just the beginning."

"Alasdair!"

"Aye, Lara, come in." Alasdair released Maeve and stepped back, turning from her to greet his sister, and all Maeve could do was sit there in shock. His kiss was not what she remembered. It was more. So much more. It was a swirling wind and crashing waves. It was searing heat on the hottest of days, and a storm that swept you up and changed you forever. Her fantasy of their kiss had been wrong because it had been lacking. His kiss had unleashed something uncontainable within her, a wanting to be loved, touched, needed by someone who wanted only her.

She swallowed, but it was useless. Her heart was in her throat. Her da was barely in his grave, and what had she done? Allowed his enemy to nearly ravish her while she gloried in every moment of it. And she couldn't even conjure shame. Guilt, aye. Shame, no. What was she going to do? She was supposed to be turning his lust from her, keeping her innocence intact to dissolve this marriage, but all she could think in this moment was when his hands would next be on her again.

He turned and smiled, and it was the smile of a man who had conquered something—no, someone. She clenched her teeth with a wave of realization and frustration. She'd made herself easy to defeat. No, she'd invited him to do so. She was a fool, and he was a master seducer.

Chapter Twelve

*A*lasdair's sister entered the bedchamber and swept her gaze over Maeve, her eyebrows arching up and her mouth forming a knowing smirk. "Well, someone's been properly kissed."

An unwelcome blush heated Maeve's cheeks. "I dunnae—"

"Dunnae try to deny it," Lara said with a snicker. "Yer face and chest are flushed in a way that only a thorough kiss can cause. And yer hair is a mess!"

Maeve's hand went involuntarily to her head, and she patted it and winced. It *was* a bee hive!

Lara came to Maeve's bed and sat in the same spot Alasdair had just vacated and studied Maeve. After a moment, she said, "Am I to take it that ye have decided ye rather like being wed to Alasdair?"

"I—Nay! He's my enemy."

"Is he?" Lara asked, cocking her head. "It dunnae seem so at the moment. Yer lips are swollen as if a hundred bees stung them."

Maeve's hand fluttered from her hair to her lips, and she gasped. They did feel swollen. "I kinnae believe I kissed yer brother." She purposely left out that she had practically asked him to kiss her.

"Whyever nae? All the lasses say he's verra handsome, and he's so thoughtful on top of that."

"My da has only just died," Maeve murmured, feeling the grief she'd shoved down rise up to fill her eyes with unexpected tears. "And I'm allowing his enemy to kiss me."

Lara's expression went from slightly amused to understanding. She reached out, took Maeve's hand, and gave it a squeeze. "Sometimes when we lose someone close to us, what we need most is to feel alive, and there is nae anything quite like being in love to make ye feel alive."

"I'm nae in love!" Maeve protested. "I dunnae even ken yer brother."

Lara winked. "Nae yet, but ye're learning him already. Was he kind to ye? Gentle? Understanding?"

God's blood, he was all those things! But was it real or a deception to get what he wanted? She'd painted him barbaric in her mind because of the feud between their clans, and then when he'd taken her, she'd assumed she'd been right, but all of a sudden, doubt was there. Did that make her a traitor to her own clan and the memory of her father?

"Nay, Maeve," Lara said, a look of understanding in her expression. "It dunnae make ye a traitor to yer clan to be possibly changing yer mind about my brother—about us. We are nae horrid. It means ye are making judgments based on the true facts ye see afore ye."

"Ye consider all in my clan yer enemy, aye?" Maeve asked, trying to understand herself and what was happening to her. She pressed her fingertips to her temples. She didn't know if she could believe Lara. It was likely she could not, but questioning the woman, talking to her, could possibly reveal lies. Though, she honestly didn't even understand why she cared, since she was going to flee Alasdair and his entire family anyway.

"I did," Lara admitted, "but I think I, too, am changing

my opinion since meeting ye. Mayhap," Lara said with a shrug, "we both made sweeping judgments we should nae have made."

"Mayhap," Maeve replied. "I would venture to say yer mother dunnae feel as ye do, nor yer brother who lost his toe."

"Ye would have had to be the one to injure my younger brother for him to lay the blame on ye, but my mama is a different sort. She loved my da greatly, as we all did, and she blames all MacKenzies for his death. But we all did, so give her time."

A knock came at the bedchamber door, and Lara stood. "Enter."

A woman came in carrying an armful of fresh gowns. Behind her entered servants toting a large bath basin, and behind them were eight women carrying pails of steaming water. The last woman to enter the room carried fresh rushes for the floor.

Maeve stared in amazement as appreciation flooded her. If Lara MacRae could show such a kindness to someone she believed was the daughter of the man responsible for her da's death, then Maeve certainly could give Lara the benefit of the doubt. "Lara, thank ye!" Maeve called across the room.

Lara swung toward her from the servant she'd been directing and smiled at her. "'Tis nae me ye need to thank, Maeve. I wish I could say I had thought of all this, but I did nae."

"Then who?" Maeve asked.

"Alasdair," Lara replied. Maeve felt her lips part with surprise, and Lara chuckled. "Everything ye see here—" Lara indicated the servants with her hand "—is Alasdair's doing. I told ye he was thoughtful."

"Is he this thoughtful to all women?" Maeve asked, thinking of Anise, her jealousy stirring.

"Nay. But I kenned he would be to ye after Brodick told me yer history with Alasdair a wee bit ago."

Maeve frowned. Had Alasdair told Brodick of the kiss? She certainly did not want to ask the question for all the ears in the room to hear and then spread castle gossip, so she motioned Lara over. When Lara was standing by the bed, Maeve asked, "What history did Brodick tell ye of?"

"Well, how Alasdair was obsessed with ye some years ago, of course. I did nae even ken he'd met ye afore recently. Imagine Alasdair, and Brodick for that matter, keeping that secret for so long."

Maeve sat back, confused. "What do ye mean he was obsessed with me?"

"I mean the way he saw ye in the woods and started tracking ye daily! Do ye nae call that obsession?" Lara grinned. "I always said there was a reason Alasdair would nae commit to a lass and get wed, but I could nae ever have guessed ye were the reason. I mean, he'll deny it of course, but..."

Maeve no longer heard Lara's words. Alasdair had seen her in the woods and tracked her? She had to press her lips together to keep from smiling. Clearing her throat, she said, "Ye think just because he tracked me for a bit, he was obsessed with me?"

"A bit?" Lara gasped. "Brodick said he tracked ye for weeks! He said Alasdair told him it had been to ensure ye were safe since ye were a lass hunting alone in the woods sometimes close to twilight. But Brodick also said if I could have seen the way Alasdair's face looked when he relayed the story of seeing ye fell a deer with one shot of yer arrow, I would have seen what Brodick did that day."

"And what was that?" Maeve asked, her mind spinning with what Lara was telling her.

Lara set her hands on her hips. "Why, that he was smitten with ye, of course."

The smile Maeve had been trying to contain broke its confinement, and she felt her lips curl upward. Good heaven! She was smiling over the enemy!

Lara let out a rich laugh. "I see by yer face he affected ye in much the same way."

Maeve bit her lip, hesitant to reveal such private things and to a stranger, but with Bee so far away from her, she needed someone to confide in. "I did build sort of a fantasy of what I wanted my husband to be around yer brother, which was foolish," she said self-consciously. "I did nae even ken him."

"Well, it seems he did the same with ye. Brodick said Alasdair told him of seeing ye take the head of a snake off with one throw of yer dagger and killing the famed Black Boar, and how it was the most amazing thing he'd ever witnessed a lass do."

Maeve could hardly believe she'd never known someone was following her in those woods or that he'd been so impressed by her. Her feelings toward him were warm and confusing.

Lara fumbled in a pouch and pulled out a ruby ribbon. Maeve gasped and reached for it. She would recognize that ribbon anywhere. Her da had spent hours staining it with berries for her, and it was the ribbon Alasdair had taken from her hair the day he'd kissed her in the woods.

"Where did ye find this?" Maeve asked.

"I took it from Alasdair's room years ago. I saw it on his table one day when I was snooping in there, and I thought I'd bribe him with it. I assumed it belonged to a lass at the castle that he held a tendre for and that he'd do what I asked of him to get it back so I'd nae blab about it and embarrass him, but when I tried to bribe him, he laughed and said I could do what I pleased with the ribbon because the lass who was the owner of it was as likely to step foot in this castle as the Devil was."

"I kinnae believe it," Maeve murmured, sliding the silky ribbon between her fingers. Alasdair had followed her. Had spoken about her. Had kept her ribbon. He'd been affected by her every bit as much as she had been affected by him. She'd not created a fantasy out of nothing. There had been something once. There was something still. Hope rose swift and sudden, making her throat tighten.

Lara set a hand on Maeve's shoulder and gave her an earnest look. "May I give ye some advice?"

Maeve nodded.

"If I were in yer stead I would be plotting to escape as soon as I could." Lara's words made Maeve go very still. "But ye should allow yerself a chance to discover him and us," she said. "Besides," she continued with a bright smile, "ye'd nae get verra far with that ankle."

"True," Maeve agreed, thinking on what Lara had said. Escape now would be impossible so Maeve might as well take this time to truly learn who Alasdair was as a man and a laird. She would need to make a decision when she returned home—if she was going to ask Colin to call a truce with Alasdair's clan—and this time would help her know her mind and what she was going to do. And what if she discovered Alasdair was everything her fanciful young mind had once imagined? She could not allow such hope because with it came hard choices or even possible heartbreak.

Chapter Thirteen

*A*lasdair could not get his wife—and the kisses and touches they had shared—out of his thoughts. His sleep had suffered, his appetite had suffered, and his training had been suffering all day long. Instead of giving Darby good instruction, he'd been absentminded and short. And later, with his rampart guards, he'd lost his thoughts in mid-sentence. Now Alasdair's head was not where it should be with Brodick. He frequently trained all day and could usually keep his thoughts upon the task, but not today. Instead, his mind was on Maeve's sweet lips, the spicy scent of her, the tangy taste of her mouth, the silkiness of her hair between his fingers, the sound of her soft little moans as he had suckled her breast, the warmness of her skin, and smoothness of the curves of her body. He groaned, failing to see Brodick's sword coming at him until the blade was under Alasdair's weapon and the man had relieved him of his own.

Brodick didn't crow his victory. He shook his head and plunged the tip of his sword into the ground before leaning on the hilt and staring expectantly at Alasdair. His friend did not need to say a word. Alasdair knew Brodick was waiting for him to explain what the devil was occurring with him. "I'm distracted," Alasdair muttered.

"Aye," Brodick replied, leaning down to pick up Alasdair's sword and handing it to him. "I can see that. 'Tis because ye have nae bedded yer wife."

"I'm nae discussing this with ye," Alasdair snapped.

Brodick chuckled. "Ye dunnae have to. 'Tis plain to see in yer tenseness. Go find yer wife."

It wouldn't do his state of distraction any good to find Maeve, but he didn't bother to say that to Brodick. In fact, finding Maeve would likely only worsen his yearning. Instead, he took his sword and said, "Ye're fine to train the men for the rest of the day?"

"Aye. So go settle matters."

"'Tis nae that simple, Brodick," Alasdair replied. The sense of protectiveness he'd immediately felt for Maeve had been joined by other emotions last night. Concern for her safety, anger at Anise for goading Maeve—because he had no doubt that's what had occurred—and desire like he'd never known before. He strode up the stairs from the loch, through the back outer courtyard gate, and into the castle. He passed a few servants on the way, nodding as he went. He needed to be alone to think, and the only place where that would be possible was his bedchamber.

He made his way up the stairs to the bedchambers, pausing when he got to Maeve's. He raised his hand to knock, then lowered it. He'd not seen her since last night, but he'd made certain she was taken care of. Anise had said she should rest with her ankle up today, so he'd enlisted Lara to check on her and ordered the servants to bring her trays of food to break her fast and for the nooning meal. He would see if she wished to come to supper later, and would aid her down if she did, but right now, he needed time to figure out what was occurring within him in regard to her.

He moved on from her door, eager to get to his own bedchamber and cast off his sweaty, dusty clothing from training. He was already peeling off his plaid as he walked through his bedchamber door and kicked it shut behind him, guiding himself into the room by memory, as his plaid was covering his eyes. He pulled it the rest of the way off, intending to toss it on his chair, but when he turned he froze.

"What the devil are ye doing in my bed?" he demanded of Anise.

She smiled slowly and pulled back the coverlet to reveal her completely naked form. "This." Her tone was every bit as seductive as the look she gave him.

Glancing around, he located her gown crumpled on the floor at the other side of the bed, went around and gathered it up, and tossed it to her, turning his back so she could get dressed. "I'm wed now, Anise. And even if I was nae, I already told ye—"

Her hands were suddenly coming around his waist, and she was pressing her body against his back. He stiffened, unhooked her arms from him, and turned to face her, glancing away when he realized she was still naked. "Anise—"

She rubbed herself against his front. "Dunnae tell me that ye dunnae desire me."

"I dunnae any longer," he replied and realized it was the absolute truth. He didn't feel even a sliver of want.

"Ye're so honorable, Alasdair," she said, reaching for him to twine her arms around his neck, but he stepped back and locked his gaze with hers.

"Listen to me," he said. "I want my wife. I only want my wife." God's blood, it was the truth. From the first moment he'd seen Maeve in the woods so many years ago, she'd affected him in a way no other woman had. "Get dressed and leave, please. I'm sorry to hurt ye, but I thought ye understood that what was between us was nae permanent. Ye said that's what ye wanted, too."

"I lied, Alasdair," she snapped, shoving her arms into her gown. "I had hoped—" She paused when her voice caught, and he felt awful but didn't reach for her to soothe her. He was certain doing so would only make matters worse. She finished setting her gown to rights and then met his gaze once more. "If I kinnae be yer wife, I will be yer mistress," she said, reaching for him yet again.

This time, he gently took her by the wrists to stop her and pushed her arms back toward her before releasing her. "I dunnae want a mistress. I'd nae dishonor Maeve so."

"Ye say that now, but she'll nae make ye happy."

If his time with Maeve last night was any indication of how they could make each other feel, they could be very happy if they could learn to trust each other and not judge each other on their families or the past. He didn't know what the truth was when it came to her da and her clan— what she believed or what he did—and he was beginning to suspect there was more to the discrepancy than simply each of them stubbornly believing their clan was the first victim. He needed time to try to discern the truth, but even if it was how he believed, he was realizing that did not mean Maeve was at fault. She had not raided his family or ordered his da killed. His thinking of her as his enemy for nothing she did was as bad as her thinking him her enemy for things he knew his clan had not done.

"Maeve and I will likely have times we dunnae make each other happy," he replied slowly, thinking how having to leave her last night after touching her so intimately had not made him happy in the least, "but regardless of what happens between me and her, it is just the two of us in our marriage. There is nae room for another, so I need ye to go."

"I dunnae doubt ye'll change yer mind, Alasdair, but ye best make haste and do it. Men want me."

"I'm certain they do," he said, going to his door and opening it wide for her to leave. "And if ye want one of them, ye should nae let our past stop ye. What we had is done."

"We shall see," she said, breezing past him, and as he watched her stalk away he had a certainty that Anise was going to somehow cause him trouble with Maeve.

Maeve tried to turn and flee the hall before Anise saw her, but she was far too slow with her hurt ankle to do so. As Alasdair shut his bedroom door, Anise's gaze locked on Maeve standing in the shadows of the alcove. Maeve's face burned with her embarrassment, and she wished to God she'd not ventured from her room to seek out some fresh air in the courtyard.

On second thought, if she hadn't ventured out of her bedchamber, she would not have seen Anise coming out of Alasdair's bedchamber, and her husband—that made her sneer—standing there with nary on but his braies. God above knew what they'd been doing. As Anise strode toward her with a smug, almost challenging look, Maeve brought herself to her full height and squared her shoulders. She refused to let this woman think the scene had caused her a moment's fretting. More than anything, she was vexed at herself for allowing her pride to goad her into eliciting that kiss from Alasdair, and then actually letting herself consider that he may be honorable, as Lara had claimed. Maeve gritted her teeth. It wouldn't surprise her one bit to learn Lara was in on a plan to deceive Maeve. The whole lot of MacRaes were liars!

"I told ye Alasdair wanted me," Anise said, stopping in front of Maeve.

It took all Maeve's willpower not to spit at the woman that she had no intention of keeping that dishonorable man as her husband. Instead, she forced herself to take a slow breath to calm her temper, and she considered carefully how she should respond. It seemed to her the best thing, the wisest thing, was to respond in a way that a woman intending to keep a husband would so she would not rouse any suspicion about trying to escape again. But Anise was likely the very last person who would stop her. In fact— Maeve nearly gasped in excitedness at the idea that had just come to her—Anise would surely be more than glad to help her escape if it meant the woman would get another chance to be Alasdair's wife.

"Ye can have him," Maeve said, switching courses from earlier. "I dunnae want him."

The woman gave her a disbelieving, almost hostile look. "Dunnae try to play games with me," Anise said. "He dunnae want ye." Maeve opened her mouth to assure Anise she was not playing games, but the woman spoke again. "He contrived a whole plan to make ye think he does, but he dunnae. He persuaded his sister to aid him in convincing ye," she said. "Lara told me how she was going to give ye a story that he followed ye years ago because he was besotted, and he kept yer ribbon all these years." Anise snorted. "Lies. He followed ye to see if he could find a secret way into yer castle in case we needed to raid it, and it was Lara herself who kept that ribbon."

Maeve's cheeks and neck burned with the mortification of knowing she had partly—no, more than partly—believed Lara. Maeve was the biggest sort of fool. There was no way

Anise could have known what Lara had told her unless Lara had told Anise what she was going to say first. Maeve felt her nostrils flare as she struggled to find a calming breath, but there was no calm to be found. It was as if she had been dropped into the middle of a turbulent ocean. Damn Alasdair MacRae for having the unexpected ability to inspire hope in her for a foolish girlhood dream she'd forgotten and then make her feel embarrassment on top of that.

"As I said, ye can have him."

Anise's brows dipped together for a moment, and then her eyes slowly widened. "Ye mean that," she whispered.

"Aye," Maeve said. "I only kissed him so that he'd nae suspect I wanted to escape him still. He kidnapped me from my home. I love another, and I have every intention of wedding Colin Fraser if I can escape here." She allowed her words to sink into this woman's skull for a moment before Maeve spoke again. "It seems to me it would behoove us both for ye to aid me in escaping."

Anise cocked her head, her lips parted, and then she expelled a long breath before biting down on her lower lip. After what seemed like an eternity, she nodded. "I'll aid ye, but I kinnae be kenned by any to have done so."

"'Tis fine by me," Maeve said, meaning it.

"We must both act just as we would had we nae had this conversation," Anise said.

Maeve nodded and glanced around her to ensure they were indeed still alone. "Do ye ken a way to aid me?"

The woman smiled slowly, triumphantly. "Aye. 'Tis simple enough. When yer ankle is healed, ye will say ye're going to ride with me to fetch herbs. Then ye will flee, and I will ensure they think ye overcame me."

There was the slightest hesitation not to accept this woman's word, or even a deep sense that she would somehow later regret doing so, but given her choices, she nodded and prayed she'd not come to regret the decision.

As the supper horn rang later that day, Alasdair made his way from his bedchamber to Maeve's but found it empty. Assuming Lara had seen Maeve to supper, he hurried down to the great hall, which was already teeming with his clanspeople. At the dais, Maeve sat with Lara on one side of her and his empty seat on the other.

Her posture was ramrod straight, and he could tell right away that whatever good feeling she'd had for him had been forgotten once again. With a sigh, he started toward the dais, but every few steps he was stopped by someone, making it take much longer than he wished to get to her. By the time he reached her, she had a flush on her face and a goblet raised to her lips, and she was exclaiming that Atholl Brose was the best drink she'd ever tasted.

He started to remind her how the drink had taken hold of her so quickly last night, but then he thought of her warm eagerness in his arms after she'd imbibed a bit, and instead, he said, "Wife, ye are the bonniest creature in the room." *Wife.* It had slipped out. It had been on his mind, but he hadn't intended to say it aloud.

She looked as if she was deciding between whether to plant another dagger in him or hold her tongue on what had stirred her ire. "Thank ye," she said, the words sharp as jagged rocks.

He didn't know what had transpired between this moment and the one when he'd left her, but something had. And by Lara's surprised look, he knew his sister didn't know what was wrong with Maeve, either. He made his way up the dais, aware everyone from Lara to Father Bernard to his scowling mother and younger brother was listening to their conversation. He sat down beside her, his arm accidentally brushing hers, and he felt her body stiffen.

She turned her attention immediately away from him to attacking her trencher. He watched her for a moment, trying to decide what to say that would not anger her more, and thought to jest with her. "Do ye fear this is the only meal we will feed ye?" he teased.

She froze with a piece of bread drenched in gravy halfway to her mouth, and a worried expression crossed her face. She popped the bread in her mouth and said, "Certainly nae."

Something was amiss, but he had no idea what. She wasn't just vexed with him. She seemed on edge with her daring gaze, and he could feel her bouncing her leg underneath the table as if she was trying to control nervous energy.

"I was just telling Maeve how ye apprenticed with the king as a young lad," Lara said.

"Aye," he replied, his attention catching momentarily on Anise, whom he saw out of the corner of his eye. She sat at the table to the right and nearest the dais. Sitting very near her, in fact so close Alasdair would not be surprised if a piece of parchment could not be slipped between them, was Athelston. His cousin was talking animatedly, but Anise was not looking at him. She was looking toward Maeve. But when she realized Alasdair was staring at her, she quickly looked to Athelston. Alasdair would wager a bag of coin that Anise had put venomous words in Maeve's ear.

"Did ye hear me, Alasdair?" Lara asked.

He glanced away from Anise toward his sister, but his attention was caught now by Maeve, who was staring at him with open contempt. Damn Anise for whatever she'd said. "Maeve," he said, leaning toward her, "'tis nae as it appears."

Maeve picked up her goblet, and her fingers gripped it so tightly that her knuckles reddened slightly over her delicate bones. "I dunnae ken what ye mean," she replied.

"I—" He scrubbed a hand across his face wondering how to best explain to his wife, or if he should at all, that he'd had a relationship with Anise, but that he had most assuredly ended it. And even if he could think of the words, this was definitely not the time to give them. "Did Anise say something more to ye?" he whispered.

"Aye," Maeve replied, her gaze burning into him like a fire poker. "The woman offered her apologies for her behavior and explained it was because she loved ye, and begged my forgiveness for how she'd acted toward me, which I gave after she promised that for her part, she'd nae dishonor our union going forward." Maeve hitched an eyebrow at him. "Can ye say the same?"

"I vow it to ye, Maeve."

She nodded, but when she turned away, he heard her murmur under her breath, "Lies from the serpent's lips."

Chapter Fourteen

*M*aeve took another gulp of the wine. She needed it to calm the fire burning in her. His wife! He threw the term around awfully casually, but why wouldn't he? He had tricked her into wedding him after snatching her, and then he'd filled her head with lies, and gotten his sister to as well, and he'd dishonored their marriage before it was even consummated. She hated him. It was all she could do to sit here calmly and think logically. She was proud of herself for planting the seed that she'd forgiven Anise. She'd have to tell the woman.

Maeve purposely turned her attention back to her trencher, though she was not in the least bit hungry, but if she had food stuffed in her mouth, she did not have to talk to Alasdair; not that he had attempted to speak to her again. He seemed to realize she was vexed. Probably that should worry her, but she was too angry to care. And she was irritated that the man's ability to affect her emotions would not loosen its grip on her.

Supper passed in tense silence, until the great hall door opened, and a young man came strolling in slowly. Excited chatter erupted in the room, and Lara said, "Well, well. It looks like Tavish has finally risen from his sick bed."

Maeve frowned as she watched the young man, who resembled Alasdair in coloring and height, approach the dais. She looked between Tavish MacRae to Alasdair. "I thought yer brother lost a leg from supposedly being shot by my clan."

"I lost a toe," the man said, stopping in front of her and looking sheepish.

"A toe! A toe," she sputtered and turned to glare at Alasdair. "Ye," she seethed.

"I was just as surprised as ye are," he said.

"Ye made a plan to kidnap me over a lost toe!"

"Nay. The plan to take ye was already formulated after yer da left us to starve for the winter."

"I told ye my da would nae have done that!"

"Either Laird MacKenzie was a liar or ye are," said Alasdair's mother.

Maeve met Lady MacRae's hostile gaze. She understood it, though, so she tried not to let it vex her. If Maeve had believed Alasdair's father had been responsible for her father's death, she would have certainly been hostile to Alasdair and everyone else at this table. "My da was nae a liar, and neither am I."

"Lies from the serpent's lips," Lady MacRae said, letting Maeve know she had indeed mumbled that statement too loudly.

Her cheeks instantly burned. "My da would nae have left innocent people to starve any more than he would have ordered yer husband's murder. Those are cowardly acts, and my da was nae a coward."

"Then how do ye explain the plaid clutched in my husband's fist?" the woman demanded.

"I kinnae," Maeve said helplessly. She had been thinking upon it, and she did not understand it herself.

"Nay?" the woman replied, her tone dramatic. "I'm so verra surprised. I would have imagined a clever lass like yerself would have come up with a good excuse by now."

"I have a thought," Father Bernard said.

"What is it, Father?" Alasdair asked.

"I believe the Frasers may have plotted to frame yer da."

She gawked at the priest. He was a man of God, but he'd already proven himself a cunning liar, so she certainly was not inclined to believe him now. "The Frasers would nae have done such a thing."

"How do ye ken?" Father Bernard asked. "It makes sense. Fraser would want there to be strife between our clans so that his clan would remain in favor with yer da, and he'd want to do something that would make our clan hate yers so that our laird and yer da never became allies. Because if they were to do so and ye still had failed to wed his son, there was a perfectly healthy son here for ye to wed, and if ye did so, Fraser would nae obtain Eilean Donan."

If that were true, then did that mean the Frasers could have murdered her father? No, it made no sense. Her father had kept her betrothal to Colin intact. There would have been no reason for them to kill him. "Colin would have told me," she said, but the smallest doubt touched her, remembering how certain Bee had been that the Frasers had killed her da.

"Are ye so naive that ye think men tell women every sin they commit?" Alasdair's mother demanded.

Maeve's gaze slid to Alasdair before she could stop herself. He had touched her body. He'd had her breast in his mouth. He had given her pleasure and then turned around and given pleasure to Anise. Maeve felt horrid, filthy, and as if she had somehow betrayed her father's memory. She'd intended to wed Colin because that was what her father had wanted and because it was good for her clan, and it had taken one kiss from this Highlander—one!—and she had lost her senses and once again had been the silly lass he'd kissed in the woods years before.

Her nose began to tingle furiously, indicating she was on the verge of crying. She rose suddenly, knocking over her goblet in her haste to get away before the tears fell, and without a word of apology or excuse, she gritted her teeth against the pain in her screaming ankle and fled off the dais and out of the great hall.

It took all Alasdair's self-restraint not to follow Maeve, but he knew she would not welcome him in this moment and he needed to speak to his mother about her behavior. "Mama," he said slowly, not wanting to make matters worse. But he had to ensure she understood he would not accept her poisonous behavior toward Maeve. "Maeve is my wife now."

"An accident could befall her," his mother said. "Ye would still be the rightful laird of Eilean Donan."

"Mama," he tried again. "I ken ye dunnae mean that. I ken ye. Ye're nae a murderer."

"I wish I were," she muttered.

Alasdair nodded. "I feel that, too. We all want to avenge Da, but Maeve did nae kill him."

"She's a MacKenzie," his mother said.

"Aye, and I'm a MacRae. Did our clan start the feud with the Frasers and the MacKenzies?"

"Ye ken well we did nae," his mother said with vehemence.

"Aye, I do, but Maeve dunnae. She was made to believe we started the feud. It will take time to convince her otherwise, and ye treating her poorly dunnae help matters."

"Why should I treat her with respect when ye dunnae?"

"What do ye mean?" he demanded.

His mother smirked. "The servants talk, Alasdair."

"And what are they saying?"

"They are saying that Anise was seen going into yer bedchamber, and she did nae come back out with any haste."

He clenched his teeth at the news. Maeve must have heard similar talk. He needed to explain things to her.

"I did nae bed Anise. Ye reared me, Mama. Ye should ken I have honor and would nae break my vows."

She blanched at that, but then she shrugged. "I believe ye honorable, Son, but ye did say ye did nae have any intentions of having a true marriage."

There was no arguing his mother's words. He had said that about his marriage to Maeve. "Just dunnae be spiteful to her, aye? Give her a chance."

His mother inhaled a deep breath and nodded slowly albeit begrudgingly.

He felt a little of his own tension dissipate. At least one problem was temporarily taken care of. Now to try to address another. He turned to Brodick. "I believe there's something to what Father Bernard says."

"I do, too," Brodick said, "but the question is how to prove it."

"That I dunnae ken," Alasdair admitted, rising. He needed to find Maeve, to explain, and he thought, perhaps, to comfort her. Sadness had shadowed her bright eyes before she'd fled, and he could well remember his own grief when his father had died. "Mama, I need to go to Maeve. Ye will keep yer word nae to be spiteful, aye?"

"Did I give my word?" she asked innocently.

He smiled slowly. "Nay, but I'm certain ye meant to."

An undeniably disgruntled look settled on his mother's face. "Fine. Ye have my word for now. But if she gives me any reason to doubt her—"

"She will nae," he interrupted, praying it was true.

He hoped this would be like a new start for him and Maeve. There had been something between them that first time he'd kissed her, and for his part, the first time he'd seen her. He hoped they could untangle the lies and build a life of peace and happiness together.

He didn't expect she'd answer the knock on her bedchamber door, so when she didn't, he tested the knob, surprised to find it open. He entered the room, and she immediately sat up, dashing her hands across her cheeks, but it was no use. Her red eyes and red nose could not be hidden.

"I locked that door!" she exclaimed, shoving up into a sitting position and drawing her knees to her chest with a wince. She straightened her leg of her hurt ankle and clutched her other one tightly.

She looked so vulnerable, and he wanted nothing more than to wrap his arms around her, but his instincts told him to take it very slowly. "I think mayhap in yer irritation with me, ye forgot to slide the bar in place."

She scowled at him. "I'm nae irritated. I dunnae care what ye do."

He crossed the room and sat at the edge of her bed, giving her space yet bringing himself closer to her. "I would be livid if I were ye."

She hitched her brows. "Well ye're nae me," she bit out. This was going to be difficult.

"I dunnae ken what ye heard about Anise and me..." He

allowed his words to trail off, wanting to give her a chance to tell him instead of his filling her head with unnecessary gossip if she hadn't heard it and she was actually vexed about something else.

For a breath, an uncertain look crossed her face, but then she said, "Well, the servants do talk, and I have two ears, so…" She shrugged as if it didn't matter, but he could see the vein at her right temple bulge.

"I vow to ye that I did nae bed Anise," he said, moving a bit closer as he spoke. He saw her stiffen, but she did not put distance between them. Instead, she speared him with a gaze bright with ire.

"I could drown in all the vows ye make," she replied.

He closed a bit more distance. "I understand ye must feel that way."

"Ye dunnae understand a thing about me, Alasdair."

Oh, but he did. She was hurting. She was scared. She was mourning. She was confused. She hated him, but she was attracted to him, just as he was to her. He could abandon trying to explain Anise to her because she clearly did not believe him, but he had to say his piece. It seemed important. "I did have a relationship with Anise in the past."

She arched her eyebrows at him. "I think ye dunnae understand what the past is, *Laird*." If she hadn't been so vexed, he would have smiled. She professed she didn't care, and yet, he could sense her jealousy. "I put an end to my entanglement with her afore I came for ye."

"If ye say so," she replied. She might as well have called him a liar for the tone in her voice.

The best course of action was to simply finish his explanation and then hope they could move on eventually, or that she would come to see he was being truthful through his actions. He moved even closer so that her foot touched his thigh. Her gaze darted to where their bodies made contact, but she neither protested nor moved. "Earlier today, I returned to my bedchamber to find Anise in it." Maeve snorted at that. He inhaled a breath to keep his own temper cool. "I did nae invite her in, but I did invite her out, immediately, and I explained to her again that what we had shared was over. I kinnae make ye believe me, Maeve, but I vow 'tis true," he added, edging still closer to where he could embrace her.

"Ye're right, ye kinnae make me believe ye. I suppose only time will tell if ye are a snake or an honorable man."

That was likely the best he was going to get from her now, so he decided to turn her attention to another topic. "Maeve, what if there is something to what Father Bernard said?"

"Colin would nae lie to me."

Her obvious absolute belief in Colin Fraser made jealously course through Alasdair. Did she love the man? He rejected the notion, vaguely aware his pride was part of the reason why, but also, she could have wed Colin Fraser, and she hadn't. That meant something. It had to.

"I would nae lie to ye, Maeve."

She laid her forehead on her knees so that her expression was concealed from him. "I kinnae believe ye." Her voice was suddenly heavy with unshed tears. "I'm alone," she whispered. "Ye took me from my home. My family. Ye bring me here and expect me to believe ye, but why should I when ye have acted dishonorably toward me? Ye tricked me into wedding ye! And ye all call my da a murderer!"

His head pounded harder with each of her words, and his chest felt as if someone had plunged a fist into the center of it and twisted out his heart. His plan had seemed simple, yet it was anything but. "I'm sorry. I did what I thought I had to do." He shoved a hand through his hair, frustration mounting with every beat of his heart. "What would ye have me to do?"

She looked up, and the unshed tears that glistened in her eyes made it almost impossible for him to breathe. "Release me. Let me go home. My da is gone. I need to go to my clan and lead them. I need to be with my family."

"I am yer family now," he said with a vehemence that surprised him. What had she done to him? He felt almost bewitched.

Tears began to spill over her lower lashes to track down her cheeks, and he could not restrain himself any longer. He brushed at her cheeks, then pulled her to him, enfolding her in his embrace. "I'm sorry, Maeve," he whispered. "I would release ye if I could." But he could not deny the part of him that was glad he felt he couldn't, and that part did make him feel dishonorable. "I vow to ye, I'll prove my honor and I'll be a good husband to ye."

Her shoulders began to shake as the tears took her, and he pressed her head to his chest. She sat stiff in his embrace for the longest time, but then, with a shuddering sigh, she finally wrapped her arms around him and clung to him as if she had no choice, as if she would drown in a sea of pain and she was relenting to grasping him in her turbulence of misery simply to survive. He'd take the moment of her weakness, and he'd do his best to prove his words true to her, to protect her instead of hurt her more. As she cried, his own chest ached with an intensity that shocked him. Her pain felt like his own. He kissed the top of her head, offering soothing words of comfort, and after a while, her tears slowed, then subsided. He expected her to immediately pull away, but she did not. She turned her head so that her cheek was resting on his chest, and eventually, her eyelashes fluttered shut and she softly began to snore. He watched her sleep until his muscles burned from holding the position. Then ever so carefully, he laid her down and covered her up. When he looked at her, his chest grew tighter.

"I think ye bewitched me the day I first saw ye, Maeve," he whispered and, leaning down, placed one more kiss upon her forehead before he rose to leave. But halfway to the door, he changed his mind, came back to the bed, and lay beside her with care. Tomorrow, he would move her to his bedchamber where she belonged.

Chapter Fifteen

*T*here were six council members on the MacRae advising board, and they were all trying to talk at once. Alasdair felt his right eye begin to twitch. He'd not gotten enough sleep—again. He'd lain awake half the night staring at Maeve while she slept. She was just as lovely asleep as she was awake. He'd memorized the slope of her cheekbones, the way her upper lip was slightly fuller than her lower, the sprinkle of freckles across her nose, the way her lashes brushed her cheeks when her eyes were closed, the way her red hair tumbled over her shoulders and beckoned him to touch it, and the even rise and fall of her breathing. She'd slept as if she were dead, and he was glad of it. She needed it. He remembered all too vividly the sadness that filled him after his own da's death.

"Alasdair!"

Alasdair snapped his gaze to Father Bernard while noting the silence in the room and cursed himself for being distracted, yet again, by Maeve. He had to take better control of his thoughts. He could tell by the questioning way Father Bernard and the other council advisors were staring expectantly at him, that they were waiting on him to answer the complaint the head of the kitchens, Tess, had lodged. He cleared his throat, not wishing to admit he'd not been listening, but he could not very well give his opinion on proposed solutions when he'd not heard any of them.

"What were the solutions again?"

Father Bernard shook his head. "We could nae agree on any, remember? 'Tis why we want yer thoughts, which ye seem to be lost in."

"Aye," Alasdair agreed and looked to Tess. The older woman appeared bone weary. Dark circles shadowed bloodshot eyes, her silver hair was half down out of updo, and a splattering of food covered her aprons. "Did ye ask for volunteers from the womenfolk as I suggested last council day?"

"Aye, Laird, I did, but what with our losing warriors, many of the women have taken on men's jobs that needed to be done, so they are seeing to their homes, their children, and doing the labor their fallen husbands used to do. They dunnae have time to help cook in the kitchens."

"I can help cook."

Alasdair followed the throaty tone to the doorway from whence it had come, and warmness filled his chest. Maeve stood in the doorway looking fresh and well rested. From his seat at the table, he could see the shadows were gone from underneath her eyes, and her blue gaze was clear and bright.

"Have ye ever worked in a kitchen?" he asked, rising and moving down the dais to aid her, but she waved him off with a wary look.

"I walked down here on my own," she said, a stubborn note in her voice. "I can walk to a chair." She limped slowly into the now quiet room. He wanted to go to her and aid her, but he could see by the determination etched on her face that it was important to her to stand on her own two feet. She wanted to show strength, and he understood that desire.

She stopped in front of the dais and gave an awkward

curtsy to the council members. Alasdair cleared his throat, thinking quickly how best to introduce her, not having foreseen this moment. There was only one acceptable way in his mind.

"This is Maeve, my wife," he said, though he knew good and well everyone sitting at the dais knew who she was by now. He hoped introducing her this way would dissuade any of the men from holding an unnecessary grudge against her.

"Of course, I wed ye, so I ken who ye are," Father Bernard replied jovially.

Maeve smirked at him. "Ah, aye, the cunning priest who duped me. Such a man of God ye are!"

"God calls me to work in many different ways, child," Father Bernard said smoothly.

"How convenient of ye to think so," Maeve shot back.

Alasdair cleared his throat, aware their interaction was quickly getting heated. He motioned to the other men on the council and launched into introducing them, but before he could finish with Athelston, his cousin said, "I ken the MacKenzie lass."

Maeve's spine stiffened visibly at Athelston's derisive tone. Alasdair had known his cousin would be none too pleased with the addition of Maeve into the clan, even if her presence as Alasdair's wife was going to be the thing to keep them all from starving this winter and gain much-needed warriors, but the man would simply have to accustom himself to her. He did understand Athelston's wariness, given his father had died in one of the raids by the Frasers and MacKenzies, but he needed to know Alasdair would not tolerate disrespect to Maeve.

He narrowed his gaze upon his cousin. "She *was* a Mac-Kenzie. She's a MacRae now, just like ye." Alasdair could see the man tense his jaw and then release it.

"Why is she in the council meeting?" Athelston asked, his tone no friendlier than a moment ago, but Alasdair was pleased the man had let the argument of Maeve being a MacKenzie go.

"I asked her to join us." More precisely, he'd told Lara to tell Maeve when she awoke that if she wished to find him, he would be in the great hall most of the day hearing of his clanspeople's needs. Those clanspeople were currently lined up outside the door awaiting their turn, except for Tess, who still stood in front of the council table, awaiting a solution to her problem in the kitchen. Except now she no longer stood alone since Maeve had moved back beside her, and the woman no longer appeared bone weary. She was staring at Maeve with a look of admiration that made the warmth in his chest grow.

"This is nae a place for a woman to be," Athelston said. And then, sparing a look for Tess, he added, "Unless, of course, the woman is here to seek our advice."

Alasdair saw Maeve's gaze narrow from the corner of his eyes, but he kept his own gaze focused on Athelston. "I disagree," he replied. The room seemed to grow even quieter than it had been. "This clan is nae made up of only men. Women are a big part of our clan; therefore, I've decided women should have a representative on the council." Truthfully, the idea had just come to him, but he believed it, he liked it, and it would be a good way to bring Maeve into his life and show her she had a voice, which he suspected would be particularly important to her.

Now he did look to Maeve who stared slack-jawed at him. Beside her, Tess was grinning. "Would ye consider sitting on the council?" he asked Maeve.

"I, well I—" She bit her lip, stood there a moment longer, and finally nodded. Alasdair was surprised, given how independent she seemed, that she'd not immediately jumped at the chance, but he supposed she was still very wary of his intentions. "Also," she added, offering a faint smile, "to answer yer other question, I helped in the kitchen at my home."

"If memory serves," Athelston said in a victorious tone, "we have to vote all new members onto this council. Or are we nae holding to our tradition since this woman is yer supposed wife."

Alasdair held in his ire with ruthless control, though his nostrils flared. "I'll forgive yer disrespect to Maeve this time, Athelston, but this is the only time I'll do so. If it occurs again, ye and I will meet one on one in combat. Do ye ken me?"

"Aye," Athelston bit out. "And I dunnae mean disrespect now, Laird, but how are we to ken for certain that she's yer wife since he have nae yet held a public bedding? Will there be one tonight?"

Maeve's outraged gasp filled the great hall, but he kept his focus on Athelston. "I dunnae hold with the tradition. I find it barbaric—"

"Agreed!" Maeve cried out.

His wife certainly was never going to have a problem voicing her opinion on certain matters, it seemed.

"I second that!" Tess blurted. Alasdair did glance to the women then and found Tess grinning so widely at Maeve that the head of the kitchen's eyes almost disappeared in her wrinkles. She looked to him, and her smile faltered somewhat. "I...I'm sorry, Laird. 'Tis just—"

"Ye dunnae ever need to apologize for telling me how ye feel, Tess. And I ken well enough from Lara that the women were nae ever a fan of the tradition."

"I demand a vote on it," Athelston said.

Father Bernard raised a hand and spoke. "I'm in agreement that going forward there nae be a public bedding by the lairds. They should be taken on their word as they are anointed by God to serve this clan."

Alasdair was more impressed by Father Bernard daily. The man was not only cunning but he had a way with words.

"I second the agreement," Brodick called out, as did two of the other council members, leaving Athelston the only one who did not support the change.

Alasdair smiled approvingly at his council members. "The vote is finished, and it's passed by majority. Now, on to a lass, Maeve, serving on the council. But afore ye men vote, I urge ye to think what yer wives would like and what ye would want for them."

"I'm wed to God," Father Bernard said with a wink, "but I feel confident in saying he wants us to treat women fairly and give them a say, so I'm an aye for yer lady being on our council."

Maeve beamed at Father Bernard, and her display of true happiness made Alasdair insanely pleased.

"I dunnae have a wife, either," Brodick said, "but I've been with a great many women"—the council members erupted into laughter at that—"and I get an earful from them, as well as Lara."

"Lara gives everybody an earful!" Father Bernard said.

"Aye!" came a chorus of agreement.

"So I say aye, we should have the lass sit on our council."

Three more ayes came and one nay from Athelston. Alasdair didn't hesitate. "'Tis passed. Brodick, get another chair for yerself. Maeve, ye can sit by me." Before she could protest, he was down the dais and taking her by the arm to help her to her seat.

If he'd had any concerns, which he didn't, the way she looked at him, her eyes so full of amazed appreciation, would have wiped them away. But there were none. The decisions felt good and right, and when Maeve slipped her arm through his and leaned willingly on him for support, her arm pressing against his, he knew in his heart he'd taken the right action.

She couldn't believe everything that had just occurred, nor that she had agreed to take a seat on the council when she was planning on leaving. But she could not flee until her ankle mended so she might as well busy herself. Never mind that she was almost giddy with the prospect of it. She turned her thoughts for a moment to Alasdair. He was confounding her, and she could see how easy it would be to believe his lies. She knew the truth of him, didn't she? Anise had told her all his actions were simply to seduce her and seal the marriage so he could get what he wanted, and yet, it didn't feel that way in this moment.

He had pushed for women to have an equal footing in his clan and for her to be the one to represent them. That he had known it would mean something to her astonished her. It meant he understood something about her most people did not, and that was very confusing for her. She hated him, and yet, she didn't. His actions conjured her old fantasies of finding and wedding a man who would want her to be his equal, and most especially, it brought to the forefront of her mind the fantasies she'd built around this man. She stole a sideways glance at him and sucked in a low, appreciative breath.

His strong features held a certain sensuality to them, which brought back all the memories of his lips on her body. And when he slid his arm around her waist so that she could lean into him because of her ankle, white-hot yearning for him streaked through her. She was almost relieved when he settled her beside him and they were no longer touching because at the rate she'd been heating up, she would have been burning with desire and unable to think, and she needed to have a clear head.

She was certainly not making choices as if she was not going to be part of this clan for long, but she could not bring herself to turn down his astonishing offer. To sit on a council that made decisions for the welfare of her clan—no, *his* clan. Hers only temporarily—well, that was something she'd always dreamed of. He poured a goblet of wine and handed it to her. Leaning over, he whispered, "These meetings can run long, and I'd nae want ye to have a thirst."

It felt suddenly like there was a band around her chest, and she could not pull her gaze from his eyes, which bore into hers. She felt funny. Warm and full and tingly, and—By the gods, she could fall for this man if she didn't know the truth of what he was doing. She had once fallen for him after just one kiss, and she feared she could again. She swallowed and forced herself to focus as they had an audience that consisted not only of the men on the dais with them but the woman from the kitchens, who was still standing there. "Thank ye," she said, taking the goblet, sipping the wine, and then setting it down before her. She had a flash of memory of watching her father do something similar in his own council meeting, and her throat tightened painfully. She swallowed and then addressed Tess.

"Tell me, Tess, what other problems plague the kitchens besides needing more hands?"

"The meat storage is low, and the men demand full trenchers of meat with every meal."

"I'd say the solution to that problem is simple."

"Aye, I would, too," Tess agreed.

Maeve arched her eyebrows. "Less meat at the meals until the storages are replenished?" Tess gave a confirming nod, and as Brodick started to protest, Alasdair held his hand up for the man to be silent. Maeve appreciated Alasdair's immediate show of support.

Maeve looked to Alasdair and the other men. "I assume the storages have nae been replenished yet because there are nae enough men available to hunt?" Alasdair nodded, and the other men confirmed her suspicions with grunts of agreements and nods. "I could teach a group of women to hunt." She bit her lip the moment the impulsive offer left her mouth. Whatever was she doing? It was one thing to accept an offer to sit and hear problems, but it was quite another to offer to teach women to hunt. Yet, if she could give the women some power before she left them, what harm was there in that? Of course, she was, in a sense, empowering her enemy, but it didn't feel that way. Her father was likely turning over in his grave!

"Preposterous!" Athelston blurted.

Maeve didn't know much about the man, but she disliked what she had discovered so far. She started to respond, but Alasdair spoke. "'Tis actually a sound suggestion," he said, to Maeve's instant pleasure and surprise. "Maeve is an excellent hunter. She killed the Black Boar with one shot of her bow when she was but a lass of fifteen summers." He looked to her then, and the smile in his eyes contained a sensuous flame. He gave her a smile that sent her pulse racing before he looked back to Athelston. "I've also been privy to seeing her lop off a snake's head with one throw of her dagger."

"I believe there are a good number of women who'd like to learn to hunt," Tess said, drawing Maeve's attention to her. "I'll inquire around the kitchens, but when should I tell them the lessons will begin?"

"I could start tomorrow," Maeve said, "And I can meet ye in the kitchens after the council meeting to learn my way around them." Only because she didn't want to sit idle. Not because she liked the woman—a MacRae.

Tess beamed at her. Well, maybe Maeve liked the woman a little. "Our laird can show ye the way I imagine?" Tess arched her eyebrows at Alasdair.

"I'd be happy to." He frowned in an obvious thought. "Maeve, ye'll need to give lessons on horseback, do ye nae think, because of yer ankle?"

It occurred to her that he was unknowingly presenting her with a chance to possibly escape sooner. "Are ye going to allow me to have a horse?" She'd assumed he had instructed the guards to keep her away from the stables.

His brows dipped together. "Aye. Of course. Is there a reason I should nae?"

Now she'd gone and raised his suspicion. She could tell in his question and the way his expression had darkened.

"Nay, of course nae," she rushed to reply. "I'd like to go down to the stables and see which one might best suit me." When a suspicious look replaced the dark expression, she wanted to curse. "My da always said ye have to be a beast's friend afore ye ride him." A sudden wave of grief hit Maeve as she heard her father's voice in her head. She picked up her goblet and raised it to her lips to disguise her expression. Her eyes stung, and she feared they glistened with unshed tears. Tess did not seem to take note. She gave a little curtsy before turning to depart the great hall.

Suddenly, Alasdair was taking her hand under the table and giving it a gentle squeeze. Surprised, she turned toward him as he was leaning toward her. He brought his mouth to her ear. "It will get better," he whispered. "I still miss my da, but the sadness lessens with each day. Now it only blankets me on rare occasions."

Maeve inhaled a long, steadying breath to try to get her emotions under control so she could thank him, but it was difficult. Not only was she battling her sadness for the loss of her father, but she was overcome with such tenderness for Alasdair, such appreciation for his words, that those emotions, too, filled her eyes with tears and made talking hard. Finally, she swallowed and turned her head just enough so he would perfectly hear her whisper under the talking in the great hall. The next clansman with a problem was being let in, and the men on the dais were talking among themselves.

"Ye're a surprising man, Alasdair," she said, meaning it. Then she blurted, "I'm uncertain how to proceed." If she fled, they most definitely could never be allies, but she was doubting everything. What if Father Bernard's theory had merit? What if she could discover the truth behind who started the clan wars and then their clans could be allies?

He ran one finger down the side of her cheekbone, and his touch made her shiver. "Slowly," he said. "We proceed slowly with each other."

She blinked. He thought she'd been talking of them, and in a way, she had, but not as he believed. Shocking, unexpected guilt overcame her. Why the devil she should feel guilt was baffling, but she did. Blast the man for showing her kindness and honor this morning. It was far easier to just hate him and think him dishonorable, which suited her best given if all worked out as she hoped, she'd be gone before the supper horn blew.

Chapter Sixteen

Alasdair's instincts had never failed him, and his gut was telling him that his wife was lying to him. He didn't want to be right. He wanted to be wrong so much that he tried to shove the feeling down and ignore it through the long council meeting, but when it finally ended, and Maeve rose quickly saying she'd make her way to the stables to familiarize herself with one of his horses, he knew he was right. It stung. It stung his pride, and she sparked his ire. He was giving and trying, and she was weaving lies around them, and yet, he couldn't blame her totally. He had kidnapped her. He had tricked her into wedding him.

So now what to do? Watch and wait? See what action she took? Based on her request to go to the stables alone, he didn't think it would be wrong until his gut was proven right, but he hoped he was wrong, because if he wasn't, how were they supposed to build anything on lies? And he was to blame because he'd been the one to start it this way.

He glanced at his wife, standing there waiting for him to answer her request to proceed to the stables alone, and his chest tightened. She had her head tilted down and her fiery locks cascaded across her right cheek in a bright wave. She brushed a hand across her face, wiggled her nose as if her hair had tickled it, and tucked her locks behind her ear. It wasn't an exceptional gesture, but he felt himself eagerly committing it to memory. It was one of her many unguarded gestures that would tell him who she was and what she liked, and for now, he suspected he'd only learn about her this way, and he found himself eager to do so.

"Ye promised yer presence in the kitchen," he reminded her, even as he decided it was the gentlest way momentarily to stop her from trying to take a horse from his stables and escape. Not that she'd get very far. He'd given orders this morning for her not to be allowed to ride out alone until he said it was all right. Caution was a way of life for him.

"Oh, aye, aye," she said. "I planned on going there right after the stables," she said, flushing.

His wife blushed when she lied. He put the fact in his mind for future guidance. "Well, I dunnae have time to take ye to the stables right now, but I can do so tomorrow."

"Oh, ye dunnae need to take time for me." Her face and neck were red as berries. Could she feel it? Did she wonder if he noticed it? He stared long and hard at her, trying to tell her without telling her and hoping it would be the thing to get her to abandon her plan to flee him.

"But I do," he finally replied. "So I'll take ye tomorrow, and now I'll show ye where the kitchens are."

He saw the war of emotions on her face immediately—the desire to keep protesting with the intuition that it would do more harm than good. When she finally gave a jerky nod, he found himself exhaling a breath of relief that she chose to follow her instincts. She winced as she put her full weight on her foot, and he held out his arm to her. "Lean on me."

"That is nae nec—"

Oh, but it was. When he touched her, her body responded very positively, so the more he could touch her, hopefully the more she would grow to trust him and them. "Aye, Maeve, it is," he interrupted, cutting off her protest as the other men on the dais rose and departed, leaving just him and his new wife in the great hall. He wanted her to understand one thing about him and never have a doubt about it. "Ye're my wife now; therefore, ye're my responsibility. I will ensure always ye're safe. If I ken ye're hurt, I'll do all in my power to aid ye. If ye're threatened, I'll protect ye. Slandered, then I'll defend ye. And if ye're somehow ever taken from me"—though he would not allow that to happen—"I'd find ye. It dunnae matter how long it would take. How far I had to go. What I had to risk to get ye back. I'd find ye." He was shocked with just how true his words were.

Astonishment flickered across her face. "Ye mean that," she whispered. And when he nodded, she took his arm. It felt like a triumph, and he wanted to test the limits of the moment, so he tugged her toward him until his lips touched hers, and he claimed her mouth as he fitted her so close to him that the length of her soft, lush body was pressed to his. The desire it unleashed in him made him kiss her faster and harder, and the way she responded with little moans and rocking her hips against him made him want to sweep her off her feet, take her to his bedchamber, and seal their marriage. But it was far too soon, and this was simply his first move in the battle to come. So he gentled the kiss with some effort while running his hands over her round bottom, up her spine, and to her slender neck.

He cupped her there to tilt her head back ever so slightly so he could explore the delectable recesses of her mouth. She was spicy and savory, and she gave with abandon, twirling her tongue with his, then retreating, nipping at his lips, running her tongue over the creases of his, and coming back once again for more. He slid his hands from her neck to her breasts, rubbing his fingers over the material restraining her hard nipples, and the need that gripped him nearly stole what was left of his control.

He broke the kiss, pleased to see her eyes heavy-lidded with desire, her chest rising and falling with her fast breaths, and a protest on her swollen, red lips. "If I dunnae stop now, I fear I'll nae be able to," he admitted. "I desire ye that much."

The smile that turned up the corners of her mouth was of such a triumphant nature that he laughed. "Do my words please ye?"

A lovely blush stained her cheeks. "Aye. 'Tis probably sinful how much, but aye. 'Tis heady to feel like I have some measure of power over a man like ye."

He felt his eyebrows arch. "A man like me?"

Her blush deepened, and his breath hitched at his wife's beauty. She fidgeted with her hands, and he stared, fascinated. Maeve fidgeted when embarrassed. He'd have not guessed it of her, but here it was, yet another piece of who his wife was. She bit her lip, and he had to clench his fists to keep from grabbing her and tugging her to him once more. "Ye're verra, er, powerful." Her gaze swept him from head to toe so that he knew instantly what she meant, but it was too irresistible not to tease her a bit.

"Ye mean because I'm a laird."

Her brows dipped together, and her eyes went to his chest, then back up to meet his gaze. "I—Nay. I mean because ye're—"

"Tall?"

Her frown deepened, and he barely contained the desire to laugh. "Nay, I mean, ye have—Or, that is, ye're built rather—"

"Proportioned?" He lifted his arm and flexed his bicep.

She smacked him there with a laugh. "Ye are teasing

me," she said, her merriment making her voice husky and so enticing.

"Aye, lass." He slipped his arm around her waist to lead her to the kitchens, but the moment his fingers settled on the gentle curve of her waist, he was struck with how incredibly right and natural it felt to be holding her so. "Come," he said, his own voice husky with the nameless emotion he was feeling. "I'll show ye the way. Then I need to go train for a bit afore supper. But tomorrow I'll aid ye in the training of the women." It was a spur-of-the-moment decision. He didn't have the time, but he'd make it. The battle for his wife's trust and affection would not be won if he didn't make the time.

She glanced at him in surprise as he led her down the stairs. "Ye're going to aid me?" He nodded, guiding them out of the great hall and to the right toward the door that led to the path outside through the inner courtyard that would take her to the kitchens. "Do ye have time for that? What, with nae having enough men for the tasks at hand as it is?"

"Aye," he replied, leading her outside into the courtyard. Above, the sky was a multitude of shades—blues, purples, golds, and oranges—and a steady wind blew from the direction of the loch, making her visibly shiver. He tugged her closer and wrapped his arm more tightly around her. "I'll ensure ye have a proper cloak by tomorrow."

"Why are ye being so thoughtful?" she asked, obvious suspicion in her tone and voice that made him want to chuckle.

"Ye do a funny thing to me, Maeve," he said, walking them through the courtyard, under the stone arches, and down the pebbled path. The scent of baking bread filled the air, becoming stronger the closer they drew to the kitchens.

She paused, so he did the same. He glanced down at her. She was nibbling on her lip, looking troubled. "I do a funny thing to ye, too," he blurted.

Her brows dipped into a deep frown, and then she gave a reluctant nod.

Based on the severe scowl now settled on her face, he added, "Ye dunnae like the way I make ye feel."

"Aye and nay," she replied, sounding exasperated. Her gaze shone in the twilight, and the last vestiges of sunlight filtered through her hair, making it look as if it were on fire. He wanted to thread his hands through the strands and let them slide through his fingers. "I'm confused. I—Well, I dunnae ken what to believe!" she nearly wailed.

He pressed a hand to her heart and said, "Trust what ye feel here, Maeve. The rest will work out."

Just then, the kitchen door swung open, and Tess appeared with a pail. She threw out some water, started to turn, and smiled at them, raising her hand to wave. "A woman of her word," Tess said.

Maeve bit her lip and darted a guilty glance at him. He knew why, but he managed to keep a straight face. "Usually," she grumbled under her breath.

"Well, come on, come on. The lasses are excited to meet ye. Eight wish to learn to hunt tomorrow, and they are beside themselves that ye are giving them this opportunity. I have to tell ye, we were nae too excited to learn our laird wed ye at first, but I must admit, I feel I judged ye too quickly and without knowing ye."

A troubled look swept over Maeve's face, and he suspected it was because she'd planned to be gone by tomorrow, and yet she now was faced with the knowledge that women were counting upon her. "I, I may have judged things too quickly as well," she said softly as she gave him a sideways glance under her lashes, a half-smile, and then she turned and walked toward Tess. He watched the enticing sway of her hips as she moved away, and right as the door shut, Father Bernard said from behind him, "I'm glad to see I was nae wrong in my judgment."

Alasdair turned around at the sound of Father Bernard behind him. The man wore a satisfied smile. "And what are ye judging yerself correct upon?"

Father Bernard waved his hand toward the now closed kitchen door. "Yer wife. I believed ye did nae ever forget her and had a strong attraction toward her. 'Twas why I concocted the plan to wed ye to her and then told ye that ye needed to woo her in truth."

For a moment, he was speechless with confusion. "What do ye mean ye believed I did nae ever forget her?"

"Oh, Brodick told me some years ago about ye following her in the woods for many a sennight. I caught him stealing a sweet treat from the kitchen and made him sit for confession." Father Bernard shrugged. "In his desire to nae be labeled a thief, he gave me all the secrets he could think of that he was holding. He said he thought ye had a tendre for the enemy's daughter and wondered if he should tell her da. I, of course, advised him nae to since he said ye quit going to the woods where she hunted after ye discovered who she was."

"Why did ye nae ever say anything to me?"

"In truth, I did nae think it worth saying anything about at the time. But as the years passed and ye did nae wed, nor seem interested in any lass beyond a bedding, I did wonder. And when I saw the way ye looked at yer wife afore ye were wed—"

"And how do ye think I looked at Maeve, Father?" Alasdair asked.

Father Bernard smiled. "Like a man besotted. I kenned then that I needed to intervene afore ye mucked it all up with a desire for vengeance."

"I should be vexed," Alasdair said, hardly believing how Father Bernard had duped him.

"But ye're nae, are ye?"

"Nay," Alasdair said with a shake of his head. "And I'm nae certain why."

"Because in yer heart ye ken I've given ye a chance ye would nae have had with the plan ye had concocted of revenge. So dunnae muck it up," he said.

"I'd say now it's up to Maeve. I believe I am doing what I can to prove I will be a good husband."

"Ah," Father Bernard said, his tone suddenly serious. "Strange are the chambers of a woman's heart, Alasdair. I dunnae think just proving ye'll be a good husband will be enough for a lass like her. Her eyes shine with longing."

"And what do ye think she's yearning for?"

"What we all secretly desire... True love."

Chapter Seventeen

*M*aeve was so confused. One minute she was certain Alasdair was a liar and only acting as if he cared about her to get her to lie with him to make their marriage complete, and then in the next breath, she wasn't certain. She found it nearly impossible to concentrate on Tess and the things she was telling Maeve about the kitchens, and the women she was introducing her to, because Alasdair was taking up all the space in her head.

She contemplated what she knew, or thought she knew, or what had actually occurred, as she nodded at what she hoped were appropriate times to Tess. If Alasdair was simply trying to dupe her to consummate their marriage, he was going to extreme measures, though she supposed that made him cunning, and he had a silver tongue what with the speech that he'd go to any lengths to find her. She nibbled on her lip as her emotions swirled. Why was she even thinking about this? She was not staying. It did not matter, and yet in a way, it mattered for future relations between their clans, but that bit she'd have to work through after she was away.

She willed herself to hush the part of her mind that was concentrating on Alasdair and turn her attention to Tess, who was leading her now to a table covered with flour so that they could make bread. They stood for a bit in companionable silence before Tess finally asked, "How is it that a lady such as ye kens her way around a kitchen?"

It seemed to Maeve that the women nearby paused in what they were doing to listen. She supposed she understood their curiosity. They had been friendly yet slightly guarded when she'd been introduced, and she found herself suddenly as surprisingly eager to learn about the women in the kitchens as they seemed to be to learn of her. Women were the keepers of secrets, and who better to apprise her of Alasdair and his family than these women?

"The woman who was my caretaker as a child became head of the kitchens. When she did, she insisted I learn to cook, though, in truth, I was eager to do so. I've nae ever been one for idleness."

"'Tis a good quality to wish to learn things," Tess said to murmurs of agreement from the women working near them, which confirmed Maeve's suspicion that they had been listening.

"What of the laird's mother and sister? Do they nae ever join ye in the kitchens?"

"Oh, aye," Tess said, rolling out some dough for the bread. "Lara dunnae care to cook, but if we need an extra hand, she's more than willing to aid us."

"She burns everything, though, when she does," a blond woman cutting vegetables said. The statement was made in a cheerful tone, so Maeve knew the woman was simply adding to the conversation and not trying to be cruel.

Tess nodded. "Aye, that she does. Lara has nae ever shown much of an aptitude for more feminine tasks, to her mother's dismay. I think Laird and Lady MacRae did nae ken what to do with her. She kinnae sew a stitch, she nearly burned down the healing room trying to learn to make potions, and she dunnae sing or dance, but she always followed Alasdair around wanting to do what he did."

"I recall her begging him to teach her to throw a dagger," a woman with silver hair said. "He wanted to, but Lady MacRae would nae allow it. She said it was unnatural."

"But one day, a few years ago, Alasdair came home from hunting in the woods, and he said he'd seen a lass kill the Black Boar everyone had been hunting!"

Maeve stilled in shock that she'd so impressed Alasdair that he'd returned here talking about her.

"I was in the solar serving Alasdair's da a repast. 'Tis why I heard the conversation," Tess explained. "I vow I dunnae eavesdrop."

"I do," Maeve said cheerfully. "'Tis my worst habit. It drives my da—" A hard lump formed in her throat. She swallowed it away with some effort. "It used to drive my da to distraction."

A smile turned up the corners of Tess's mouth. "I can see on yer face ye loved yer da greatly."

Maeve nodded. "I did, and I do." His loss was still so raw, and talking of him made her feel as if she was about to cry, so she said, "So what did Alasdair seeing the woman kill the Black Boar have to do with Lara?"

"Oh! He used it to convince his da that it was nae unnatural. Different, but nae unnatural. He also suggested that this other lass's da was more openminded than his own to allow his daughter to pursue hunting. 'Twas quite clever. Laird MacRae did always try to be accepting of other ideas and ways, so once he was convinced, he persuaded Alasdair's mama to allow it. That was all the encouragement Alasdair and Lara needed. From then on, she went hunting with him, learned to shoot a bow and arrow, throw a dagger, and wield a sword. But that all changed when Lara and Alasdair's da died. Their mama has lived in fear of losing another person she loves, the poor soul. She forbade Lara to hunt or practice weapons anymore, and she's become rather sharp-tongued, but I vow she's a wonderful woman."

"I appreciate ye telling me this," Maeve said. "I must admit our first meeting was nae the best."

Nor the second...

And this information about Alasdair made her like him, which added to her confusion and uncertainty about what and who to believe.

"Nay, it was nae," came a new voice.

Maeve turned from the dough toward the sound of the voice and blinked at the sight of Alasdair's mother standing in the doorway with a resigned look upon her face. She walked slowly into the room and stopped at the table where Maeve was working. The women curtsied as she moved through the room, and her warm smile showed Maeve a different side of the woman she'd met. She was not unkind, just hurting, and Maeve understood that.

"Alasdair has asked me to give ye a chance and judge ye on yer own merit."

Either Alasdair was the cleverest man in the Highlands, who knew exactly how to get a woman to warm to him, or his mother was the clever one who knew what to say to persuade Maeve to her son's side, or Anise was not telling her the truth that something had occurred between her and Alasdair. Maeve ground her teeth in frustration at how much this was needling her when it should not at all as Alasdair's mother crossed her arms over her chest and studied Maeve. "He, Brodick, and Father Bernard are convinced the Frasers are trying to keep our clans in strife with each other so that ye would wed the Fraser's son, and they would inherit Eilean Donan."

"Colin would nae do that to me," Maeve said.

"Men have betrayed women for much less than a stronghold," the woman replied. She tilted her head as her gaze bore into Maeve. "Ye need to think upon that. Ye are the heiress to a strategic castle. Ye think ye ken Colin Fraser, but ye also believed ye kenned my son, I imagine." Lady MacRae's words hit a nerve. The woman pursed her lips at Maeve. "I dunnae see why I honestly have to give ye any chance, but I will nae be purposely cruel for Alasdair's sake and because ye are his wife...for now." Had Alasdair told her they'd not lain together? "Ye'll have to make a choice soon, lass," Lady MacRae continued. "Loyalty to my son or loyalty to Colin Fraser. And I tell ye now yer choice will be all the proof I need of who ye really are."

The door to the kitchens opened, and Anise stepped in holding two sacks. Maeve could not help but note that none of the other women in the kitchens greeted Anise. Tess looked up and offered the smallest of smiles, but everyone else went about their business as if Anise had not even entered. Maeve frowned. Did they dislike the woman because she'd lain with Alasdair out of wedlock? Maeve could not help but think of Bee and her da. They had loved each other, so it seemed to Maeve that their joining without being wed was not sinful, and that was no different from why Anise had joined with Alasdair. Maeve believed the woman must truly love him, and mayhap he truly loved her, too. Something burned in her chest at the thought, and her stomach felt suddenly knotted. A realization struck her, and her lips parted with shock. She was jealous.

"I need someone to aid me in gathering herbs for the healing room," Anise said.

Before Maeve could even open her mouth to offer herself, Lady MacRae said, "Maeve can aid ye."

Maeve had to clench her teeth on her snort. Lady MacRae's dislike of her had just proved very useful for Maeve. The woman had removed all obstacles from getting out of the kitchens to escape.

Once they were outside and the kitchen door had shut behind them, Maeve fell into step beside Anise but could not keep up because her ankle began to throb. "Can ye slow please?"

Anise glanced back at her, and her gaze fell to Maeve's ankle. "Aye." As they started once more, at a much slower pace, all of Maeve's thoughts turned to her doubts about whether or not Anise was telling her the truth about her and Alasdair. It shouldn't matter, but it did. "Alasdair told me that he found ye in his bedchamber and asked ye to leave," Maeve blurted.

Anise paused at a pebbled path and turned to Maeve with her hands on her hips. "I imagine he'd say just about anything to get ye to consummate the marriage so he can provide for us MacRaes. I should be vexed that he said that, except he told me he was going to if the need arose. He told me right after he gave me this." Anise pulled her hair back from her neck and there was a love mark on her fair skin. She offered an apologetic smile. "I'm sorry to hurt ye, Maeve. I love him, and he loves me."

Maeve tried to decide if Anise was telling the truth or not, but she simply couldn't yet. "Ye love him so much, ye want him so much for yer own, that ye're willing to aid me in escaping so that ye can have him even though it will cost him being laird of Eilean Donan?"

Anise arched her eyebrows at Maeve. "Aye. He dunnae need to be laird with ye as his ally." Maeve didn't know what to say to that. "He's honorable. Ye've seen it. And I've seen enough of ye to ken ye'll nae simply go back and allow yer men to attack us again. I wager that ye'll even aid us with obtaining food for the winter and mayhap even send a contingency of yer own warriors to help guard us against further attacks. Perhaps," Anise said with a knowing look, "ye'll even convince Colin Fraser nae to attack us again. Does he love ye as ye love him?"

Maeve couldn't correct Anise on how she felt for Colin. Instead, she swallowed the knot that had lodged in her throat. She'd planned on ensuring the MacRaes had food for the winter and speaking to Colin, but she'd not thought of sending warriors to aid them. That could be an option, she supposed. "He loves me," she finally answered because she believed it to be true. Why else would he have waited so patiently for her to decide to wed him? "And I believe he will listen to me regarding yer clan."

"Then Alasdair will come to see I saved him."

"From me as his wife?"

"From having to wed for something other than love," Anise said, smiling at her. "We're lucky that we will both get to do that."

"Aye," Maeve said faintly and followed Anise as she started down the path.

"I hope yer plan involves a horse because I'll nae ever get away from here on this ankle."

"Aye," Anise said. "It does. There's one tied in the woods awaiting us."

"Is it yers?" Maeve asked.

"Nay," Anise said, moving from the pebbled path and into the woods where there was, indeed, a black horse waiting.

"Whose is it?" she asked, curious how the woman could procure another horse.

"'Tis the guard Darby's. He left it tied outside the stables like a lazy oaf, and I took it when nae anyone was watching."

"I hope he will nae get into too much trouble for that mistake."

Anise looked at her with surprise. "Ye're worried for Darby?"

"Well, aye," she acknowledged, her cheeks warming.

"Dunnae be. The man deserves this trouble and much more."

Maeve held her hand out to the horse for the beast to sniff and become familiar with her. Once the animal did that, she untied him as she asked Anise, "Did Darby do something to ye?"

A dark look crossed the woman's face that gave Maeve a chill. "It dunnae matter," Anise said, "and ye need to go. Nae anyone will look for ye afore supper, and ye should be too far gone by then for Alasdair to catch."

Maeve nodded and mounted, then looked down at the woman. "What of ye?" she asked. "How will ye convince them ye did nae have a hand in aiding me to escape?"

"Dunnae vex yerself about that," Anise replied. "I've a plan."

"Where's Maeve?" Alasdair asked, looking around the almost empty kitchen. His mother and Tess were the only two women there. The supper horn had blown a bit ago, but he'd had to go to Lara's bedchamber to borrow a cloak first. He held the fur-lined cloak in his hands.

"I sent her with Anise to collect herbs for the healing room a good while ago," his mother said with a maddening-ly innocent air. "Likely she went with her to the healing room."

Alasdair narrowed his eyes upon his mother. "Are ye trying to stir trouble?" God above only knew what lies Anise might feed Maeve while they were together.

"If ye're nae doing anything with Anise anymore, then there's nae any trouble to be stirred. Yer wife should have the utmost faith in ye."

"Aye," Alasdair snapped. "My wife, whom I recently kidnapped, who thinks our clan started scrimmages with her clan, who already halfway believed I was still bedding Anise because of the damned castle gossip—"

"Alasdair!" his mother cried out at his crass choice of words.

"Which Anise undoubtedly started," he continued, ignoring his mother's reprimand. "Aye, 'tis perfectly reasonable to think Maeve should have unwavering faith in me." He stalked to his mother until he was right in front of her. "Cease this, Mama. Ye gave me yer word."

"I—"

He held up his hand to silence her. "I miss him, too," he said, referring to his father. "But this will nae bring him back, and Maeve was nae the one to kill him. And it just may be that her clan was nae, either. Ye heard Father Bernard."

"Aye," his mother said on a sigh.

"Ye are making things harder for me, and they are already difficult enough."

A stricken look settled on his mother's face. "I'm sorry, Son. I just dunnae want to see ye wed to a woman ye dunnae love and who loves another."

Alasdair stilled. "Did she say she loved Colin Fraser?"

"Nae exactly," his mother said, "but she said the man would nae ever lie to her. She clearly believes in him."

Alasdair scrubbed a hand across his face. He had taken Maeve to save his clan and for revenge, but it wasn't like that now. The short time he'd been with her had shown him his desire for her was still strong and that she still drew him to her. Father Bernard had said Alasdair looked at her as if he was besotted. There was caring there, for certain, and because of that, he wasn't sure he could keep her here if she was truly in love with Colin Fraser.

He left his mother and made his way to the healing room only to find it empty. He went from there to the great hall, where the clan was gathering for supper. Maeve was not sitting at the dais, and he didn't readily see either woman in the great hall. He made his way to the dais, where Lara and Brodick were seated. "Have either of ye seen Maeve or Anise?"

"Nay," they answered in near unison, glancing at each other and bursting out laughing as if what they'd done was the most amusing thing in the world. These two were acting odd, but he didn't have time to contemplate why. He was starting to get a bad feeling in his gut, and he knew well to trust that instinct.

"Lara, ye go to Maeve's bedchamber and see if she's there now, and then Anise's, and Brodick, ye go to the kitchens and ask Tess if she's seen her. Meet me at the stables."

"Is something amiss?" Lara asked, no longer smiling with her amusement of a moment ago.

"I hope nae," he said, "but I've a feeling in my gut, and I ken well Maeve still wanted to flee us. Mama apparently sent her with Anise to gather herbs in the woods."

"Unguarded?" Brodick asked.

"Aye," Alasdair said. If Maeve had a mind to flee once they got to the woods, he had no doubt his canny wife would make it happen, and the thought of her alone, at night, in the woods with a hurt ankle, washed cold fear over him. Wolves dwelled in those woods, and there were many places to fall and break her pretty little neck.

They all exited the great hall together and then went their separate ways. Alasdair kept an eye out for both women as he strode through the mostly empty castle halls and into the courtyard, where only a half dozen people remained that had not made their way to supper, and down the path to the stables, where he found the stable master, George, looking frantic.

"What's amiss, George?"

"Darby left his horse tied outside of the stables, and now the beast is gone, and he's blaming it on me."

Maeve. That icy fear that had washed over him shoved a hard, cold sliver into his heart. "Fetch my horse," he barked.

A moment later, George came out leading Alasdair's horse. Alasdair took the reins from the surprised stable master, mounted, and took off toward the woods without waiting for Brodick and Lara to appear and tell him they had not located her. He knew she was gone. He just prayed he found her before trouble did.

She saw her clansmen before they saw her. The shards of the day's fading light shone down on them as they crested a hill in the woods, and she noticed their plaids—the blue, green, red, and white of her clan's colors—before she even noted the number of men. *Two.* She hadn't made much progress toward her home, given Darby's stallion had taken an immediate disliking to her once she started off in the woods, so she was confused as to what two of her warriors were doing so close to Alasdair's home, but then it hit her: they were likely coming to inquire if the MacRaes had seen her. Though, sending only two warriors into enemy territory did seem strange. Still, she'd not argue it. She'd been turned around for a while and struggling with the foul beast she was upon.

"Here!" she called out, raising her hand and waving it excitedly. "'Tis me, Lady MacKenzie." She gave Darby's horse a little nudge to move faster toward the hill to meet the oncoming warriors. As she drew closer to them, she frowned. She didn't recognize their faces, but then again, her clan was made up of over a thousand people. She couldn't know everyone. The man in the front looked to be close to her age with his unlined skin and full head of brown hair, but the warrior riding behind him was bald with dark, slitted eyes and an unpleasant downward turn to his mouth.

"Why did nae Alfred come with ye to inquire of me?" she asked. It seemed to her that her father's former right hand would have seen to the matter of her disappearance personally.

"She's as bonny as ye thought," the older man said, turning his head slightly to look at the younger warrior. The odd statement made the hairs on the back of Maeve's neck stand up.

She opened her mouth to inform them both that they should not speak of her, their leader, as if she were not there, nor should they speak of her in such personal terms.

"I saw her first," the younger man replied, and the hungry expression on his face made the hairs on her arms join the hairs on her neck to stand at attention. She gripped her reins tightly as her heartbeat increased, and the flow of blood through her veins moved at a more rapid pace. "I get her first," he added, and he moved his reins as if to edge closer to her.

"Alfred will carve out yer hearts if ye put a finger on me," she said, hating that her voice trembled.

"Who the devil is Alfred?" the older man sneered.

She didn't need anything more than that. They could not be MacKenzie warriors, despite the MacKenzie plaids they wore. If they were her clansmen, there was no way they would not know who Alfred was. He'd been head of guards for fifteen summers.

She gave a swift jerk of her reins to swing Darby's horse around, but the obstinate animal refused to obey, and that was going to cost her. She knew it with a dread that filled every place in her body, and it was a breath before the dread turned to black fright. The younger man grabbed her reins as the older man came beside her and yanked her off her horse. He slid off his own, threw her to the ground with a force that knocked the wind out of her and set stars dancing in her line of vision, and he was on top of her as she released a bloodcurdling scream.

Maeve's scream ripped through the silence of the twilight calm, and it tore into Alasdair, shredding what little calm he'd managed to maintain. He stilled as his blood rushed hard through his veins, and he tried to decide which way the scream had come from. She was in trouble! She screamed again, louder, more terror filled, and a red sort of haze instantly covered his vision as he turned his horse to the north in the direction of her scream.

He urged the beast into an all-out gallop that was heedless of his own safety. He didn't matter. All that mattered was getting to Maeve before she was hurt, or worse. As he rode up the hill, following the echoes of yet another frightened scream, terrible scenarios filled his head, and he gripped his reins so hard that they cut into his palms. When he crested the hill, his heart stopped. Moonlight shone down on Maeve, who was lying on the ground with a man holding her arms over her head and another straddling her.

Rage gripped him in an iron hold, and the world around him disappeared except for her. There was no noise, no feeling, just methodical actions. He let out a war cry as he drew his sword and galloped toward his wife and the men who were daring to touch her. The man holding her arms scrambled up and started to reach behind him to, no doubt, draw his own sword, but Alasdair was upon them before the man could even reach all the way back to where the weapon was sheathed. As Alasdair brought his horse right up to the side of Maeve, he sent his sword deep into the standing man's chest and drove it all the way to the hilt, before he yanked it out and jumped off his beast to face the other man now standing.

Alasdair could not look to Maeve yet and risk being distracted. "Ye," he thundered, pointing his sword at the man who was drawing his own weapon, "are going to die for touching my wife."

"I dunnae think so," the younger man said, and as he stepped toward Alasdair and Alasdair prepared to fight him, the man's eyes suddenly grew large, his face slack, and he began to stagger. Alasdair frowned, unsure what was happening, until the man tilted forward to land almost on top of his fallen comrade, and when he did, Alasdair saw the dagger planted deep in the back of the man's neck. Behind him, Maeve stood, panting, fists by her sides, gown torn, blood streaked across her cheek from her busted lip, and tears streaming down her beautiful face.

His heart squeezed so hard in his chest that pain vibrated out from it to every part of his body. He closed the distance between them in two long strides, gathered her to him, and she crumbled into his arms, clinging to him as the tears took her.

Chapter Eighteen

She clung to him as the world turned violently around her. He was no longer her enemy or a man she could not trust. He'd cut down the men trying to hurt her with no care for his own safety. He had risked himself to protect her. She would not forget it, ever. And he held her now with such tenderness, whispering soothing sounds in her ear, running his large hand gently down the back of her head, even as he embraced her with his other arm. She could not see how this man did not care for her, despite what Anise had told her.

Maeve tried and failed to stop crying, which was out of shock and relief that Alasdair had come before the men had defiled her or worse. The thought of the men had her pulling back from Alasdair and looking toward the fallen dead men. "Those are nae my men," she said, her voice clogged with tears and her lingering fear.

"Nay," he agreed, turning ever so slightly to look behind him at the men. "They wear yer plaid, though."

They both stood in silence for a long breath, she supposed letting that fact sink in. Father Bernard's suggestion that the Frasers were behind the attacks immediately came to mind. She didn't know who these men were, but they were not her men, and yet, they had her clan's plaid on, which meant they had to know someone who had access to plaids from her clan.

"They did nae ken me," she said, the hairs on her arms prickling. Alasdair immediately began to rub his hands gently over her skin. She looked up at him, their gazes clashing and holding, and the tenderness, the concern, that was in his gaze made her breath hitch. There was no denying what she saw, nor was there denying the warmness that grew inside her.

"Maeve," he said, his voice husky with worry. "Did they hurt ye?"

"Nay, nae really. Ye got to me afore they could do anything, thank god."

His arms grew tighter around her; his muscles flex and bunching against her skin. Being held by him, she felt safe, comforted, and cared for. She pressed her cheek to his chest, listening for a long moment to the still thunderous beat of his heart. She could not believe, given his reactions this night, that he was not honorable, nor that he'd been lying to her about Anise.

"I'm sorry," she whispered.

His finger came under her chin to tilt it to him once more so that they were again looking at each other. "'Tis I who should be sorry," he replied. "I take it ye believed the castle gossip about Anise and me?"

She nodded but held her tongue on revealing that Anise herself had told her it was true and that everything he said to Maeve was simply a ruse to get her to bed him. She thought of telling him, but it served no purpose except to create trouble for Anise, and Maeve could somewhat understand the powerful desperation that had driven the woman to trick her.

"I kinnae make ye believe I have ended things with Anise, and that I dunnae hold feelings for the woman, but—"

"I believe ye," she said, thinking of how he'd charged in,

heedless of his own safety to save her and of the fear and tenderness she'd seen in his gaze. What she was going to do with this new belief, she did not know.

"How did ye get away from Anise?" Alasdair suddenly asked. "Or did the woman simply let ye go?"

"'Twas nae so difficult," she said, avoiding giving an exact answer because she had no idea what Anise was saying. And when he opened his mouth as if he was going to question her again, she gave a little shiver, which was not entirely an act. She was cold and weary. "Do ye think ye could take me back to the castle now?"

"Aye," he said, glancing back at the dead men once more. "I'll send some of my men back to bury these two. Did they say anything to indicate who they were or what they were doing here?"

"Nay," she said. "I suppose it would have been wise to leave one of them alive to question."

"Mayhap," he agreed, "but I could nae think properly when I saw them attacking ye."

At that moment, Darby's horse came galloping up to them and tried to nudge Maeve. She glared at the animal. "Yer horrid disposition almost got me ravaged," she informed the beast.

"In case ye try to flee on horseback again, ye should ken that all the warriors' horses have been trained to be agreeable only to their masters."

"That would have been helpful to know," she said, wondering why Anise had sent her on this horse, then.

"Nae anyone outside the warriors ken it. Nae even the wives. Only my warriors and my family."

"Then why are ye telling me?" she asked.

His hand came to cup her chin, and the look he got in his eyes sent a shiver of yearning down her spine. "Because,

Maeve, ye are now my family, if only ye will give me a chance. Give us a chance."

"Alasdair!" came a man's cry from down the hill.

Alasdair took her by the hand, and they turned just as a half dozen warrior-manned horses galloped up the hill. Brodick led the charge, and he came to a shuddering stop in front of Alasdair and Maeve. He glanced at the dead men, then back to him. "I see ye took care of things," he said.

"Aye," Alasdair replied, squeezing Maeve's hand. "I retrieved my wife."

Brodick gave Maeve a disapproving look. "Yer wife knocked Anise out to get away from her."

Brodick's words so shocked Maeve that her mouth slipped open. She clamped it shut as soon as she realized it, but not before Alasdair saw her with it gaping open. She hoped he didn't read her utter surprise in her expression; though, currently, she had half a mind to tell him everything. She could hardly believe Anise's duplicity. Then again, thinking on the woman's desire for Alasdair, it made perfect sense to paint Maeve as a villain.

It was well into the night before Alasdair was finished dealing with the repercussions of Maeve's attempted escape and the attack on her. He got Maeve back to her bedchamber, and then he called an emergency council meeting to discuss the men and theories. They all had the same one— that it was the Frasers—except Alasdair, who didn't seem as convinced, but who also didn't seem to have a good reason why. Alasdair instructed the guards to be doubled around the castle, and then he had to sit on the dais in the great hall and listen to a whole host of his clansmen and women state the opinion that he should send her back to whence she came, which included his mother and Anise—who sported a black eye—which did not at all go with her story that Maeve had knocked her out by hitting her in the head. Lara, Brodick, and Father Bernard had spoken in favor of Maeve by attempting to convince him that she understandably needed time to become accustomed to their clan.

He sat through it all silently, nodding now and then so everyone would think he was considering what they said. He wasn't. He'd known the minute he held Maeve in his arms as she cried that the only thing that would make him give her up was Maeve herself. He thought of what his mother had said about thinking Maeve loved Colin Fraser, and he knew he needed to speak with her frankly about it, but he also thought about how she had lied to protect Anise. He knew it in his gut. He had no doubt that Anise had willingly helped Maeve escape, and when the council meeting ended and Anise appeared at the doorway with only him and Brodick left in the great hall, he motioned for Brodick to stay. He didn't want to add more fire to the flames of gossip about the two of them.

"What is it, Anise?" he asked, moving toward the door where she stood with Brodick by his side.

"Can I speak with ye alone, Laird?"

"Nae now. I'm going to see Maeve and ensure she's well after her ordeal."

"'Tis about her," Anise said.

He wasn't surprised. "Say yer piece."

"Ye may wish to hear this alone."

"I dunnae."

A look of irritation flittered across Anise's face. "Fine. Yer wife told me she loves Colin Fraser."

It was said matter-of-fact, without the slightest hesitation or any normal indications that Anise was lying, so he suspected she wasn't, and it felt rather like a punch in the gut. "Fine. Ye've said what ye came to say, now off with ye."

"But—"

"Goodnight," he snapped, having lost all patience.

When she was gone, and he and Brodick exited the great hall, Brodick put a hand to Alasdair's arm. "Do ye wish to talk?"

"Aye," he said, "to my wife. So, if ye'll excuse me..."

"Aye. Good luck."

A few short moments later, he was knocking on her door. "Aye?" came her voice, and the weariness in her tone roused his concern for her, even as his mind was turning over what Anise had just told him.

"May I come in?"

"Aye. 'Tis nae barred."

He opened her door and paused at the sight of her. She stood at the washbasin splashing water on her face. The bodice of her gown was loosened to reveal the swell of her breasts, and rivulets of water ran down her chest. Her hair was piled on top of her head, except for a few loose tendrils that hung around her face. Her eyes were closed, and she straightened at the creak of her door, he assumed, as she patted around on the washbasin stand.

"The cloth fell," he said, assuming it's what she was looking for. He strode to her, bent down, and handed it to her.

"Thank ye," she murmured, wiping the water from her eyes before she opened them, and her gaze met his. When their eyes locked, desire jolted through him, but not just desire but a wanting to discover her likes and dislikes, fears and joys, dreams and hopes.

He stood there a moment, not only drinking in her loveliness but carefully considering how to proceed. "Anise tells me ye spoke of loving Colin Fraser."

She scowled but did not deny it. An ache sprang in his chest, and he forced himself to continue. "Ye clearly wish to keep some things to yerself regarding tonight. Details that seem to be forgotten about ye, Anise, and yer escape and how it all came to be and occurred." He paused to allow her to understand that he knew the truth, and he saw the minute she realized it. Her eyes grew big, and her face lost its rosiness. "I accept that," he continued, not wanting to cause her more worry than necessary, "and I even understand what yer reasons may be, but I kinnae accept nae kenning if ye have a true affection for another man. So, do ye?"

"What if I did?" she asked.

He did not miss the tone in her voice. It wasn't challenging but more like probing, testing.

"Then I suppose I'd be obliged to let ye return to him."

"Ye expect me to believe that after ye took me against my will, ye would allow me to return to Colin if I told ye I loved him?"

He sighed. He'd made a grave mistake. It was so clear now. He'd wanted to aid his clan, but the way he'd gone about it had possibly made it nearly impossible for Maeve to ever trust him because he had not thought he'd want her trust. He had not thought he would want a real marriage with her. He had simply not thought. "I dunnae expect ye to believe me, but 'tis true. I will."

She took a deep breath and then let it out very slowly. "Women dunnae ever have choices, nae really, so 'tis hard for me to believe ye are giving me one now."

"If ye truly love him, why have ye nae wed him?"

She tossed the towel onto the wash table and then sat on the edge of the bed. He walked to her, inclined his head in silent question, and waited for her to indicate that he could sit before he did so. The bed creaked under his weight, and she tilted toward him just a bit. He expected her to move when their legs touched, but she didn't. That she trusted him enough to stay where she was made him feel oddly choked with emotion.

"I am nae in love with him, but my da wanted me to wed him so that I would be protected when my da was gone." He wanted to tell her he'd protect her, but he stayed silent so she would continue. "My da was in love with my former companion, Beitris, who is now head of the kitchens, yet he did nae wed her because he promised my mama I would have the choice to wed for love." She bit her lip and glanced at his mouth. He caught the rosy blush that stained her cheeks now. "I did nae ken about my da and Bee until recently. I was thrilled, of course, and I told my da he could nae go on sacrificing his and Bee's happiness for me. He hesitated to wed her because if I did nae end up wedding Colin, my da believed it would fall to him to take a wife from a strong clan to gain an alliance. When I discovered this, I told him to go to the Fraser and set the date for my wedding. Bee was livid. She loved my da and wanted to wed him, but she's so good and giving that she was willing to sacrifice her own happiness for me. She told Da to break my betrothal. She told me so after he left, but when he did nae return and Colin brought him home dead, Colin told me that Da did nae break the betrothal. So, I thought my da believed Colin the right match for me. Now, I dunnae ken what to think."

"Ye're amazing," he said.

She frowned. "How so?"

"Ye were willing to wed a man ye dunnae love so yer da could wed the woman he did."

She shrugged. "'Tis nae any more selfless than ye being willing to wed me to save yer clan."

Her words made him uncomfortable because her motivation with her da had been much purer than his own. "Ye were nae motivated by revenge at all. I was."

"And now?" she asked, studying him.

"And now," he said, unable to keep himself from touching her and running one finger over her hand that lay on her thigh. She shivered under his touch. "I dunnae care about revenge at all."

"What do ye care about?"

"Discovering who ye are," he answered honestly. "Will ye give me that chance?"

A shy look came across her face, but she nodded. "I'd like to ken ye better as well."

"Then let's get comfortable and talk," he said, scooting to the back of her bed, kicking his legs out in front of him, and leaning against the headboard.

She looked at him warily from the foot of the bed.

He patted the space beside him. "I'll nac touch ye I vow it. Unless," he said, his voice going husky, "ye want me to touch ye. And then I will."

"I think it best," she said, scooting backward in such an adorable fashion that he smiled watching her, "that we keep our hands to ourselves."

"I vow it," he agreed, crossing his hands in his lap, trying to tamp down the already near overwhelming urge to run them all over her body. When she settled beside him, he said, "I dunnae wish to bring up a topic that causes ye pain, but will ye tell me how yer da died?"

Her brows dipped together, and she nibbled on her lip.

"Aye. But why do ye wish to ken that?"

"Because I kinnae get Father Bernard's theory on the Frasers out of my mind—especially after tonight—and ye said yer da's mistress—"

"Beitris," Maeve said.

It was then he recalled what Father Bernard had told him about Beitris, so he quickly told Maeve.

"I kinnae believe it!" she exclaimed.

"Aye," he agreed. "'Tis strange but true. So," he continued, "ye said Beitris believed yer da was going to the Fraser stronghold to break yer betrothal."

"Aye," she said, wariness in her tone now. "But it could have been that Da just did nae want to argue with Bee afore he left because he kenned she would wish to sacrifice them for me."

"What did Colin tell ye happened?"

Maeve sucked in a lower portion of her lip for a moment, and Alasdair knew she was thinking upon it now. "He said that Da had gone hunting with them to celebrate the upcoming wedding and that he had fallen from his horse and the injury killed him."

"Was yer da a careless rider?"

"Nay! But accidents do happen."

"Aye, they do." But the more Alasdair thought about it, the more certain he became that Father Bernard was correct. "But from what I've deduced of yer da, he would have given his life for ye."

"Oh aye," she said, a smile curving her beautiful mouth. "He would have."

"Then I think, Maeve," he said gently, "he would have gladly given his happiness to try to ensure ye had yers."

"Aye. I'm thinking the same thing, but that means either Colin kenned my da was murdered and lied to me or he did nae ken at all." Her eyes filled with tears and a few spilled over to run down her cheek.

He wasn't supposed to touch her, but some promises were meant to be broken. He cupped her cheek gently in his palm and ran his thumb over her wet, smooth skin. She sighed and leaned into his palm. Her trust in this moment was the greatest gift of his life.

"If the Frasers killed my da, whether Colin kenned or nae, then it's my fault my da is dead," she said in a choked whisper as more tears spilled down her cheeks.

Her pain made him ache, and he found himself cupping her cheeks and kissing her tears away, and before he knew it, his mouth was on hers and her hands were twining about his neck as she twisted toward him, moaning. He pulled her to him and onto his lap to hold her. As good as she felt and tasted, he did not want to let the kiss get out of hand. Breaking his promise to her was one thing; obliterating it was another. He allowed his hands to explore the hollows of her back for one moment as his tongue explored her mouth, but as he felt his desire growing hotter, he reluctantly pulled back.

She settled her head against his shoulder with a contented sound that made him smile. And then she said, "Tess told me ye were the reason yer sister was allowed to learn to hunt. And that it came about because ye came home speaking of a lass ye saw kill the Black Boar. I kinnae believe I made such an impression on ye."

There was no point denying it now. "Well, ye did."

"Ye made an impression on me, too," she said, her tone almost shy.

"Did I?" He was looking down at her when she tilted her face upward to him. Dampness still clung to her thick lashes.

"Aye. Ye were the reason I was nae so keen to wed."

"I was?" he asked, shocked.

She nodded. "I foolishly believed I could choose the man I wished to wed, but women do nae have choices."

She looked away, but he cupped her chin and brought her gaze back to him. "Ye do. I took it from ye, but I vow I'm giving it back. I will let ye make the choice."

She did not look at all convinced. "Ye say that now, but they are pretty words until actions prove them false or true."

He didn't know how to prove it to her, other than offering to take her home once again, but he was loathe to make it so easy for her to leave him. But if she asked, he would see her home and find another way to save his clan. She yawned, and he could see the tiredness in her eyes. "I should go and let ye sleep."

"Will ye stay? I dunnae want to be all alone."

"Aye, I'm verra glad to stay."

"I'm nae scairt," she said.

"Nay, of course ye're nae," he agreed, recognizing instinctually this was important to her.

"It's just that, well, I'm feeling sad after our conversation."

She scooted down until her head was resting on her feather pillow and looked up at him. Her red hair fanned out around her fair skin, and she looked at him with eyes void of guile. Her loose bodice fell open even more so that he could see the perfect swell of her breasts, and as his gaze was riveted there, he saw the fast beat of her heart underneath her skin. He was hit forcefully by emotion, but it was not lust. It was respect and a deep liking for her. She was brave and candid, and those were two things he very much admired.

He lay beside her and slipped an arm around her waist. When she scooted back to fit herself against him, his muscles tightened with desire but also contentment. He had the strangest sensation that he was home in a way he'd never been before, but his mind would not settle. Worry invaded his thoughts, and it was a concern he was not accustomed to. Maeve was led by her concern for her clan and her need to fulfill what she believed her father wished for her, and in that regard, they were alike.

He knew what he would do if he were her. He'd return home and wed as his father had wished, unless he was convinced he'd been betrayed by the Frasers. She was doubting the Frasers now, but he knew if she heard a confession that would be best. Her chest began to rise and fall slowly, and when the sound of her steady breathing filled the silence, he knew she had fallen asleep, and it was not long before he succumbed himself.

Chapter Nineteen

Maeve awoke to Alasdair already up and gone. She dressed and made her way to the great hall where she discovered Lara, who waved her over. "Ye ken the gossip about Alasdair and Anise is just that. Aye? Dunnae fash yerself with it any longer."

Clearly, Lara thought the gossip was the reason Maeve had fled, and that was embarrassing. "I'm nae fashed," Maeve said. And she wasn't really any longer, but she was greatly vexed with Anise and wary of what the woman might do next.

Lara chuckled. "Oh aye, the scowl on yer face proves how little ye care."

"I did nae say I dunnae care," Maeve muttered. "But Alasdair can do as he wishes," she added, uncertain why she had said that, beyond pride.

Lara arched her eyebrows. "Oh aye?"

Maeve nodded.

"Well, I'll nae be letting my husband do as he wishes when I'm wed. But I suppose…"

"What?" Maeve prompted as Lara let her words dwindle.

"Well, I suppose ye did nae wish for my brother as a husband, and that's the difference. Ye dunnae want him, nor do ye care for him."

Maeve opened her mouth to object, but what could she

say? She had wanted him once, then considered him an enemy, and now? She did feel something for him, but what? And did it even matter what she felt? Her da had made his wishes for her clear, and she needed to abide by them to honor his memory.

"I care for him," she said quietly. "It's just—"

"Confusing?"

Maeve nodded.

"Hopefully it will become less confusing for the two of ye afore it's too late."

Maeve frowned. "What do ye mean?"

"'Tis nae anything. Just castle gossip."

Before Maeve could ask what Lara meant, Father Bernard appeared. "Maeve, allow me to show ye around the castle so ye can become familiar with it." Maeve didn't have a chance to agree or disagree. Father Bernard linked his arm through hers and was tugging her toward the door before she could blink. She cast a look over her shoulder and found Lara staring at them with a concerned expression on her face, and the feeling that something was brewing lingered with Maeve all morning. It felt as if servants were casting odd looks her way, but when she asked Father Bernard about it, he waved off her concerns.

"'Tis nae more than idle castle gossip," he said, repeating Lara's explanation.

Maeve was eager to find Tess because if anyone knew what was being said, she thought it would be her, but when she got to the courtyard where they were supposed to train that afternoon, the crowd of women was already there, as well as Alasdair. He paused for a moment in his talk and gave her a smile that warmed her through. That the man had such an effect on her bothered her, but she was helpless to stop it. She wound her way through the women until she got to Tess.

Tess acknowledged her with a smile, and Maeve thought to wait to speak to her when Alasdair was done talking, but it seemed he would never be done speaking because the women had so many questions for him, most of them silly. Maeve found herself growing impatient, but not Alasdair. He answered each question with care, though some of them didn't deserve his time.

How had he gotten so muscular? That one had been asked by the blonde woman beside him as she batted her eyelashes and giggled. *Was it bow hunting that made him cut of stone?* Maeve rolled her eyes, but as they went on, mostly asked by a group of three younger lasses huddled together, Maeve began to have suspicions about their intentions. She turned to Tess, who was beside her, and whispered, "It seems the women have forgotten Alasdair is wed."

Her words, as well as her snappy tone, surprised her, and they clearly surprised Tess, too, because the woman gaped at her for a moment before responding. "Castles are full of gossip, which ye stirred to a frenzy with yer escape attempt," she said, eyeing Maeve. That was the third time this day that the word "gossip" had been used.

Maeve frowned. "What exactly is the gossip?" she whispered.

"Well, my lady, the gossip is that ye and the laird have nae...er, made yer marriage true, and the lasses ken well the laird has...er, *had* a healthy appetite for the bedding, so..."

Heat singed Maeve's cheeks. "They think he dunnae have an appetite for me." Tess nodded, and though Maeve would not have thought it possible, her embarrassment grew as well as her offense. "Why would they even be talking of...of—"

"The servants change yer bed linens," Tess whispered.

"And there's nae been any proof of yer innocence being taken. And the two of ye slept in the same bed last night, so they are saying either he dunnae want ye or ye were nae innocent. Either way, a sinful wager has started."

"What sort of wager?" Maeve asked, her pulse ticking upward.

"The lasses ken now that the laird is ready and willing to take a wife, so they are fighting to replace ye."

"Do they expect me to leave again?"

"Aye." Tess darted her gaze toward Alasdair, who was still answering ridiculous questions. "And if ye dunnae, they expect he'll have Father Bernard dissolve the marriage. I ken it's ridiculous."

It was. She knew it was. But the smallest part of her tightened in fear, which shocked her, but before she could consider it, Anise appeared at the far end of the courtyard, strolling toward them with a demure smile upon her face.

"Ye best watch that one," Tess whispered.

Didn't she know it. But instead of releasing that comment, she addressed what she knew Tess was referring to. "Alasdair is too smart to fall prey to any scheme she may be conjuring," Maeve said.

"If ye say so," Tess replied.

By that afternoon, Maeve was ready to kill Anise and shake Alasdair senseless. She seethed inwardly as he stood behind the healer and guided her yet again on how to properly line up her arrow. Maeve distractedly finished helping the lass she had agree to aid, and then she marched over to Alasdair and Anise. She forced a bright smile to her face, though she would have cheerfully smacked the woman if it wouldn't have made her look jealous. But she *was* jealous. Shockingly so.

"Should nae ye be in the healing room?" she asked Anise. "Mayhap putting a poultice on that black eye I gave ye?"

Anise's gaze widened.

"My eye feels better."

"How does yer head feel where my gentle wife hit ye?"

His pointed question made Maeve a little less irritated with him.

"Er, better, laird, thank ye. Could ye show me how to place my arms again?" Anise asked. "I just dunnae feel I understand how to hold the arrow."

The woman backed herself into Alasdair's chest before he could even answer if he'd show her or not. She wiggled her behind at him, and Maeve grabbed his hand. It was one thing not to tell the truth of what the woman had done because Maeve knew it had been done out of desperate love for her husband, but it was quite another to stand here and watch the woman flirt with Alasdair. Anise clearly thought Maeve's return to the castle was short-lived, and Maeve could not blame her for her confusion on exactly how Maeve did feel about Alasdair, since she was only starting to sort through her complicated feelings herself. "Might I have a moment of yer time, Husband?"

He didn't look the least bit surprised, the devil.

Maeve strode to the other side of the courtyard where they could be alone, then swung around to speak to Alasdair. "What are ye doing?"

"Teaching Anise how to hunt," he said.

"Do ye nae realize that she's flirting with ye?"

"I do, but it dunnae matter. I've only got eyes for ye, Maeve."

She didn't mean to grin, but she did. "Will ye let me instruct her instead of ye?"

"Aye," he said to her relief. "If ye wish it."

"I wish it," she replied, wincing at how eager she sounded.

The smile that graced his lips could only be described as smug.

"What?" she snapped. His smile grew larger and more dazzling, which increased her vexation with the jealousy gripping her.

"Why do ye wish it?"

He was baiting her. She knew it, and yet she answered. "I dunnae like it."

He leaned closer until his presence was nearly overwhelming. She could feel the heat radiating from his skin, see the perspiration on his brow, smell the faint scent of smoke upon him from a fire. "Why do ye nae like it? Are ye jealous?"

"Certainly nae," she lied. "I'd have to care to be jealous."

"And here I had judged ye honest," he said, his voice like silk. "Well," he amended, "mostly honest."

Her cheeks burned at that truth. She had lied about Anise. "Fine. I may be a wee bit jealous."

Before she knew what was happening, his hand slid around the back of her neck, and he claimed her mouth for a thorough kiss that left her breathless. When he released her, she had trouble forming a proper sentence. "What— what was that for?"

"So ye dunnae feel the need to be jealous. I'm yers, if ye want me."

She cleared her throat, her nerves feeling knotted. "Do ye ken what the women in the castle are saying?"

A shadow of annoyance crossed his face. "Aye. Brodick told me. There's an easy way to put a stop to the gossip, ye ken…"

She knew he was teasing, but her emotions were taut as a bow. "'Tis nae as simple as that."

All the levity left his face, and she wished she'd responded better. "Dunnae I ken it," he muttered. "Come. Let's turn our attention to a less complicated matter."

‧⟊⟊⟊‧

"Lara tells me ye may need an extra body on the hunt today," Brodick said a sennight later as he strode up to Alasdair. The courtyard around them was chaotic as the women he and Maeve had been training were getting ready for their first test hunt to see what skills they had mastered and what they needed to practice further.

Alasdair paused in restringing Maeve's bow for her while she was instructing Tess on the proper way to throw a dagger. "When did ye see Lara?"

"I stopped in to visit her in the healing room. Yer mama has put her in there once again, in fear for Lara to be out and about, given the men who attacked Maeve."

"Why would ye stop in to see my sister?" Alasdair asked, lowering Maeve's bow he'd been holding to his side.

"Because she's bored in the healing room, Alasdair, and I had a free moment."

"And how do ye ken my sister is bored in the healing room?"

"We had a conversation at supper," Brodick replied, but he was avoiding Alasdair's gaze.

Alasdair had been so busy with running the clan in the last two weeks and training the women with Maeve that he had dragged himself to supper at night, almost too exhausted to eat. But he had wanted to spend the time with Maeve. They had fallen into deep conversations about their morning training nearly every night, so he had to admit he had not taken note of his sister talking to Brodick.

Of course, they'd grown up together, and he knew they thought of each other almost as brother and sister. Or he thought they did. "Ye ken I think of ye as a brother."

"Aye," Brodick said, his tone wary. "But ye dunnae want me pursuing yer sister."

Alasdair stood speechless for a moment, and before he could think of a proper reply, Maeve said from behind him, "Of course Alasdair would be thrilled if ye and Lara end up together."

Alasdair turned to Maeve, who was giving him an encouraging look. "Why do ye sound as if ye ken what's going on between my sister and Brodick?"

"Because I have two eyes," Maeve said. "Ye fail to see what's right in front of ye, or ye are ignoring it."

"There's nae anything occurring yet, Alasdair," Brodick said.

"Well if it does," Maeve said, "Alasdair will approve." With that, she flounced past them toward her horse, which was tethered with the others on the far side of the courtyard.

"Yer wife is bold."

"Aye," Alasdair agreed. She was sneaky, too, but with the best intentions. He'd seen her talking in private to Anise, flailing her hands, her expression angry, and he would have wagered all the coin he had left that she'd been giving the woman hell for lying about her hitting Anise to get away, but Maeve, being the bighearted lass he'd come to discover she was, had hugged an astonished-looking Anise after her lecture and then left her standing there gawking.

"Are ye happy ye took her?" Brodick quietly asked Alasdair.

Alasdair looked at his friend. "Aye."

"Because it will be good for the clan?"

"Nay," Alasdair answered honestly. It wasn't even a consideration anymore.

"I did nae think so."

Alasdair arched his eyebrows. "What makes ye say that?"

"Ye could have made a move to take over her clan by now, but ye're waiting, giving her time to become accustomed to ye, considering her feelings. That is nae something a man who wed just for revenge would do."

It had changed. He had changed. And it was because of Maeve. When he was with her, he felt—Well... He looked to her, trying to sort out his thoughts, and that was when Anise screamed, and her horse shot forward toward Maeve's. Maeve did nae have hold of her reins! The realization echoed through his mind. He lunged forward, but he'd never close the distance. He knew it. And he yelled out to her, but it was too late. Her horse reared up and threw her backward. Maeve flew off the beast to land on the ground. Her head just missed hitting a rock, and instead she whacked it against the ground. It bounced forward, and then backward, and she lay still as death.

A roar ripped out of him as he raced across the court-yard and dropped to the ground beside Maeve. His heart pounded as he gathered her in his arms, and her eyes fluttered open. "What happened?" she said.

He scooped her up and to his chest as he stood, but he could not catch a true breath. It felt as if a fist had been plunged into his chest and squeezed his heart.

"What happened?" she asked again, looking utterly dazed.

"I'm so sorry, my lady," Anise said, worry etched on her face, but Alasdair was in no mood for her apologies. Fury choked him. He wasn't certain Anise had purposely tried to injure Maeve, but he'd had enough. "She could have been killed," he said to Anise, his voice cold. The thought resounded through him. Maeve could have been killed, and he loved her. Shock reverberated through him. He had fallen in love with Maeve. He didn't know exactly when, but the feeling was so complete, so strong, he trembled with it. He held her close. "Anise," he said, ready to denounce the healer.

"Accidents can happen to anyone," Maeve inserted, surprising him. He would have thought this would have been the last thing she was willing to tolerate.

He looked at her, about to protest, but the pleading look in her eyes had him holding his tongue. He trusted her. She was doing what she was for a reason, and he'd hold his tongue until he knew. "I'm taking ye to lie down," he said, ignoring Anise now.

Maeve nodded, and after he gave Brodick instructions for the practice hunt, Alasdair started out of the courtyard and toward the castle. When they were far enough away not to be overheard, he paused and looked down at Maeve. "Why are ye protecting her? I ken she aided ye on the night ye tried to escape."

"I ken ye do, and I appreciate ye nae questioning me about it. I kenned she did what she did out of love for ye, so I let it pass, and I'm nae certain today was on purpose."

"Maeve, I kinnae allow her to attempt to hurt ye."

"Believe me, I dunnae wish to let her hurt me. I'll speak to her, and if I'm nae satisfied, ye can take action. Will ye allow me that?"

"Aye," he said, though it was begrudgingly. His instinct was to protect Maeve, but he knew how important it was for her to have a voice equal to his, and he wanted to give her that.

Chapter Twenty

The funniest feeling had been plaguing Maeve since yesterday when Alasdair had roared and run across the courtyard to scoop her into his arms, but she could not quite work out what it was. It was on her mind as they rode out for another practice hunt with the women they had trained, and it distracted her as they rode back toward the castle after the hunt. They rode side by side with Brodick behind them leading the women, and as they neared the edge of the woods, horns sounded and Tavish and Alasdair's mother rode hard toward them.

"'Tis the horns to announce a visitor," Alasdair told Maeve, but before she could even wonder aloud who, Tavish and Lady MacRae appeared.

"Colin Fraser is here," she said between gasps of air. "I came to stop ye from coming to the castle with her."

Lady MacRae gave Maeve a narrow-eyed look.

"We'll take her back into the woods and keep her hidden," Lady MacRae said. "'Tis why Tavish is with me. In case she tries anything."

"Mama ordered me," he said to Maeve, and the helpless look he gave her made Maeve smile. Tavish was a kind soul.

Lady MacRae scowled at her younger son before focusing once more on Alasdair. "Ye can deal with Fraser. He's demanding to search the castle for her. He says he has it on good authority that we have her."

"I wonder if there were other men with the ones who attacked ye that may have gone back and told him," Alasdair said, looking to Maeve.

"Nay, they did nae ken who I was, so if anyone was with them, I doubt they recognized me from a distance, if at all. Could there be a betrayer amongst yer men? Someone who would possibly be working with the Frasers to lay blame for the raid on yer clan?"

"I kinnae think of any man who would wish to hurt their own clan, but 'tis a possibility I'll nae rule out," he said. He stared deep into her eyes. "Does this mean ye believe the Frasers did connive against us?"

"This means," she said, her pulse pounding furiously through her, "I think it a possibility, and I dunnae believe ye would lie to me about yer own clan's guilt in the starting of the raids."

"Ye trust me," he said.

She heard the happiness in his voice, and it filled her with a joy that made her want to weep. There was just one thing left to know for her. "What will ye do now, Alasdair? Will ye force me to stay here and hide me away from Colin?" she asked him quietly, ignoring everyone else with them.

He reached over and took her hand to squeeze it. "Yer future is nae my choice." Maeve's breath caught in her chest that he was giving her the exact words she had hoped he would. "'Tis yers. I love ye, Maeve."

"What?" She could not have heard him correctly.

The smile he gave her was so gentle that tears filled her eyes. "I love ye. I want ye to stay with me but nae because I force ye to. I told ye afore, and I meant it, the choice has to be yers."

She stared wordlessly at him for a moment as her heart

pounded in her chest. He loved her. A shock ran through her as she realized she loved him, too. He was everything she had once imagined and more. "Well, come on," she finally managed to say. "Let us go inform Colin that we're wed good and true."

A slow, wolfish grin spread across Alasdair's face. "Good and true?"

"Aye. We will be."

A cheer went up around them, and heat flooded Maeve's face as she realized everyone had been listening. Even Alasdair's mother was smiling at Maeve. They rode into the courtyard hand in hand, and when Colin saw her, he broke away from the contingency of men with him, which appeared to be two dozen or so. He rode toward her, meeting them before they got past the guard tower.

"Maeve!" he said, bringing his horse to a halt beside her. "My God, Maeve, I've been worried sick. I " His sentence stopped as his gaze fell to her hand, which still held Alasdair's.

"Ye took her against her will!" Colin said, starting to draw his sword, but Maeve released Alasdair's hand to reach for Colin's sword arm.

"We're wed!" she said, grabbing Colin's forearm.

"By force!" he growled and moved as if to take her, but Alasdair was between her and Colin with his sword raised before Colin could finish drawing his weapon.

His warriors started to move, but Brodick said in a loud, clear voice, "If ye so much as blink, the archers will shoot ye." Brodick motioned above them, and that's when Maeve saw the men lining the rampart. Though the MacRaes looked to have a mighty force, it was not true, and she had to stop a war from occurring. She loved Alasdair, and though her father had kept her betrothal intact to Colin, and she felt guilty about that, she could not deny her heart any longer.

"I'm nae wed by force, Colin," she said. "I love him. I love him, and I think I have for a verra long time." She caught Alasdair's gaze upon her, and the warmth in his eyes told her he felt the same way.

"I dunnae ken what he's done to ye, Maeve, but—"

"He loves me," she said simply. "He loves me for me, and nae Eilean Donan."

A bark of laughter came from Colin. "He's fooled ye, Maeve. Do ye nae think he planned what to do, what to say, so ye would accept him?"

Colin's words sent a sliver of doubt through her that she refused to accept. "We're wed good and true."

"Dunnae be afeared, Maeve," Colin said. "Whatever he's convinced ye of—"

"Did my da tell ye he wished to break my betrothal with ye?" she demanded, staring hard at Colin, looking for any sign that he was lying. "Did yer clan start the scrimmages purposely with mine and Alasdair's to set us at war with each other so yer family could obtain Eilean Donan one day? Was my da's death really an accident?"

"My God, Maeve!" Colin said, and the horror on his face told her he was astounded by what she was implying. "Ye ken me! Ye have kenned me all my life. Do ye think I'd do that to ye?"

Confusion buffeted her for a moment. She didn't think he would, but if his family didn't do it, then who had? Who had started the scrimmages and stolen her family's plaids to do so? No one else would gain from it, not that she could think of. She frowned and cast a look at Alasdair.

"Maeve," he said, his tone grave, "I vow to ye, my family did nae strike first."

"I ken it," she assured him.

"He'd say anything to win Eilean Donan, Maeve!" Colin bit out.

She shook her head. "Nay, he would nae. He would give up Eilean Donan for my happiness."

"He's muddled yer head, Maeve." He held his hand out to her. "Come with me."

"She told ye," Alasdair said, his words hard, "she loves me, and she is my wife."

Alasdair gave her a long, searching look, and she knew he was offering her one last chance to change her mind, but it was made up. She reached for his hand and held Colin's gaze. "Ye need to go. I'll be returning to Eilean Donan with Alasdair within the sennight. As my husband. He is the new and rightful laird. And together we will uncover who tried to lay blame at his clan's feet, and if it is yer clan, Colin, and ye kenned it, I will consider ye my enemy."

Real grief twisted Colin's face, and her heart squeezed. She'd never meant to hurt him.

He looked as if he was going to say more, but Alasdair spoke. "Ye have my word of safe passage off my land, and ye are welcome back if ye wish to be allies, but if ye ever return again trying to take Maeve, I will kill ye."

"I'll nae forget this," Colin swore.

"I'm certain ye will nae. Maeve is a great treasure to lose."

Colin gave her one last look before he motioned for his men to follow him. She watched him go, afraid he'd change his mind and start a fight. But he did not pause, and he did not turn back. She breathed a sigh of relief when he was finally out of sight. "He's gone," she murmured.

"Aye, for now," Alasdair said, his tone grim.

"Someone betrayed us, Laird," Athelston said from

Alasdair's right.

"Aye. It seems it's a possibility."

"I'll personally question each man now," Brodick said.

"I'll aid him, Laird," Athelston offered. "I owe ye that and more for my disrespect toward yer wife." Athelston looked at Maeve. "I judged ye as our enemy, but ye have proven true." The man shocked her by kneeling. "I offer ye my fealty, as the lady of the clan." The man bowed his head, and Maeve wasn't certain what to do.

"If ye accept it," Alasdair said, his voice low, "place yer hand upon his shoulder. If ye dunnae, then tell him he needs to prove he is truly loyal to ye."

She was inclined to demand he prove his loyalty further, but with everyone looking on expectantly, from Alasdair's mother to his brother and the men and women gathered, she decided to let bygones be bygones. She placed a hand on his shoulder, and a roar of approval went up in the crowd. Then, to her utter astonishment, one by one, Alasdair's men offered her their fealty, and then the women she'd taught to hunt did the same. The last person to come up to her was Anise. The courtyard grew very quiet.

"My lady," Anise said, kneeling. "I beg yer forgiveness for everything I have done." Anise gave her a beseeching look. "I—" The woman darted a look between Alasdair and Maeve before she whispered, "I had a bit of trouble letting go, so I may have been a tad deceitful." A tad was generous of the woman. She was very deceitful, and yet, Maeve did want to forgive her. That didn't mean she was ready to trust her, but holding a grudge against someone was harder on the person holding it than anyone. "Will ye take my pledge of fealty?"

Maeve nodded and placed her hand on Anise's shoulder. After the woman rose, the supper horn rang, and Alasdair's mother came forward, holding out her arm to Maeve. "Come, let us celebrate ye truly now being a MacRae."

Maeve started to accept Lady MacRae's offer, but Alasdair took her by the hand. "That particular celebration will have to wait. Maeve and I have business."

Lady MacRae frowned. "What business?"

"Husband and wife business, Mama," Alasdair said, his voice low.

Maeve could feel the heat in her face and neck. Lady MacRae grinned and nodded. "Off with ye, then. We'll celebrate on the morrow."

Maeve let Alasdair lead her toward the castle door. It wasn't until they stepped into the castle and they were alone that he spoke. "Ye did nae have to take Anise's apology, Maeve. I would have backed ye had ye demanded she prove her loyalty first."

"'Tis nae good for a body to hold grudges."

Alasdair grinned at her. "I dunnae. It has worked out pretty well for me." He took her by the shoulders and turned her to face him, and then he reached up and traced a finger over her forehead. "My grudge brought me ye, and for that I thank the gods."

His touch made her shiver even as his words warmed her. She skimmed her hands up his chest, tilting her face up to his and entwining her hands around his neck. "Ye best take me to our bedchamber now and show me how thankful ye are."

Gladly, lass," he said, then swept her into his arms to take the stairs two at a time toward the bedchambers.

When they passed servants midflight and the women all started giggling, Maeve whispered, "Set me down! They ken what we're up to!"

"Aye," he said, winking. "But setting ye down will nae

keep it a secret. I plan to make ye scream with pleasure."

"'Tis rather boastful," she said with a giggle as he brought them to the top of the stairs and strode down the passage toward his bedchamber.

"Nae boastful," he assured her, pausing to open his door and take her inside. "Hopeful."

He gave her a look that made her burst with such love. Even after all the time she'd made him wait for them to lie together, she could see on his face that he would continue to wait if she said the word.

"'Tis hope well-placed," she assured him. "I dunnae want anything more than to become yer wife this night."

"I dunnae think I've ever heard such sweet words," Alasdair replied before his mouth descended on hers. The kiss he gave her was unlike any she'd received from him yet. It was the kiss of a man who had been holding back his passion. It was unbridled, searing, and hungry. His hand tangled in her hair as they traded kisses, tugging and pulling at each other's lips as he moved them toward the bed.

He lowered them to the bed as one, the mattress giving under their combined weight so that she sunk into the feathery softness. His heavy body came on top of her, but she didn't mind it at all. She felt safe, protected, and loved. His mouth left hers to trail kisses over her jaw, down her neck, and lower. In search of what, she didn't know until his tongue moved hot over the sensitive skin of her chest, and then his teeth were tugging her bodice down so his tongue could circle her nipple, eliciting a hiss of excitement and anticipation from her.

He circled her nipple once, twice, and she cried out, arching toward him, wanting him to take her into his mouth. He was more than happy to oblige. He suckled her then as if he had been starving himself of her. His tugs and pulls on her nipple, his frantic hands over her back and then her bottom were those of a man who'd been waiting all his life for this moment. She gloried in it and returned it with touches of her own, through his hair, to the back of his neck, and around his shoulders to the bunched muscle of his back.

His mouth left her nipple as his hands slid under her skirts to relieve her of her undergarments, and then warm fingers found the center of her, where she pulsed in a strange and wonderful way. When he parted her and his fingers grazed her nub there, she moaned, gripped by insatiable need. He pulled back for a moment, rounded off the bed, and rid himself of his clothes. He was beautiful. He reminded her of the conquering warriors the bards would speak of around her father's fires. She wanted to tell him this, but she didn't want him to wait to come to her, over her, in her, a breath longer.

He came back over her, the bed creaking again, and his hands finding her knees, which she had pressed together without even realizing it until he was parting her with a gentleness that put a knot in her throat. His large hands trailed down the inside of her thighs, then one hand splayed across her belly while the other parted her core once more. With a long suckle of the throbbing nub, she understood at once what drew men and women into sin. This was heaven.

She threw her head back and tilted her pelvis up, not even caring that she was pressing into his face. He sucked harder, sending deep waves of intense pleasure through her until she thought she would burst with it. She was panting, clawing at the covers, then alternately scraping her nails across the ridges of his back as the need in her built until all she could hear was the pounding of her heart in her ears and all she could feel was the pulsing of her core and the rushing of her blood through her veins. All she could smell was him—sweaty sin. And all she could see was the top of his head, dark and glistening and moving in the same motion his mouth was.

Her body seemed to clench all the way to her bones, and then everything came apart—her senses, her world, her mind. All that was left was the rolling pleasure and so much heat she cried out from it. He came up then between her thighs, bringing his hands under her bottom and entered her in a slow movement, stopping for a breath when he met her barrier. She knew what was to come. Bee had been very blunt about what occurred between a man and a woman, not wanting Maeve to be naive.

She was glad of it at this moment. His gaze found hers, questioning. "Go on, then," she said, her voice hoarse from her cries of pleasure. "I ken the pain will nae last and the pleasure will be worth it."

"God, I hope so," he said, entering her to the hilt. He stilled to give her a moment, which she took, adjusting to his size, his heat, the two of them joined as one.

As one. Tears pricked her eyes.

"My God, did I hurt ye that bad? I'll—"

He started to pull out, and she grabbed his arse to hold him in her and still. "Dunnae ye dare. I took the pain. Now I want the pleasure."

He grinned down at her with a look of raw love and kissed each of her wet cheeks where a few tears had leaked out. "That's the least I can do for ye, lass."

And then he began to move in languorous strokes, and as the uncomfortableness gave way to a budding pleasure, she understood that he was warming her from the inside. His strokes became faster as she encouraged him, and that same sensation of pulsing built within her but deeper, seeming to wind around the very core of who she was. It grew until she was taut as a bow, and then she had to clench her thighs and squeeze her eyes shut as ecstasy shot through her hotter than any fire she'd ever felt. He growled out her name and stilled as who he was joined with who she was.

She opened her eyes to find him looking at her, and he leaned forward and caught her lips in a reverent kiss. "I love ye, lass. With every breath I possess and every beat of my heart."

"I love ye, too," she said, kissing his stubbly jaw, his neck, and finally his chest. He lowered himself all the way to her and rolled to the right, bringing her with him until she was snug against his side, and then he lifted his arm up and under her neck so that she could rest her head on the bulge of the muscle at his shoulder and chest. She threw her leg over his torso, and put her hand on his chest, inadvertently over his heart, which thundered beneath his skin

"I did this," she whispered, awed as she glanced up at him with a grin.

He smiled down at her. "Aye, lass." His fingers found her nipple and immediately drew a moan of pleasure from her lips. "And I did this. And I intend to do it again and again for the rest of our lives."

"Again tonight as well, aye?" she said, her back arching toward him and her body becoming greedy for more.

"Aye," he said on a chuckle before he complied.

Chapter Twenty-One

"Did ye make me a grandbairn last night?" Lady MacRae asked Maeve as she entered the kitchen the next afternoon to help with supper.

"If nae last night, then mayhap ye did today since ye and Alasdair have been abed all day long!" Lara teased.

The kitchen erupted with laughter from all the women. "Come," Lara said, "work aside me. We were just discussing Anise."

"Anise?" Maeve replied, going to where Lara was rolling dough.

"Aye. Nae any of the women in the kitchen wish to work with her, and Mama and I were trying to think where to put her."

"Do they nae wish to work with her because of me?" Maeve asked.

"Nay," Lady MacRae replied. "'Tis her own doing. She was nae well-liked afore ye came here. She'd floated from bed to bed afore she and Alasdair, well…" Lady MacRae gave Maeve an apologetic look.

"Dunnae fash yerself. I ken they had a, um, relationship." And hearing this made Maeve understand Anise a bit better. She had been searching for love, likely, and she had thought she'd possibly found it with Alasdair and then along came Maeve.

Lady MacRae nodded. "The women are weary of what

man's bed she will end up in to try to steal next, now that it's obvious Alasdair has eyes only for ye."

"I feel a bit sorry for her," Lara said.

"Lara has a soft heart," Lady MacRae said in an admonishing voice.

"'Tis nae it, Mama! I feel sorry for her because I think she does the things she does because she dunnae feel she truly belongs."

"Why would she nae feel as if she truly belonged?" Maeve asked, trying to find answers to what made Anise do the things she did.

"Because her mama could nae say who Anise's da was, and the women of the clan have nae ever let Anise forget it," Lady MacRae said. "Lara and I did try to aid her, but if I'm to be honest, I did nae want her wedding Alasdair."

"Because of her unknown birth?" Maeve asked, hoping that was not why, and she was relieved when Lady MacRae shook her head.

"Nay," she said. "Because I could see plainly he did nae love her."

"And if I'm being honest, I did nae make a huge effort to include her or get other ladies to because I was holding a grudge," Lara admitted.

"Over what?"

Lara nibbled on her lip for a moment and once more dashed a look at her mother. "She held Brodick's attention for a number of years, but I think it was merely to get close to Alasdair, but still..." She shrugged.

Lady MacRae was looking at her daughter with a frown. "Why would ye care if she held Brodick's att—" Her eyes went wide, and then she grinned. "Do ye have a tendre for Brodick?"

"Aye, Mama," Lara said, blushing.

"Since when?" the woman demanded.

"Since I could walk." Lara said on a laugh.

"Whyever did ye hide it, then?"

Lara rolled her eyes at her mother. "Because he treated me like his little sister and nae a lass he had any interest in. Until recently."

As those two started chattering nonstop about Broderick, the door to the kitchen opened and Anise walked in, and the women were just as unwelcoming to her as the time before when Maeve went with her to gather the herbs. Maeve watched Anise's reaction as table after table of women gave Anise hostile stares as she approached and left each worktable. Her shoulders drew back, her chin notched up, and her lips pressed together, and then she walked to the far side of the room to a table where no one was at and settled in to do her work.

Maeve watched her at supper that night as well. At the first three tables Anise approached, she went to sit down and the women on the bench closed the space that had been empty. At the fourth table, a woman waved her away. Anise finally settled at the last table where Athelston and a group of other warriors sat. She and Athelston spoke the entire time.

The next day the same thing occurred in the kitchens and at supper that night as well. After a sennight, Maeve made a decision, and that night, as she and Alasdair lay sweaty and in each other's arms, she brought up her plan. She turned on her left side and faced her husband. "The women of yer clan are nae kind to Anise."

He rolled over to face her as well. "I ken," he said on a sigh.

"I want to show the women by example that she is worthy of their friendship."

"Even after all she did to ye?"

"Aye," Maeve said. "I see the truth of why she did the things she did, and it was nae malicious."

"What truth is that, Wife?" Alasdair asked her, running his finger down her breast until he was teasing her nipple. Her belly immediately tightened and her blood heated, making it hard for her to think, but she concentrated and said, "She was desperate to belong, and they would nae let her, nae truly, so I imagine she thought as yer wife, they'd be forced to accept her. But then I came along and ye abandoned her."

His brows dipped together. "I did tell her from the beginning what we were and that it was a mutual pleasurable pastime."

"I ken ye did," Maeve replied, "but that dunnae mean she believed it."

"I feel like an arse now," Alasdair replied, turning over on his back and settling his head in his intertwined hands.

Maeve climbed on top of him to straddle him, then bent over and kissed his chest before kissing his lips. "That's what I love about ye. Ye truly care."

"'Tis that all ye love about me?" he asked, wiggling his eyebrows at her.

"Nay," she said, on a chuckle. "Ye do have a magical way with yer tongue and yer hands."

He slid his right hand down between them and began to stroke her. "Is this the magic way?" he asked, his voice rough.

Her core tightened as all the blood in her body seemed to go straight to where his fingers were stroking her. "Aye," she assured him. "So can I?"

"Can ye what?" he asked, pulling himself halfway up to suckle one of her breasts as his fingers drove her to madness.

Her thoughts were lost to the pleasure he was giving her. Her body began to vibrate with liquid fire as she came to the edge of her release. "Come in me," she whispered, wanting to feel him deep inside her as the spasms took her. She did not have to ask twice.

He slid in her, filling her in a way only he could. Both his hands found her breasts, and he teased her nipples as she soared to shuddering ecstasy. He joined her at the height, grunting his pleasure and gripping her as he surrendered to her completely. She loved the moment after they came together. He collapsed on top of her, his body covering hers completely, their hearts pounding the same furious rhythm, and their breaths mingling as one. They lay that way for a long stretch of silence, soft to hard, flesh to flesh, husband to wife, enemies to lovers. Never had she been so happy or glad that they had both been willing to get to know each other aside from their families and the old feuds that bound them.

He eventually rolled off her, and she settled in the crook of his arm, as had become their custom. When she didn't immediately throw her leg over his, he grabbed her leg and gently set it over his. She slid her hand over his heart, and the last question she'd meant to ask him returned. "Do ye think it's a good plan to attempt to truly befriend her?"

He brushed aside the hair that had fallen over her eyes, and she tilted her head back until their gazes met. "I think ye have the biggest heart of anyone I have ever kenned."

Maeve smiled. "Ye're avoiding my question."

"Aye." He pressed a kiss to the top of her head. She loved it when he did that. "I think," he said slowly, "ye should hold yer trust back until ye are certain she's earned it."

"I will. I vow it."

Chapter Twenty-Two

*T*he next day the chatter in the kitchen stopped as Maeve made her way past the working women to the table where Anise once again worked alone. She briefly looked at Maeve before staring quickly down at her almost formed dough once more, but she was not fast enough that Maeve did not notice the woman's surprise.

"If I were ye, if I had lived yer life with the hardships ye have endured, I would nae truly like me, either, and I would have done the things ye did," Maeve said quietly so that none of the other women in the kitchen would hear.

Anise glanced up again, and this time the wariness in her gaze was obvious. "I gave ye my fealty," she said, her tone strained. "What more do ye want? Have ye come over here to rub in that ye won Alasdair?"

"Nay," Maeve said honestly. "I wish for us to be friends truly."

Anise's lips pressed together in a hard, firm line. "Ye wish to be friends with me and nae just a ruse?"

"Aye," Maeve replied. "I see when ye look at Alasdair that ye must have truly cared for him, and I ken it must be hard."

The woman swallowed audibly. "Ye dunnae ken anything about how hard my life has been."

"I do, a little," Maeve said.

Anise gave her a smirk. "Ah, let me guess, I was being

gossiped about."

"Nay, nae really gossip. Lara told me about yer mama nae kenning who yer da was. I'm sorry for how ye have been treated because of something that is nae yer fault, nor should have mattered in the first place."

"Stop it," Anise said almost vehemently.

Maeve frowned. "Stop trying to talk to ye?"

"Aye," the woman said, pounding her dough as if she were trying to kill it. "'Tis too late for us to be friends."

"'Tis nae too late, Anise. I dunnae hold any grudges toward ye."

The woman was gripping the edge of the table so hard that her knuckles were white. "I hold a grudge toward ye," she hissed under her breath. "If ye had nae come along, he would have eventually wed me. I would have gotten with child, and he would have wed me."

"If ye were with child, he probably would have," Maeve agreed because Alasdair was not the sort of man to turn away from a duty like a child or let a child be born a bastard.

"He only wed ye for yer land," Anise spat.

"Nay," Maeve said gently. "He took me for revenge and was going to wed me for my land to save yer clan, but he wed me because he loves me. I'm sorry to say it, but he did nae love ye."

Anise's eyes narrowed, but Maeve quickly placed her hand over Anise's to try to get her to let her finish. "There will be a man that comes along and loves ye, and that will be the right man for ye. Ye would nae wish a man as yer husband who did nae give ye his full heart. Settled love is nae the sort of love ye deserve."

"Nae any man here will ever see me as any more than a fatherless woman with nae anything to bring to a marriage. I dunnae have worth, except as a healer, but being a healer is nae a reason for a man to wed me."

"The right man will nae care if ye bring anything to the marriage."

Anise made a derisive noise. "The men here have sisters and mamas who tell them to keep away from me."

"What of Athelston?"

A wary look crossed Anise's face. "I…I dunnae wish a man like Athelston as my husband." She sounded almost fearful.

"Has he done something to hurt ye?" Maeve asked.

Anise's glance darted to the door, as if she feared Athelston would somehow appear there, but then she looked back to Maeve and quickly shook her head. "Nay. He's nae hurt me. Now leave me be." With that, Anise flounced away, but that simply made Maeve more determined to be her friend.

The next day, she enlisted the help of Lady MacRae and Lara, who agreed to come to the table in the kitchens and work alongside Maeve and Anise. The look of shock on Anise's face when the three of them came to work with her, followed by the small smile that tipped up the corners of her lips before she ducked her head, increased Maeve's belief that this was the way to aid Anise so the need to belong didn't drive her to desperate acts any longer.

It took several days for Maeve to see any effects of her efforts, but on the fourth day in the kitchen, Tess joined them at the worktable, and on the seventh day, two more women joined them. When Maeve entered the kitchens on the ninth day, Anise was at a table full of women talking and laughing with them, and when she spotted Maeve, she waved and smiled. But then a worried look settled on her features for a moment before Lady MacRae said something to her and she was laughing again.

That night, when Maeve was going to the great hall for supper, she saw Anise and Athelston standing in the courtyard arguing, and she planned to ask her about it after supper that night, but Anise did not appear for supper.

"What has ye worrying yer lip, Wife?" Alasdair asked later that night as they were lying in bed in the aftermath of coming together.

Maeve rolled onto her side to tell Alasdair her concerns. It had become their habit to talk that way after joining, and in the last sennight, all her talk had been about their return to Eilean Donan for her clan to meet their new laird. She'd sent a missive to the council and Beitris, so that they knew she was all right and had wed. They intended to leave for her home at week's end, so when she blurted, "Anise," she wondered if the surprised look on Alasdair's face was because she was worried about Anise or because she was not speaking of their trip.

"What ails ye about the lass? I thought ye said things were going well with her."

"They are as far as the women accepting her, but I saw her in the courtyard arguing with Athelston tonight."

Alasdair did not look the least bit concerned, and when he shrugged, she knew she'd judged correctly. "Mayhap she's taken to his bed? Lovers argue sometimes, Maeve. Ye dunnae ken this because ye did nae ever have a lover, except for me, and I worship ye; therefore, ye dunnae have cause to argue with me."

"Ye dunnae think he'd harm her, do ye? She seemed almost scared of him when she spoke of him in the kitchen a few days ago."

Alasdair shook his head. "Nay. But I'll speak to my cousin if it will bring ye peace."

"Athelston is yer cousin?" Maeve asked, astonished.

"Aye. I thought ye kenned."

"I did nae."

Alasdair turned fully toward her and began to trace his finger back and forth over her collarbone, which sent chills racing across her body. "He's the only son of my da's younger brother."

"I did nae ken ye had an uncle, either. How come I've nae met him?"

"He passed years ago. He and my da did nae get along, and he went off to make his own fortunes. But things did nae work out well for him. I dunnae remember him much. He died when I was a boy of six summers. He had to come back here to live because the clan he tried to start broke up. Athelston's mama refused to return with my uncle, and she abandoned Athelston to my da's care."

"Oh, that's horrid," Maeve said. "I feel a little more warmth toward Athelston kenning this."

"He's an odd one," Alasdair said, "but he's harmless enough. Except I did nae care at all for him trying to force me into a public bedding with ye."

"I'm glad ye changed that for me."

Alasdair rolled over her and had her cradled between his powerful thighs in a flash. He cupped her breast, and a wicked gleam lit his eyes. "I'm nae about to ever let another man drink in yer perfection."

She pursed her lips at him. "Here I thought ye did what ye did because ye recognized the practice is barbaric."

"Oh, aye, that's why I did it," he said, chuckling.

She smacked his arm even as a grin turned her lips up. "Ye're a barbarian, after all."

"Let me show ye just how much of a barbarian I truly am," he growled.

After being kept awake half the night by her voracious husband, Maeve did not rouse until Alasdair threw open the door and demanded, "What?" in an irate tone.

She opened one eye, saw Alasdair standing there, naked, talking to someone. She let out a sigh of appreciation as he closed the door and turned back to her. The sunlight streamed in and hit him to accentuate the glorious sculpting of his muscled body.

"Good morning," he said, striding across the room, kneeling on the bed, and kissing her full on the mouth.

When he pulled away, she eyed his very exposed male parts. "I certainly hope ye were talking to a blind man at our door."

"I was talking to Brodick, and if he's going to rouse me from yer arms, then he needs to look away."

"What's the matter?" she asked, starting to rise when he pulled away to grab his braies off the floor.

He came up with his braies in hand. "Stay under the covers until ye have to rise."

She scowled at him and threw the heavy coverlet back, hissing between her teeth as the cool air hit her naked body. They'd enjoyed another night entwined in each other's arms. "One of the guards spotted a fire on the outskirts of the land," he explained. "We're going to investigate, but I'll leave guards."

Their gazes met, and she knew he was thinking, just as she was, of the last time there was a fire on his land. It was when her father and Laird Fraser had planned the mission to strike at the MacRaes to make it harder for them to raid Fraser and MacKenzie lands.

"It will nae be my clan," she said, certain. Her council

had been informed she'd wed Alasdair and that he was now their laird, so to strike at him would be to strike at themselves.

"I dunnae think it is, Maeve."

She could tell by the gentle tone of his voice that he meant it. "I want to come with ye."

He smiled down indulgently at her. "And I'd normally happily have ye by my side, ye ken that."

She nodded because, in truth, she did. He'd treated her as an equal since the moment he'd brought her to his home, and that behavior had only increased since they'd wed. "But we leave tomorrow for yer home, and one of us needs to be here to oversee the final preparations, and there is nae anyone I trust to do that more than ye."

She beamed up at him. "Ye ken just what to say to get me to do as ye wish."

He winked down at her and then gently cupped her chin. "And ye ken just what to do to get me to do as ye wish." As he dressed, she watched him, marveling, as she had done every single day since seeing him fully unclothed, in the beauty and strength of her husband.

"Will ye return in time for supper, do ye think?" she asked.

He pulled his braies up to his hip bones. "I hope so. But if nae in time for supper, most assuredly afore ye're asleep."

She looked up at him from underneath the hair that had slid over her eyes. "Ye better," she said, her voice husky. "I wish ye to do that thing to me again tonight that ye did last night."

"My God, Maeve," he said, coming to his knees in front of her, and then reaching forward, he brushed her hair back out of her eyes. "When ye look at me that way, from behind yer hair, it guts me. I kinnae hardly think." He leaned down and kissed her hard upon her mouth. "What thing do ye wish me to do?"

"This one," she said and flipped herself over to smile coyly at him from over her shoulder.

Before she knew it, he was unclothed once more, on top of her, and spreading her legs with his own. He entered her slowly, sliding his hand under her until his fingers found her center and he parted her. As his body found a rhythm in and out of her, his fingers found one as well to tease her.

Heat grew in pace with her heartbeat, and not long later, she was screaming her pleasure at the exact moment another pounding came at the bedchamber door. "Alasdair, I have the men assembled, and we're waiting for ye," Brodick yelled. "What the devil are ye doing?"

"Pleas—"

Maeve bucked Alasdair off her and flipped over to smack a hand over his mouth. "Dunnae ye dare!" she hissed.

He peeled her hand away to reveal a devastatingly handsome smile. "Wife, by the way ye scream when ye find yer release, everyone in this castle kens when I pleasure ye."

"Ye're teasing me," she said, hoping he truly was because that would be mortifying.

He winked at her, rolled off the bed, donned his clothes, and then he strode toward the bedchamber door. "I'm nae. I'll be home afore bed to finish what we started. If ye'll see to the packing of what we'll need for the time we'll be staying at yer home—"

"Our home," she corrected him.

He smiled. "Aye, our home."

"I ken what we need, Husband. Clothing. Everything else will be provided at Eilean Donan."

"I'll see ye tonight," he said, blowing her a kiss before

exiting their bedchamber.

She lay on her back after he left, staring up at the ceiling and thinking of all she needed to do today. They would travel tomorrow, the two of them, plus Brodick and Father Bernard, to Eilean Donan, where Maeve would introduce Alasdair to her clan. The plan was for Alasdair and Maeve to oversee the running of Eilean Donan, and for Lara, Tavish, and Lady MacRae, to oversee the running of the MacRae stronghold with Brodick and the council's help. Father Bernard was going to go to Eilean Donan with them to see Beitris. Maeve suspected that Lara and Brodick would be wed before half a year was through. They'd been spending a great deal of time together and every time she caught them in the vicinity of each other, they had matching besotted looks upon their faces, and Lady MacRae seemed to approve.

And as for Tavish, if his mother had any say in it, he'd likely be wed before the year was out. Lady MacRae had turned her full attention to that endeavor since she'd decided the Frasers were fully to blame for her husband's death and not Maeve's father; therefore, she did not feel inclined to devote her time to despising Maeve anymore. Maeve intended to try to get to the bottom of who had been framing Alasdair's clan with Alasdair's help, once they were at Eilean Donan. She wasn't certain how they would do that exactly, but together they would figure it out.

Her eyes kept fluttering shut in the warmth of their bedchamber and with the lack of sleep from last night's pleasures, and though she had a great deal to do today, she allowed herself to close her eyes. Sometime later, she jerked awake to what sounded like thunder. A glance toward the window showed a blue sky and sunshine. Frowning, she rose and moved to the window to glance into the inner courtyard.

She hissed in a shocked breath as she took in the court-yard, which was teeming with warriors. She recognized the Fraser flag immediately, and searching the courtyard, she found Colin on a horse beside his father and a man she didn't recognize. But she did know the banner he flew—the king's banner—and a quick sweep of the courtyard once more revealed that over half the banners she saw were the king's and all the others, save for about two dozen, appeared to be the Fraser's men. Directly across from Colin and his father were Lady MacRae, Tavish, and Father Bernard.

Fear knotted inside her as she turned away from the window to locate her gown. She didn't know why the Frasers and the king's men were here, but she knew it had to involve her. Her hands were trembling as she yanked on her gown and clumsily tried to tie the laces. By the time she finished and was searching for her slippers, waves of apprehension were rolling over her. Just as she turned to leave her bedchamber, a pounding came at the door, and before she could take so much as a step toward it, it burst open, and Anise flew in.

Her eyes were wide with fright. "Ye must come with me quickly!" she said, rushing toward Maeve and grabbing her by the arm. "They're here for ye, and I can get ye out if ye'll come with me!"

Maeve tugged her arm out of Anise's hold and stepped back. "Calm yerself," she said, though, truthfully, a storm had erupted inside her. "Are ye saying the Frasers are here for me?"

"Aye. Nay. I mean—" She turned to look over her shoulder at Maeve's open door. "Maeve, please! I can explain after we find Alasdair and the others."

"Nay. Explain now," Maeve demanded as she moved toward the window to see into the courtyard once more. She gasped and turned, already moving toward the door. The image of the overwhelming number of Frasers and the king's men with their swords drawn facing the pitiful amount of MacRae men left to defend the stronghold, sent black fright through her. When Anise stepped in her way, Maeve shoved her aside.

She rushed out of her bedchamber door with Anise calling behind her. "Maeve! Maeve! Stop! Ye kinnae go down there. They'll take ye away!"

Maeve paused at the top of the steps just long enough to grab the rail. "They kinnae take me away. I'm Alasdair's wife good and true!"

"They think ye're nae!" Anise wailed, and that stopped Maeve short. She swung around to look at the woman whose face was a mask of twisted grief. "I did a terrible, terrible thing," she whispered. "I tried to fix it, but Athelston—" She choked on a cry. "He's a verra bad man, though I kinnae say I'm better. But the kindness ye showed me, I— If I tell the truth now, the king will have my head for lying, I imagine. I dunnae ken what to do. I—"

"Anise," Maeve hissed. Panic welled in her throat, threatening to make her unable to speak. She swallowed past it. "What did ye do?"

"Maeve!"

She jerked around at the sound of Colin's voice so near that she yelped in fright. She could see by the shocked look in his eyes that he had heard everything. "Ye lied?" He looked past Maeve to Anise, as if he knew who she was.

Maeve turned toward Anise just in time to see her nod as tears rolled down her face. "Ye kinnae take her now. I— Please, I—"

"Shut up," Colin said in a cold voice Maeve had never heard him use. "I did nae hear this, and if ye wish to keep yer life, ye'll hold yer damned tongue. Ye were right about one thing: the king dunnae take to liars. But the greater threat to ye is Athelston. Maeve will be fine."

That last sentence, the one that sounded as if he knew her future, as if he would be taking her with him, sent her skittering backward a step, but he lunged for her and caught her by the arm, twisting it behind her back and shoving her down so that her head was near the ground. "Give me the sleeping cloth," he bit out.

My God! It had all been planned. She opened her mouth to scream, but Anise, with tears streaming down her face, slapped a damp cloth over Maeve's mouth. She could hardly breathe, but when she did inhale, a sickly sweet scent filled her nose and her lungs, and within a few breaths, her world went black.

Chapter Twenty-Three

*A*lasdair rode hard through the thick woods after one of the warriors they'd seen fleeing the fire they'd started on the MacRae land. All the Frasers but this one had gotten away, and he had no intention of letting this last man, who appeared from this distance to be wearing a MacRae plaid, flee. He motioned to Brodick to go left, and Alasdair went right. Both trails led to the same opening, so if the man doubled back once he realized this, either Brodick or Alasdair would encounter him.

His horse thundered over the rough terrain, and he jumped logs and dodged branches, never slowing. Every instinct he possessed told him this man somehow had answers Alasdair needed. He turned at a sharp bend and came face-to-face with Darby, who was riding fast toward Alasdair. Shock stilled Alasdair for one moment and confusion filled him.

Stopping Darby would have been easy enough with a throw of a dagger, but he didn't want to kill him, and if he fell off the horse and landed on the dagger just so, well, he could well end up dead. The only hope for it was to knock him off the horse if he could not catch Darby's reins. When they were nearly upon each other, he leaned over as far as he dared from his horse, but he could tell the reins were going to be impossible to reach, so he released his own, scrambled onto his horse's flank as the beast thundered through the twilight, and he jumped at Darby at the last possible second.

They both tumbled to the ground hard as the horses raced past them. They went down rolling, knocked into a stone, and Alasdair came up to his feet in one jump while drawing his sword. His ears were ringing from the fall, but he brought the tip of his sword right under Darby's chin.

"Why?" he demanded. "Why did ye start a fire on our land, yer land, and why were ye aiding the Frasers?"

Darby reared a leg upward, then swept it toward Alasdair's right knee, which buckled his leg. He fell to the right, and Darby rolled to the left. By the time Alasdair gained his feet and turned toward Darby, he was bringing his sword toward Alasdair's neck. Alasdair brought his own blade up fast, meeting Darby's steel in a clash of sound and with a force that sent a vibration down the length of his forearm.

His arm muscles bulged as he struggled to shove back the blade Darby was attempting to kill him with. They battled that way for a few moments, grunting and breathing heavy in the night before Alasdair finally gained the upper hand and, with a shout, pushed Darby's blade up, slipped his own under Darby's, and sent Darby's weapon flying from his hands. Then Alasdair quickly set the tip of his blade to Darby's chest. A stain of red appeared through his clothing.

"Ye should have paid better attention on how to defend yerself during yer training," he growled. "Why, Darby? Why have ye turned traitor? Did the Frasers offer ye coin? Land?"

When the man stared stonily, Alasdair twisted the tip of the sword enough to draw a hiss of breath from Darby. "Why are ye doing this?"

"Ye'll nae kill me," Darby said. "Yer sense of honor

would nae allow ye to kill an unarmed man."

"I dunnae have near as much honor as Alasdair, so I'm happy to kill ye, armed or nae, Darby," Brodick said, riding up behind the younger man, who whirled toward the sound of Brodick's voice then turned back to look at Alasdair.

"Ye'll nae let him kill me," Darby said, a smug look coming to his face.

Alasdair offered a smile he hoped was as cold as he currently felt about Darby. "I'll nae let him kill ye unarmed, but I'll certainly let him make a go of it after I give ye my dagger." Alasdair smiled. "I'll enjoy watching ye try to keep yer life while yielding my small dagger against Brodick's formidable sword. And if he fails to kill ye, I'll finish the job. That is my vow." He finished it by digging the tip of his sword even deeper into the man until a steady stream of crimson appeared.

"Athelston," he blurted. "I'm here because of Athelston. And because I want revenge against yer family."

"Because yer da was named a coward?"

"My da was nae a coward," the man said through clenched teeth. "My da was the lone man who ever questioned yer da's orders."

"Yer da," Alasdair said slowly so the man would damned well understand the truth, "was banished because he left his position on the front line of an attack."

"Nay." Darby shook his head, but Alasdair saw doubt flicker in his gaze. "Athelston told me it was a lie that yer da made up so other men would nae question his authority as my da had done."

Dark anger stirred in Alasdair. *Keep yer enemies close.* That's what his da had always said. Alasdair had unknowingly kept an enemy close. Betrayal stung deep. "Athelston has filled yer head with lies." The question was why. "What did my cousin say he wanted ye to set the fire for?" Alasdair asked.

Brodick stepped to Alasdair's side to stand in front of Darby. "And how are the Frasers involved in all this?"

"He believes the lairdship should have gone to his da as the firstborn of the two sons—"

"His da lost the lairdship by vote of the council because he was nae running the clan well," Brodick protested. He opened his mouth to say more, but Alasdair held up a hand to silence him.

"Ye ken the history of my da and his brother, aye?" Alasdair asked.

Darby nodded. "Aye. Born on the same day, one right after the other, Athelston's da first."

"Aye, and so he was laird for a short time, but he made one disastrous decision after another. Did ye ken that?"

"Nay," Darby admitted. "I did nae ever hear anyone speak of that."

"Nay, he would nae. My da kept it verra quiet so as nae to bring shame to his brother, but Athelston conveniently left out that part of the history. And ye were only too willing to believe him and betray me."

Regret and worry settled on the man's face.

"What do the Frasers have to do with this?" Alasdair asked, repeating Brodick's question. "Why were ye here burning my land with the Frasers?" Alasdair had recognized the Fraser plaid when they'd gotten close to the fires, but all the men had gotten away except for Darby.

"Athelston made a bargain with Laird Fraser some years ago. Laird Fraser promised him he'd remove yer da as laird, and eventually ye, leaving way for Athelston to become laird."

Rage swept through Alasdair. "Do ye ken what Athelston was to give in return?"

"Fealty to the Fraser and to aid him in ensuring he obtained Eilean Donan."

Alasdair's mind swirled with what he'd learned. Athelston had been harming his own clan for years to ensure he'd one day run it. "Did Athelston kill my da?"

Fright settled in Darby's eyes, giving Alasdair his answer. After a long pause, Darby said, "Aye."

"And what of Laird MacKenzie?" Alasdair asked. "Did the Frasers kill the man, or was he in on the plan?"

"I dunnae ken what truly happened to Laird MacKenzie, but I do ken he was nae aware of what the Frasers were trying to do. They want Eilean Donan, and they did what they needed to do to ensure they got it."

"But they dunnae have it," Brodick said, speaking what Alasdair was thinking. "'Tis Alasdair's by right of marriage to Maeve, as the heiress to the land and stronghold."

"But she's nae yer true wife," Darby blurted.

The man's words, and the way he said it with such surety sent fear spiraling through Alasdair and the sinking feeling he had missed something very important. "Why did ye and the Frasers come to burn the land today?" It didn't make sense with Laird MacKenzie gone and Alasdair wed to Maeve.

"Because Athelston needed ye to continue to be seen as too weak of a laird to stop raids. Combine that with yer marriage being dissolved and—"

"What?" Alasdair demanded. "What did ye say?"

The man's face went white. "The Fraser laird has gained permission to collect Maeve to take her to the king for the king to have the final say in whether or nae to dissolve yer marriage since it has nae yet been made true."

"On whose word?" Alasdair roared.

"Athelston's, I believe, and the castle healer, Anise. She vowed she examined Maeve and she was still maiden, and—"

"Bring him with ye," Alasdair said to Brodick as he stepped back, lowered his sword, and strode toward his horse.

"What are ye going to do with me?"

Alasdair turned back toward the man. "That depends," he said, his blood rushing through his veins in fear for Maeve. "Ye best be praying Maeve is nae gone, because if she is and any harm comes to her, I'll tear out yer heart."

Because to lose Maeve would destroy him.

Muffled voices pierced Maeve's strange dreams. She tried to open her eyes, but it took a moment. Her lids felt stuck closed, and when she did finally manage to get them open, her vision was so blurry that she could not make out the details of the room she was in. Confusion blanketed her as she sat up and strained to hear the voices. Was that Alasdair?

She rubbed at her eyes as she tried to sift through the fog in her mind. She'd awoken in her and Alasdair's bedchamber, she'd heard a noise in the courtyard, and—She slapped her hand over her mouth to stifle her gasp. Anise had barged into her bedchamber, and Anise had put something over her mouth on the stairs. She'd been drugged! Colin's betrayal tore at her insides and made icy fear twist around her heart.

The room came into view, and the opulence of it caused her to gape. Heavy silk curtains hung from nearly ceiling to floor, but they were parted over stained glass windows that allowed muted sunlight to fill the room. She was in a large wooden bed piled with intricate emerald coverlets embroidered with lace. At the far end of the room was a place to sit unlike anything she'd ever seen. It looked to be almost two chairs put together upon which one could lie down.

Elaborate tapestries hung on the walls, and as she scooted to the edge of the bed, she noticed a thick rug peeking out on all sides of the bed. There was a large wooden wardrobe in the room, as well as a gleaming washstand and an ornate fireplace where a roaring fire crackled. A gown was laid out in another chair, and her heart jolted when she realized it was the gown she'd been wearing.

Looking down, she stared in mute shock at the dressing gown someone had put on her, and when her hand fluttered to her hair, she felt that it had been plaited. Where was she? She tiptoed toward the cracked bedchamber door, and in the other room, which appeared to be a receiving room every bit as elaborate as the bedchamber, Colin stood looking out a window and his father sat in a chair with a goblet in his hand.

Her stomach clenched tight as she fought to keep her control and listen to what they were saying. She needed answers, and at this point she did not expect to get the truth from Colin.

When Colin swung around suddenly from the window, the anger on his face gave her a little hope. Whatever was going on with him and his father, Colin was very unhappy about it.

"Why did ye keep me in the dark about what ye were doing?" he demanded.

His father regarded Colin over his goblet before tipping it up, taking a drink, and then slowly setting it down. Silence stretched for a moment that seemed an eternity and made Maeve want to scream at the man, but she bit down hard on her lip and stood there, heart pounding. "Ye ken why. Ye would have fought me over what had to be done."

"Maeve will nae ever forgive me," Colin said, and his forlorn tone and look of misery gave her even more hope. Colin was not a horrid person. Whatever he was involved in, there was good in him. "I thought I was rescuing her," he said, his voice low and almost throbbing with regret.

His father rose, went to Colin, and put a hand on his shoulder. "Ye would nae have gone for her had I told ye the truth."

Colin shoved his father's hand off his shoulder and glared at him with eyes blazing with anger. "Of course I would nae have! She dunnae love me if she's that man's wife now in truth!" He spat each word.

"Listen to me, Son. She was taken against her will by the MacRae." A look of disgust settled on Colin's face, and he turned away from his father and toward the window once again. "Who kens what they told her," Laird Fraser continued. "Aye, she laid with the MacRae, but he forced her to do so." Colin looked down with an expression of distress, and a triumphant look crossed his father's face for a brief moment, but when Colin glanced up once more, his father schooled his features. The man was a liar!

"Then why did ye lie? Why did ye tell me that woman, Anise, examined Maeve and pronounced her still an innocent?" Colin swung back to his father. "I took her with the belief that we could dissolve the union, and I could wed her. We kinnae do that now. She kinnae be mine."

"She can," Laird Fraser said, gripping his son by both shoulders. "I lied to ye because I kenned ye would nae take her if ye believed she could nae belong to ye, but she can."

"How?" Colin asked.

"We have the word of the MacRae healer that Maeve is still an innocent, and we have Athelston's sworn word, too, and he's a council member. The king is ill, and his right hand is a Fraser. He will grant her to ye this day."

Maeve felt ill. Athelston had lied. Anise had lied. Why was Colin still listening to his father? Surely, he could not think to go through with such a treachery.

"Ye will be saving her," Laird Fraser said. "Ye love her, dunnae ye?"

"I do," Colin said, shoving a hand through his hair. "I need the whole truth, Da. Did Maeve's da come to break the betrothal?"

When Laird Fraser did not immediately answer, Maeve knew the truth before he spoke, but as he said the word *aye*, the room swayed. She placed a hand against the wall to steady herself, and when Colin sat, she knew he was feeling as unsteady as she was. He would aid her. How could he not? He lowered his head into his palms, his elbows resting on his knees, and he sat that way for a long moment. Maeve had to slow the breath that wanted to come in short, hard gasps so they wouldn't hear her.

When Colin finally looked up, his face was marked with loathing. "Did ye kill him?"

Maeve's breath caught in her chest as she waited for Laird Fraser to answer.

"I had to," the man finally said. Maeve clenched her fists at her sides as anger seared her from the inside out. "He would nae listen to reason, and he was going to allow her to wed who she wished. I did it for our clan. We need the MacKenzie stronghold to remain the greatest clan in the Highlands."

"She did nae wish to wed me," Colin said, his face

pained. "How can we build a union on that? She'll hate me."

"Ye will be a good husband to her. Ye love her and will treat her with kindness and respect. She will come to love ye."

A scream built in Maeve's throat when she saw that Colin seemed to be considering his da's words. She bit her lip, usure what to do. Before she could make up her mind, he spoke. "She's all I ever wanted," he said. "But nae like this."

Relief flowed though Maeve.

"Then go." Laird Fraser waved toward the bedchamber door, and her heart jolted in fear. She scooted back from the cracked door to where she was certain they could not see her. "Go," he said again, his voice harder, colder. "Go and tell her all. I'll be hanged, and ye may be, too. The king will likely nae believe ye did nae ken all these years that we instigated the feuds between the MacRaes and MacKenzies."

She clenched her teeth on the raw hatred that wanted to spew out of her. He'd used his son, and now she knew what was coming. He'd demand Colin choose, and she feared the result. Her heart thundered in her chest. If she were Colin, what would she do? She didn't know. To have to decide between family and honor was the worst choice.

The Fraser continued. "And our clan will fall. Ye ken it's true. Nae to mention what it will do to yer mama and sisters, and—"

"Stop it!" Colin shouted. "I'll nae tell her. I'll make it up to her somehow."

She had to escape. She feared they'd convince the king of their lie. She turned from the door she'd been staring at, caught her toe on the rug, and went careening into the washbasin to the right of the door. It flew from the table to clatter to the floor at the same moment she hit the hard wood. Pain jolted through her knees, but she scrambled to her feet as the door behind her was thrown open. Colin stood there with his father directly behind him. His face was a mask of torture, but she didn't care.

"Dunnae come near me," she hissed.

"Good Christ, Maeve," he said, his voice breaking on her name. "I'm sorry."

And before she could ask what for, he lunged at her and covered her mouth with another cloth that smelled sickly sweet. This time, she knew darkness was coming a breath before it happened.

Chapter Twenty-Four

*H*e knew she was gone the moment he entered the courtyard. His mother and sister were there with his brother waiting for him, and their expressions were solemn. He tried to keep his heart cold and still as he dismounted, so he could make the most logical decisions, but it was impossible. The grip Maeve had on him defied logic. He would lay down his life for her, and without her, his life seemed nothing but a vast stretch of bleak years.

"Tell me," he said.

"The king's men came for her with Laird Fraser and his son," his mother said, tears filling her eyes. "They said yer marriage had nae been made complete, and we protested, but the king's men said she'd have to be taken to the king's castle in Edinburg where a decision would be made. I dunnae ken why they'd believe she was nae yer wife in truth," his mother said.

A knot of pure black rage formed in his chest, and he withdrew his sword. "I ken why they thought my marriage could be dissolved. Have ye seen Athelston and Anise?"

"Aye, Athelston," Tavish said, "but nae Anise. I wanted the men to fight to keep Maeve here, but Athelston convinced me it was a battle we'd nae win and we'd lose too many men in hand-to-hand combat. He said to wait for ye to return, and then we could strategize on how to get her back."

"Athelston is a liar," Alasdair spat as he started to stride past his family. "As well as Anise. Call the men to search for them," he said to Tavish. "And if ye find either of them afore I do, guard them well." Alasdair did not wait to explain why; he barged through the castle door and took the stairs three at a time to Athelston's bedchamber. He kicked the door open only to find it empty.

He went from there to the great hall where Tavish was gathering the warriors and giving them the orders Alasdair had passed to him. Alasdair held up his hands for quiet. "Search the castle first, then the courtyards and the land beyond. Athelston has betrayed us, but he'll nae realize we ken this, so ye should be able to—"

"Alasdair!" Lara cried from the entrance to the great hall.

He looked to his sister, then rushed toward her as fear twisted her face. "Anise is dead! I went to the healing room, and she is crumpled on the floor and nae breathing. I found this in her hand." Lara raised a potion bottle. "I think," Lara whispered, her voice cracking as she moved into the room, "she must have killed herself."

He wanted to have pity for her, but too much anger gripped him. "If she did nae, then Athelston did." He didn't doubt the man would have if he thought Anise was not going to keep their secret.

"Alasdair," came Athelston's voice from the doorway suddenly. "Ye've returned. Did ye get the fires put out?" he asked, his expression so smug, so triumphant, so damned certain of himself and the lies he'd woven.

There was no tether of reason strong enough to hold Alasdair back. With an inhuman roar, he charged toward Athelston and sent him flying out of the room and against the passage wall. The man was trying to regain his balance when Alasdair was upon him, hitting him in the face. A hit for his father. And the clan. One for betrayal and grief. He shook with rage as his fist connected with bone that broke under the power of his anger and fear for Maeve.

He was unaware of anything but the two of them. All sound stopped but that of his fist connecting yet again with bone. This time it was Athelston's jaw. "What have they planned for her?"

When Athelston tried to raise his fist to fight instead of answering, Alasdair pummeled the man harder and faster. Someone grabbed his arm from behind, but he jerked loose and drew back his fist to hit him yet again. But then he was grabbed in a firmer grip. He glanced over his shoulder to see Tavish there.

"Dunnae kill him until ye have the answers ye need," his brother said.

He faced Athelston once more. "I did nae catch any Frasers," he seethed, unsheathing his dagger and bringing the point to the man's bollocks. He pressed hard into one until Athelston cried out and slumped forward, but Alasdair pushed him upright and into the wall. He shoved his forearm under Athelston's throat and kept his dagger at the man's bollocks. "I'm nae going to kill ye, but I'll gladly take yer bollocks unless ye give me answers now." Athelston's left eye was already swollen shut, but his right eye widened as he looked at Alasdair. "I caught Darby, and I ken what ye have been up to. Now, tell me afore I lose my patience. What is the plan for my wife?"

"The king is ill," Athelston gasped.

"Go on," Alasdair said, loosening his forearm just enough so the man could speak.

"Robert Fraser is making all decisions currently."

"And?" Alasdair demanded, aware of that fact already.

"They took her to the king's castle, so Robert could pronounce yer marriage dissolved. She'll then be wed to Colin, and he'll take her to her home—their home." A smile twisted Athelston's bloody lips. "By the time ye reach her, her marriage to Colin will have been consummated. I dunnae imagine ye would want the woman once she's been bedded by another."

Alasdair sent his fist straight into Athelston's mouth and then released the man, who crumpled to the ground. He stood over his cousin and warred with himself not to plunge the dagger he held into the man's heart. "Did ye kill Anise?" he demanded.

"She was planning to reveal me," Athelston spat. "Yer damned wife and her befriending the whore." Alasdair saw red. He raised his dagger, his heart thundering, as he thought about plunging it into Athelston's black heart.

"He's nae worth yer murdering him," Father Bernard said. "We'll deal with him, Alasdair. Ye go get yer wife."

"I need ye to come with me," Alasdair said to the priest. "I'll need yer word to the king that Maeve and I are truly wed."

"I'll see that the man rots for what he's done to my daughter-in-law, Son, and to us," Alasdair's mother said. "Dunnae fear. I ken exactly where yer father would have sent him."

Alasdair did, too. The Black Isle. It was where traitors were sent to rot in hell on Earth.

The worst of the sinners had to be a priest who had turned bad, Maeve thought as she was dragged into the chapel at the king's court. Standing in front of the priest, who turned to look at her, were Colin, his father, and Robert Fraser. Other than the priest, they were the only ones in the room. She'd been given a choice of gowns to wear for her wedding. She'd traded one of them for the tattered, gray gown the servant who'd brought in the steaming water that Maeve was supposed to bathe in, was wearing. She'd also had to give the blasted woman the ribbon that Alasdair had kept all those years, but she gladly gave it up in hopes that it would give her the unbecoming gown that might be the thing to keep Colin from wanting her at least for this night. She hadn't bathed, either. She was quite certain she smelled, and the thought was the one bit of happiness she found in the moment. That, and when Colin gaped at her, she knew it was not because she looked ravishing. She'd not brushed her hair, either, and she had undone the plait. She may have been pronounced an innocent and her marriage dissolved by the corrupt Robert, but she would not go willingly into this farce, which was why she was being carried into the chapel, and she had no doubt was why there were no witnesses here, other than the ones who would lie.

Colin looked miserable. Good. She no longer felt even a sliver of pity for him. If he intended to "wed" her, then he intended to bed her, and she'd sooner kill him than allow him to touch her. The guards who had her on either side by the arms carried her up to Colin's side, and then he took her forearm in a viselike grip and pulled her snugly against his side. He turned to look at her, and while sorrow shone in his brown gaze, so did determination. He'd made up his mind to wrong her.

"Maeve, I'm sorry," he said.

She turned her head and looked up at him, her lip curling. "Ye're a liar, 'tis what ye are. But what could be expected when ye have a lying, murdering father?"

Laird Fraser stepped in front of her with his hand raised as if to slap her, but Colin moved to block his father. "Ye'll nae touch her, Da."

"Then get her in line and ensure she stays that way. She'll rouse her men to insurrection against us if ye bring her back to Eilean Donan and they think she's been coerced into this."

Maeve had a moment of hope that she would do exactly that, before Colin said, "Do ye nae think I've thought of that? Maeve will nae be doing that, though, because if she does, I will have to hurt Beitris."

Maeve's stomach dropped to the floor. "Who are ye?" she hissed. "I thought ye were honorable! I defended ye!"

"I am honorable, but I love ye."

"This is nae any sort of love I want a part of!" she cried out. She didn't care if it got her hit. "I love Alasdair. I'm wed true to Alasdair. He took my bod—"

Colin pressed his finger to her lips, and the dark, layered look he gave her made her flinch. "Every time ye say his name, every time ye claim he is yer husband true, that will be a lash Beitris will take for yer mistake. If ye do anything, anything at all, Maeve, to make anyone believe ye are anything but grateful to have been rescued and ecstatic to be my wife, I'll have to kill her. I dunnae want to, but I will. Please dunnae make me. I just want us to be happy. We can, ye ken?"

Bile had risen in her throat, but she forced herself to nod. What was she going to do? She'd have to go along with the lie until she and Bee could escape.

He smiled grimly at her, and then he tapped by her right eye. "I see yer thoughts turning, Maeve. I see I'm going to have to be extreme with ye until ye are ready to behave."

"Nay, I—"

"Wed us," he bit out to the priest, who immediately began the ceremony.

"State yer name," the priest said.

When she didn't speak, Colin said, "Shall we count this as Beitris's first lash?"

"Maeve MacKenzie," she bit out.

And thus it went. She gave the answers she knew she must in order to save Bee, and she tried not to fret. She was wed to Alasdair, and no other wedding could undo that. It was over in a matter of minutes, and when Colin bent his head to kiss her, she turned her face and nearly heaved when his lips met her cheek.

"Come on, then," he said, tugging her by arm. "Time to go to Eilean Donan so we can make our marriage official."

⚜

"Remember," Father Bernard said the next day as they rode up to the king's castle, "we are nae going in forcefully. Our best hope of seeing the king, pleading yer case, and getting Maeve back is through diplomacy."

Alasdair nodded as he rode his horse up the long, winding stone path that led to the first guard tower. He wanted to go in by force. He wanted to shove past anyone who dared to try to stop him, but he knew the foolishness and futility of that. The king's guard was large, and though Alasdair had brought nearly all the men he had available, they only numbered 253. That was nothing compared to the force the king could amass.

"Tell me the plan again?" he said as they dismounted and handed their horses off to stable boys who appeared. He turned and motioned for his men to stand by. If he was denied Maeve, he would fight to the death, as would each of his men, but for now, they would wait for him out here. If things did not go his way, Brodick would come to get them, and they would scour the castle for Maeve, if they could, and steal her away. If not, so be it. Death was preferable to a life without her.

"We'll seek an audience with the queen first," Father Bernard said.

"Because ye ken a secret of hers," Brodick supplied.

"Aye," Father Bernard said. "I dunnae think we'd be granted an audience with the king without her, but she'll get us one. Hopefully, the king will be well enough to understand that his right hand is trying to usurp his power by coming for Maeve with the Frasers."

Alasdair nodded and approached the guard tower with Father Bernard. A guard appeared. "State yer name and yer business."

"Father Bernard. I'm here to seek an audience with Her Grace."

"The queen kens the likes of ye?" the guard said in a sneering tone.

"Aye, ye young pup. We're close, personal friends, so take a care nae to offend me, lest the queen commands yer head as an apology. Now run along and tell the queen that Father Bernard is here to discuss Laird Douglas."

Alasdair thought that Laird Douglas must either be the queen's secret or somehow related to it.

"Wait here," the guard bit out. He motioned to the guard in the other tower, who came out with his sword drawn. "Watch these three," the first guard said. "I'll be back shortly."

The moment he was gone, Alasdair leaned over and whispered to Father Bernard, "Are ye certain ye're a priest?"

Father Bernard chuckled. "We men of God are some of the canniest of all, Alasdair. We have to be."

Alasdair nodded and motioned Brodick closer. "Do ye see the best way out if we have need?"

"Aye," Brodick said. "The right side of the drop-off from the castle looks less steep."

"There will nae be a need," Father Bernard protested, but even still, Alasdair and Brodick spent the time waiting for the guard to return, quietly discussing the best escape route and how to attempt it.

But when the guard returned and told them the queen would see them, there did not currently seem to be a need, after all. Alasdair found himself searching for Maeve as they walked through the castle. He looked down corridors as far as he could without leaving the party, and he studied the crowds of men and women milling in different rooms. It was on the path from the main floor to the queen's receiving chamber that a servant woman ascended the stairs toward them and caught his attention. She wore a ribbon that made his heart stop.

When she started to pass him, he looked closer and knew the green ribbon to be the one that belonged to Maeve. It was entwined with gold thread the likes of which he'd never seen before or would again. "Where did ye get that ribbon?" he demanded, causing the guard and Father Bernard to stop and turn back to look at him.

The woman's hand fluttered to her hair, and she got an uneasy look. "I did nae steal it!" she protested.

"Nay, then where did ye get it?" he asked again.

"The lady that 'twas to be wed gave it to me in exchange for my gown." The woman shrugged. "I dunnae ken why. My gown was drab and tattered, and this one was the one she was to be wed in." The servant beamed and swept her hand down the length of the lovely silk gown she wore.

"What did she look like?"

"Oh, flaming hair, unhappy blue eyes. Lovely skin, though, and verra pretty despite her unhappiness. I suppose 'tis nae all I thought to be a lass with a great castle about to wed a man who will inherit another."

"Ye ken she's a lass with a great castle?"

"Aye. I heard the other servants gossiping that she's the lady of Eilean Donan. I dunnae why she was so grim about wedding Colin Fraser. He's handsome enough."

His anger became a scalding fury that threatened to explode from him like fire. Father Bernard must have seen it because he spoke. "Did the lass wed Colin Fraser?"

"Oh, aye. This morning. They set off right away to her home after. I saw her coming out of the chapel. In truth," the woman said, leaning in, "I went there to see her. She was wed in my dress, after all. She looked even more unhappy after the ceremony."

Damned Colin Fraser, and Laird Fraser, and the priest who had wed them, who had to have known she didn't want to be wed to Colin. And damned Robert Fraser. "Thank ye," Alasdair managed.

"Do ye ken her? The flame-haired woman?" the servant asked.

"Aye," he replied, having to stop himself from saying Maeve was his wife. The walk to the queen's chamber seemed interminable knowing Maeve was no longer here but on her way to Eilean Donan where Colin would, no doubt, try to bed her. He was going to rip out Colin's heart with his bare hands. In fact, he was going to do that now. He grabbed Father Bernard, who was walking in front of him, by the arm. "I kinnae—"

"Leave it to me," the man said and smiled understandingly at him. "Take yer men and save yer wife. I'll bring the reinforcements ye need."

Alasdair nodded. "Ye'll be my voice," he asked of Brodick.

"I'd be honored, Alasdair. Dunnae fash. We'll nae fail ye."

With that, Alasdair turned on his heel and raced back the way they'd just come, praying he'd get to Maeve before Colin laid a hand on her.

Chapter Twenty-Five

*M*aeve paced the familiar length of her bedchamber unsure what to do. Her stomach turned with anxiety, and every time she heard footsteps, she stopped and tensed. She'd played her part upon arrival and given a speech to convince her clan that Colin had rescued her, and she was grateful and happy to be his wife. She'd had no choice. He'd had Beitris surrounded by his guards so that Maeve had no hope to speak to her or warn her. Besides, Maeve knew he meant to keep his vow to hurt Bee if Maeve did not comply.

He was coming. He was coming to bed her, and what choice would she have? What was wrong with him? Their joining would not make her his wife. It would only make her despise him more than she already did, which was deep down to her bones. She looked around her bedchamber for a weapon, but the room had been carefully cleared of anything that could be used to kill Colin. He had known she'd try. She could not even take cold comfort in that, his betrayal cut so deep.

Footsteps fell outside her bedchamber door once more, and this time, the handle rattled, and the lock, which had been installed by one of Colin's men when they put her in here, clicked. Her mouth went dry as the door creaked open. There, on the threshold, stood a small, hooded man. He stepped into the room and closed the door behind him.

She moved against the wall, fearful of why he might have been sent, and then he turned, and raised his arms to lower his hood that almost completely disguised his face.

"Bee!" Maeve burst out and flew toward the woman, colliding into her. They wrapped each other in loving embraces, crying, and laughing, though Bee kept shushing Maeve. "How did ye get in here?" she asked, pulling back.

Bee winked at her. "Men are simple creatures, Maeve."

"Nae Alasdair," Maeve blurted.

Bee smiled approvingly as she stared at Maeve for a moment. "I kenned it." Bee touched her heart. "I kenned it here that the speech ye gave was a lie and the missive ye sent about being happily wedded was the truth."

"Oh, Bee," Maeve said, burying her face in the woman's shoulder for one moment. "We have to flee now. Colin threatened to kill ye if I did nae comply." She gave Bee a quick explanation of what had occurred at the king's castle and what she had discovered about the MacRaes and the Frasers. As she talked, she moved to her window that overlooked the waters of Loch Duich. She and Bee stared into the dark waters below. "The waters are rough tonight," Maeve whispered.

"Aye," Bee agreed. "A storm approaches. The tide will push us against the rocks."

"We'll stay, then," Maeve said, her hope deserting her. "Alasdair will come for me eventually. I ken it. I'll keep ye safe, dunnae fash. I'll bear Colin—"

"Shush yer foolish talk. Ye'll go. I'm nae a strong swimmer, and I'll hide. Come back as quick as ye can."

"Where will ye hide?" Maeve asked.

Bee's face turned red. "There's a secret room off yer da's chambers. We used to, well—"

"Ye used to meet there," Maeve guessed, her heart

wrenching.

"Aye. It was built long ago, in case of a siege. It had a tunnel that led outside, but the tunnel collapsed, and it was deemed too dangerous to dig out again."

Maeve nodded. "Go to the room now. I'll go straight to Alasdair, and between his men and mine, we'll take back the castle." She bit her lip when she thought of the king's right hand. "I just pray I can get an audience with the king and convince him of the truth."

"Ye will with yer husband and my cousin. Bernard is a canny one."

"I ken it," Maeve said, hugging Bee to her. "Now, go afore Colin comes."

Bee hugged her back, pulled up her hood, and left with one glance back. Maeve did not waste time. She pushed the window all the way open and looked out into the dark waters. She trembled with fear as she climbed up into the window. Below she could see nothing but darkness and one lone light that came from an approaching vessel. It was odd for a birlinn to travel at night, but Maeve half wondered if Colin had sent for more of his men. She prayed not, took a deep breath, and jumped.

Icy water sucked her under into the darkness. She knew in an instant that she'd misjudged the dangers. The frigid temperatures slowed her movements and made her limbs heavy, and the loch was angry this night. It turned and swirled, and every time she tried to swim to the surface, she was pulled back under by the force of the water.

Her lungs began to burn, and her thoughts became harder to hold on to. Fear curled spindly fingers around her heart to slow its beat. She kicked at the water and pulled at it with her arms, but when she failed to reach the surface again, defeat washed a warm blanket over her. She wanted to wrap herself in that blanket and sleep. She liked the warmth. The safeness. It reminded her... Well, it reminded her of...of Alasdair.

Her heart gave a jerk as she recalled that she was trying to get to the surface to save Bee and get to Alasdair. If she never made it there, not only would she die but Alasdair would be in a dire predicament and so would Bee. Maeve kicked again, harder than she ever had, and when she broke the surface, she sucked in a greedy gulp of much-needed air, but as she did so, a wave came crashing over her to push her back under.

Again, she had to fight her way to the surface, but her arms screamed now and her legs were like the heaviest weights, soon to be useless, and her lungs squeezed so painfully that she knew she would soon be out of time. She broke through the surface once more to the roar of the water surrounding her. She sucked in a quick breath as the winter air washed over her already trembling body, and she tried to gain her bearings of where to swim so she would not be sucked under again. That's when she saw the torches in the darkness right beside her. There were six of them lit against the black night to line the length of the large birlinn.

She didn't have time to decide what to do. A wave came at her again, but something hit her in the head before she was pushed under, and when she grabbed at it as the water overcame her, she realized it was a rope.

She held on for dear life, going under once more where death was beckoning her, and she floated there with only strength enough to grasp the rope. And then, to her amazement she started to move upward. She was being pulled to the surface. When she broke through the water this time, she looked up, and leaning over the side of the boat was Brodick, grinning at her. He and two other men pulled her up, and together they brought her over the side of the birlinn and wrapped her immediately in a cloak.

Before she could even ask Brodick what was occurring, the men standing in front of her moved suddenly to the side, and Maeve saw that Father Bernard was approaching with a smile. Beside him was a man she did not know by face but by the crown he wore upon his head. Maeve stood to her full height as the king of Scotland stopped in front of her. She gave a curtsy, made awkward by her exhausted limbs and the rocking of the birlinn upon the waves.

"I'm told ye need my aid," the king said, taking her hand as she straightened.

"Aye, Sire," she replied as the wind whipped her hair and stung her face.

"Tell me yer version of the story," the king said. "These two—" he wove a hand at Brodick and Father Bernard "—have told me their views but they speak for the MacRaes. I want to hear what ye, as the current head of the MacKenzie clan, have to say."

"I'm nae the head now," she said. "I'm wed good and true to Alasdair MacRae, so he is now rightful laird." And then she quickly relayed the rest of the tale as the king listened. Just as she finished, the war horns of her home began to sound.

"We're being invaded!" she gasped.

"Nay," the king said with a smile. "Ye're being rescued by yer husband, and we're here to aid him."

"Ye believe me, then?" she asked, looking to her home, where torches flared one by one across the rampart to prepare for battle.

"Aye, lass. Yer tale matched that of these two perfectly." He motioned to Brodick and Father Bernard once more. "Come, let us vanquish my enemies and yers, and take back the home I gave yer da."

There was no way to approach Eilean Donan by stealth. That was what made the castle so coveted. So Alasdair did the only thing he could: he and his men charged full force up the bridge with swords drawn. The war horns sounded as they overcame the first set of guards assigned to keep intruders from gaining the bridge. There was nothing so effective to a warrior as the desperate need to save the woman he loved.

Alasdair didn't want to cut down men that were loyal to Maeve, men who would hopefully one day be loyal to him, so when he felled them, he did so without using lethal force. He was halfway down the bridge to the next set of guard towers when more horns sounded and the torches along the rampart that faced the Loch Duich lit. The MacKenzies were being attacked by water. Alasdair could not have asked for a timelier siege.

He charged forward with his men through the second tower, but when he got to the outer courtyard, hundreds upon hundreds of warriors swarmed toward them from all directions. MacKenzies fought alongside the Frasers under the false belief that he was the enemy. His blood roared in his ears as he met blades from his left and right, fighting toward the castle door. But there, lined up in front of the door, with Colin in the middle, was a long row of archers.

Alasdair paused. He was more than willing to give up his life for Maeve, but he did not want to lead his men to certain death without even trying to reason with Maeve's men. Colin's were a lost cause. He gave the signal for his men to hold, and he lowered his own sword to his waist.

"Maeve is my wife. I ken ye have been told she's nae, but she is," he yelled above the noise that remained, but as he spoke, a quiet descended.

"Ye took Maeve against her will," Colin bellowed.

"Aye, I did," Alasdair said truthfully, "because I thought the MacKenzies started the feud with us and killed my da, but then I learned it was yer clan." He pointed his sword at Colin. "Bring Maeve forth and let her speak the truth."

"Our lady already gave us the truth," a MacKenzie said. "And she said yer marriage was nae complete, therefore dissolved. She said she wished to be the Fraser's wife."

"She said that under duress."

Shock flew through Alasdair at the sound of Maeve's voice coming from behind him. He turned and there, in the moonlight and burning torches, stood his wife, dripping wet, holding a sword in front of her, with the King of Scotland on her right, Brodick on her left, and Father Bernard beside him. Behind them was a sea of the king's men.

Maeve and the king exchanged a look, and she nodded. The king raised his hands, and the hiss of blades being lifted in the air filled the night. "Colin Fraser, Laird Fraser, I name ye traitors to my kingdom. And any Fraser that dunnae put down their sword by my order now will also be named a traitor. And if any MacKenzie dares to raise a sword against Laird MacRae, who is the rightful laird of Eilean Donan as Lady Maeve's true husband, ye will die a traitor's death."

Swords immediately went down through the courtyard, and the king looked to Maeve. "Well, go on, lass. Go to yer husband."

Maeve flew toward him, but he met her halfway on the bridge, caught her in his arms, and hugged her to him. She buried her face in his neck, and a sob escaped her. When she looked up at him after a moment, he caught her mouth with his, pouring all his love into the kiss to the sound of cheering from his men. He pulled back after a moment, and she gave him the gut-wrenching smile only she could and pressed her hands to his cheeks. "I rescued ye," she said on a laugh.

"Aye, Wife. The day ye forgave me my wicked ways and offered me yer heart, ye saved me."

"Ye saved me, too," she said, pressing her lips to his once more. "In the woods many years ago, and in the woods the day ye took me. I just did nae realize the second time was a rescue at first."

"I suppose now 'tis time to unify our clans," he said, setting her on her feet and taking her hand.

⚜

To her left, she could see that Colin and his father had been taken by the king's men and that the Frasers seemed to be complying with the king's orders. And as they moved toward the king, someone yelled her name.

She swung toward the voice and was nearly toppled over by Beitris, who flew into her arms, hugging her.

"Are ye all right?" Bee asked. Her motherly concern had Maeve instantly thinking of her da, and it set a knot in Maeve's throat.

"I am. Are ye?"

"Aye," Bee said, grinning and looking between the two of them. "I am seeing ye with a husband ye love. Yer da would be so happy for ye, Maeve." Tears filled Maeve's eyes, which Bee brushed off Maeve's cheeks. "Quit the crying now and explain to the clan how ye have come here as the willing wife of the McRae," Bee said.

Maeve swept her gaze over her clansmen gathered in the courtyard and could see that they were all staring raptly at her. She looked to Alasdair. "Do ye wish to address them as the new laird?"

"I will, but after ye address them. We are a team, ye and I, and we will lead them together."

"I love ye," she said, and he squeezed her hand as she held up her other one for silence. "Many of ye may be confused by what has occurred since I disappeared and then returned with Colin. I want to explain everything, and I want to assure ye that I am wed true to Alasdair MacRae and verra happy about it. His clan is nae our enemy, and they did nae start the raids with us. The Frasers did." And then she launched into the tale, beginning with the day she disappeared, saying, "Ye all ken how Highlanders hold grudges, aye?"

⸎⸎⸎⸎⸎

It was very late that night by the time Maeve and Alasdair made their way to their bedchamber. They were both weary, but not so much that they did not want each other. They came together slowly and silently with Alasdair undressing her first. Each gentle slide of his hand over her body stoked a fire in her and chased away the chill from the loch so that by the time she was standing naked in front of him, she was not cold at all.

She reached for his plaid to take it off him, but he caught her hands gently with his and stilled her. "Let me look at ye for a moment. I was so scairt for ye when I returned to the castle and ye had been taken. I kinnae imagine my life without ye, Maeve. Ye are everything to me. Ye are the most amazing lass I have ever kenned."

"Flattery will get ye everywhere with me, Laird," she teased. But then she sobered, wanting him to know how she felt in this moment. "I would walk through fire for ye, Alasdair."

"I ken it, lass, and to have yer love, yer loyalty, is the greatest treasure I could ever hope for." He released her hands and pulled her gently to him, taking her mouth with his in a slow, tantalizing kiss that she knew was the beginning of a night of bliss, with a lifetime more to come.

Epilogue

"I hope I have twins," Lara said, holding Mara and cooing down at her.

The worried look on Brodick's face made Maeve and Alasdair laugh, and Maeve saw a mischievous glint come into Alasdair's eyes. He rose from the bed with Henry, whom Alasdair had been holding since the wee hours of the morning because their newborn son's favorite place was in his da's arms. Maeve couldn't say she blamed him because that was her favorite place, too.

He walked toward Brodick, who seemed to have been steadily creeping toward the door as if he wanted to escape. When he stood right in front of the man, Alasdair said, "I think twins may run in our family, Lara, so ye and Brodick will likely have them once ye're wed."

Brodick definitely looked like he wanted to flee now, which made Maeve giggle. "Hold Henry, Brodick," Maeve said. "He dunnae bite."

"Nay," Alasdair said, holding his son out to his best friend. "He only wets himself and wails so loudly that it makes yer ears ache."

"'Tis nae that bad!" Maeve chided, and just as Brodick reluctantly took the bairn—because really Alasdair gave him no choice—Henry started to wail. Maeve would have wagered it was the loudest she'd heard yet. "Bring him to me," she offered, but Alasdair shook his head.

"Nay," he said, and motioned to Brodick. "Go with Lara and ye two coo over the bairns for a while. But bring them back afore the nooning meal. They need their mother's milk."

Maeve loved how Alasdair knew just as well as she did what their children needed. He had been right by her side since the day they were born meeting all their needs as well as hers. He was amazing.

"What will ye two be doing?" Brodick demanded.

"Sleeping," Alasdair announced, guiding the man out the door Lara had already gone through. When the door shut behind them, Alasdair made his way back to the bed, but he did not sit on it. He slowly stripped his clothes as a sinful look that warmed Maeve to the core came into his eyes.

When he was completely undressed, he sat down beside her and raised her arms to take off her gown. "I thought ye said we were going to be sleeping," she teased.

"Aye," he said, giving her a wicked look that curled her toes, "and so we are. After we make another bairn."

I hope you enjoyed reading Maeve and Alasdair's story and will consider leaving a review! I appreciate your help in spreading the word about my books, including letting your friends know. Reviews help other readers find my books. Please leave one on your favorite site!

Next up in the Wicked Willful Highlanders series is Highlanders Never Surrender!

On the path of vengeance, he unwillingly collided with love.

No one desires retribution against their enemy more than Highlander Cormac MacLean. Yet his foe has the favor of the king and Cormac lacks irrefutable proof of the man's nefarious deeds, so revenge must be planned with calculated care. But when Cormac's hot-headed brother impulsively attempts to kidnap their enemy's stepsister, Cormac finds himself fleeing with the wounded beauty after she sustains an injury trying to protect him. He has every intention of returning the troublesome lass to her home, until it quickly becomes apparent that she may be the one person who can free his sister from the dark place in which she dwells. At every turn, the strong-willed woman shows bravery and loyalty, and instead of wanting to keep her at a distance as vows given and family allegiance demands he must, he aches to touch her, protect her, and possess her forever.

Desperate to escape her impending wedding to a suspected murderer, Brigid Campbell is not exactly dismayed when she's snatched from her stepbrother's clutches by a Scottish barbarian who she incidentally ends up saving from an arrow aimed at his heart. Still, when she awakens from her injury at Cormac's home, she is quite upset that her dearest companion was left behind to face the wrath of her stepbrother. So, when her overbearing captor announces he'll be keeping her to assist his sister, she makes a demand of her own—he must help her rescue her companion. When the officious man refuses, she takes matters into her own hands bringing her the startling discovery that behind the Highlander's mask of dislike for her lies a compellingly complex man who willingly charges into peril to save her. At each brush with danger that ensues, he's there to aid her, filling her with hope that despite the feud that brought them together, she may have finally found a family to belong to and a man to trust and to give her heart.

Brigid fuels Cormac's desire and makes him question his oaths, but it takes his enemy making a master move for him to face the truth that since the day he met Brigid, there could only ever be one choice for him—banish his ghosts, silence his guilt, and show the woman he loves unquestionably that she is his and he is hers—if only it's not too late.

If you love sweeping epic romance that takes you on a rollicking adventure through the highlands, then you should try out **When a Laird Loves a Lady**, which is book one in my *Highlander Vows: Entangled Hearts* series. You can read a bit about book 1 below.

Not even her careful preparations could prepare her for the barbarian who rescues her. Don't miss the USA Today bestselling *Highlander Vows: Entangled Hearts* series, starting with the critically acclaimed When a Laird Loves a Lady. Faking her death would be simple, it was escaping her home that would be difficult.

Keep In Touch

Get Julie Johnstone's Newsletter
https://juliejohnstoncauthor.com

Join her Reading Group
facebook.com/groups/1500294650186536

Like her Facebook Page
facebook.com/authorjuliejohnstone

Stalk her Instagram
instagram.com/authorjuliejohnstone

Hang out with her on Goodreads
goodreads.com/author/show/2354638.Julie_Johnstone

Hear about her sales via Bookbub
bookbub.com/authors/julie-johnstone

Follow her Amazon Page
amazon.com/Julie-Johnstone/e/B0062AW98S

Excerpt of When a Laird Loves a Lady

One

England, 1357

Faking her death would be simple. It was escaping her home that would be difficult. Marion de Lacy stared hard into the slowly darkening sky, thinking about the plan she intended to put into action tomorrow—if all went well—but growing uneasiness tightened her belly. From where she stood in the bailey, she counted the guards up in the tower. It was not her imagination: Father had tripled the knights keeping guard at all times, as if he was expecting trouble.

Taking a deep breath of the damp air, she pulled her mother's cloak tighter around her to ward off the twilight chill. A lump lodged in her throat as the wool scratched her neck. In the many years since her mother had been gone, Marion had both hated and loved this cloak for the death and life it represented. Her mother's freesia scent had long since faded from the garment, yet simply calling up a memory of her mother wearing it gave Marion comfort.

She rubbed her fingers against the rough material. When she fled, she couldn't chance taking anything with her but the clothes on her body and this cloak. Her death had to appear accidental, and the cloak that everyone knew she prized would ensure her freedom. Finding it tangled in the branches at the edge of the sea cliff ought to be just the thing to convince her father and William Froste that she'd drowned. After all, neither man thought she could swim. They didn't truly care about her anyway. Her marriage to the blackhearted knight was only about what her hand could give the two men. Her father, Baron de Lacy, wanted more power, and Froste wanted her family's prized land. A match made in Heaven, if only the match didn't involve her...but it did.

Father would set the hounds of Hell themselves to track her down if he had the slightest suspicion that she was still alive. She was an inestimable possession to be given to secure Froste's unwavering allegiance and, therefore, that of the renowned ferocious knights who served him. Whatever small sliver of hope she had that her father would grant her mercy and not marry her to Froste had been destroyed by the lashing she'd received when she'd pleaded for him to do so.

The moon crested above the watchtower, reminding her why she was out here so close to mealtime: to meet Angus. The Scotsman may have been her father's stable master, but he was *her* ally, and when he'd proposed she flee England for Scotland, she'd readily consented.

Marion looked to the west, the direction from which Angus would return from Newcastle. He should be back any minute now from meeting his cousin and clansman Neil, who was to escort her to Scotland. She prayed all was set and that Angus's kin was ready to depart. With her wedding to Froste to take place in six days, she wanted to be far away before there was even the slightest chance he'd be making his way here. And since he was set to arrive the night before the wedding, leaving tomorrow promised she'd not encounter him.

A sense of urgency enveloped her, and Marion forced herself to stroll across the bailey toward the gatehouse that led to the tunnel preceding the drawbridge. She couldn't risk raising suspicion from the tower guards. At the gatehouse, she nodded to Albert, one of the knights who operated the drawbridge mechanism. He was young and rarely questioned her excursions to pick flowers or find herbs.

"Off to get some medicine?" he inquired.

"Yes," she lied with a smile and a little pang of guilt. But this was survival, she reminded herself as she entered the tunnel. When she exited the heavy wooden door that led to freedom, she wasn't surprised to find Peter and Andrew not yet up in the twin towers that flanked the entrance to the drawbridge. It was, after all, time for the changing of the guard.

They smiled at her as they put on their helmets and demi-gauntlets. They were an imposing presence to any who crossed the drawbridge and dared to approach the castle gate. Both men were tall and looked particularly daunting in their full armor, which Father insisted upon at all times. The men were certainly a fortress in their own right.

She nodded to them. "I'll not be long. I want to gather some more flowers for the supper table." Her voice didn't even wobble with the lie.

Peter grinned at her, his kind brown eyes crinkling at the edges. "Will you pick me one of those pale winter flowers for my wife again, Marion?"

She returned his smile. "It took away her anger as I said it would, didn't it?"

"It did," he replied. "You always know just how to help with her."

"I'll get a pink one if I can find it. The colors are becoming scarcer as the weather cools."

Andrew, the younger of the two knights, smiled, displaying a set of straight teeth. He held up his covered arm. "My cut is almost healed."

Marion nodded. "I told you! Now maybe you'll listen to me sooner next time you're wounded in training."

He gave a soft laugh. "I will. Should I put more of your paste on tonight?"

"Yes, keep using it. I'll have to gather some more yarrow, if I can find any, and mix up another batch of the medicine for you." And she'd have to do it before she escaped. "I better get going if I'm going to find those things." She knew she should not have agreed to search for the flowers and offered to find the yarrow when she still had to speak to Angus and return to the castle in time for supper, but both men had been kind to her when many had not. It was her way of thanking them.

After Peter lowered the bridge and opened the door, she departed the castle grounds, considering her plan once more. Had she forgotten anything? She didn't think so. She was simply going to walk straight out of her father's castle and never come back. Tomorrow, she'd announce she was going out to collect more winter blooms, and then, instead, she would go down to the edge of the cliff overlooking the sea. She would slip off her cloak and leave it for a search party to find. Her breath caught deep in her chest at the simple yet dangerous plot. The last detail to see to was Angus.

She stared down the long dirt path that led to the sea and stilled, listening for hoofbeats. A slight vibration of the ground tingled her feet, and her heart sped in hopeful anticipation that it was Angus coming down the dirt road on his horse. When the crafty stable master appeared with a grin spread across his face, the worry that was squeezing her heart loosened. For the first time since he had ridden out that morning, she took a proper breath. He stopped his stallion alongside her and dismounted.

She tilted her head back to look up at him as he towered over her. An errant thought struck. "Angus, are all Scots as tall as you?"

"Nay, but ye ken Scots are bigger than all the wee Englishmen." Suppressed laughter filled his deep voice. "So even the ones nae as tall as me are giants compared te the scrawny men here."

"You're teasing me," she replied, even as she arched her eyebrows in uncertainty.

"A wee bit," he agreed and tousled her hair. The laughter vanished from his eyes as he rubbed a hand over his square jaw and then stared down his bumpy nose at her, fixing what he called his "lecturing look" on her. "We've nae much time. Neil is in Newcastle just as he's supposed te be, but there's been a slight change."

She frowned. "For the last month, every time I wanted to simply make haste and flee, you refused my suggestion, and now you say there's a slight change?"

His ruddy complexion darkened. She'd pricked that MacLeod temper her mother had always said Angus's clan was known for throughout the Isle of Skye, where they lived in the farthest reaches of Scotland. Marion could remember her mother chuckling and teasing Angus about how no one knew the MacLeod temperament better than their neighboring clan, the MacDonalds of Sleat, to which her mother had been born. The two clans had a history of feuding.

Angus cleared his throat and recaptured Marion's attention. Without warning, his hand closed over her shoulder, and he squeezed gently. "I'm sorry te say it so plain, but ye must die at once."

Her eyes widened as dread settled in the pit of her stomach. "What? Why?" The sudden fear she felt was unreasonable. She knew he didn't mean she was really going to die, but her palms were sweating and her lungs had tightened all the same. She sucked in air and wiped her damp hands down the length of her cotton skirts. Suddenly, the idea of going to a foreign land and living with her mother's clan, people she'd never met, made her apprehensive.

She didn't even know if the MacDonalds—her uncle, in particular, who was now the laird—would accept her or not. She was half-English, after all, and Angus had told her that when a Scot considered her English bloodline and the fact that she'd been raised there, they would most likely brand her fully English, which was not a good thing in a Scottish mind. And if her uncle was anything like her grandfather had been, the man was not going to be very reasonable. But she didn't have any other family to turn to who would dare defy her father, and Angus hadn't offered for her to go to his clan, so she'd not asked. He likely didn't want to bring trouble to his clan's doorstep, and she didn't blame him.

Panic bubbled inside her. She needed more time, even if it was only the day she'd thought she had, to gather her courage.

"Why must I flee tonight? I was to teach Eustice how to dress a wound. She might serve as a maid, but then she will be able to help the knights when I'm gone. And her little brother, Bernard, needs a few more lessons before he's mastered writing his name and reading. And Eustice's youngest sister has begged me to speak to Father about allowing her to visit her mother next week."

"Ye kinnae watch out for everyone here anymore, Marion."

She placed her hand over his on her shoulder. "Neither can you."

Their gazes locked in understanding and disagreement.

He slipped his hand from her shoulder, and then crossed his arms over his chest in a gesture that screamed stubborn, unyielding protector. "If I leave at the same time ye feign yer death," he said, changing the subject, "it could stir yer father's suspicion and make him ask questions when none need te be asked. I'll be going home te Scotland soon after ye." Angus reached into a satchel attached to his horse and pulled out a dagger, which he slipped to her. "I had this made for ye."

Marion took the weapon and turned it over, her heart pounding. "It's beautiful." She held it by its black handle while withdrawing it from the sheath and examining it. "It's much sharper than the one I have."

"Aye," he said grimly. "It is. Dunnae forget that just because I taught ye te wield a dagger does nae mean ye can defend yerself from *all* harm. Listen te my cousin and do as he says. Follow his lead."

She gave a tight nod. "I will. But why must I leave now and not tomorrow?"

Concern filled Angus's eyes. "Because I ran into Froste's brother in town and he told me that Froste sent word that he would be arriving in two days."

Marion gasped. "That's earlier than expected."

"Aye," Angus said and took her arm with gentle authority. "So ye must go now. I'd rather be trying te trick only yer father than yer father, Froste, and his savage knights. I want ye long gone and yer death accepted when Froste arrives."

She shivered as her mind began to race with all that could go wrong.

"I see the worry darkening yer green eyes," Angus said, interrupting her thoughts. He whipped off his hat and his hair, still shockingly red in spite of his years, fell down around his shoulders. He only ever wore it that way when he was riding. He said the wind in his hair reminded him of riding his own horse when he was in Scotland. "I was going to talk to ye tonight, but now that I kinnae..." He shifted from foot to foot, as if uncomfortable. "I want te offer ye something. I'd have proposed it sooner, but I did nae want ye te feel ye had te take my offer so as nae te hurt me, but I kinnae hold my tongue, even so."

She furrowed her brow. "What is it?"

"I'd be proud if ye wanted te stay with the MacLeod clan instead of going te the MacDonalds. Then ye'd nae have te leave everyone ye ken behind. Ye'd have me."

A surge of relief filled her. She threw her arms around Angus, and he returned her hug quick and hard before setting her away. Her eyes misted at once. "I had hoped you would ask me," she admitted.

For a moment, he looked astonished, but then he spoke. "Yer mother risked her life te come into MacLeod territory at a time when we were fighting terrible with the MacDonalds, as ye well ken."

Marion nodded. She knew the story of how Angus had ended up here. He'd told her many times. Her mother had been somewhat of a renowned healer from a young age, and when Angus's wife had a hard birthing, her mother had gone to help. The knowledge that his wife and child had died anyway still made Marion want to cry.

"I pledged my life te keep yer mother safe for the kindness she'd done me, which brought me here, but, lass, long ago ye became like a daughter te me, and I pledge the rest of my miserable life te defending ye."

She gripped Angus's hand. "I wish you were my father."

He gave her a proud yet smug look, one she was used to seeing. She chortled to herself. The man did have a terrible streak of pride. She'd have to give Father John another coin for penance for Angus, since the Scot refused to take up the custom himself.

Angus hooked his thumb in his gray tunic. "Ye'll make a fine MacLeod because ye already ken we're the best clan in Scotland."

Mentally, she added another coin to her dues. "Do you think they'll let me become a MacLeod, though, since my mother was the daughter of the previous MacDonald laird and I've an English father?"

"They will," he answered without hesitation, but she heard the slight catch in his voice.

"Angus." She narrowed her eyes. "You said you would never lie to me."

His brows dipped together, and he gave her a long, disgruntled look. "They may be a bit wary," he finally admitted. "But I'll nae let them turn ye away. Dunnae worry," he finished, his Scottish brogue becoming thick with emotion.

She bit her lip. "Yes, but you won't be with me when I first get there. What should I do to make certain that they will let me stay?"

He quirked his mouth as he considered her question. "Ye must first get the laird te like ye. Tell Neil te take ye directly te the MacLeod te get his consent for ye te live there. I kinnae vouch for the man myself as I've never met him, but Neil says he's verra honorable, fierce in battle, patient, and reasonable." Angus cocked his head as if in thought. "Now that I think about it, I'm sure the MacLeod can get ye a husband, and then the clan will more readily accept ye. Aye." He nodded. "Get in the laird's good graces as soon as ye meet him and ask him te find ye a husband." A scowl twisted his lips. "Preferably one who will accept yer acting like a man sometimes."

She frowned at him. "*You* are the one who taught me how to ride bareback, wield a dagger, and shoot an arrow true."

"Aye." He nodded. "I did. But when I started teaching ye, I thought yer mama would be around te add her woman's touch. I did nae ken at the time that she'd pass when ye'd only seen eight summers in yer life."

"You're lying again," Marion said. "You continued those lessons long after Mama's death. You weren't a bit worried how I'd turn out."

"I sure was!" he objected, even as a guilty look crossed his face. "But what could I do? Ye insisted on hunting for the widows so they'd have food in the winter, and ye insisted on going out in the dark te help injured knights when I could nae go with ye. I had te teach ye te hunt and defend yerself. Plus, you were a sad, lonely thing, and I could nae verra well overlook ye when ye came te the stables and asked me te teach ye things."

"Oh, you could have," she replied. "Father overlooked me all the time, but your heart is too big to treat someone like that." She patted him on the chest. "I think you taught me the best things in the world, and it seems to me any man would want his woman to be able to defend herself."

"Shows how much ye ken about men," Angus muttered with a shake of his head. "Men like te think a woman needs *them*."

"I dunnae need a man," she said in her best Scottish

accent.

He threw up his hands. "Ye do. Ye're just afeared."

The fear was true enough. Part of her longed for love, to feel as if she belonged to a family. For so long she'd wanted those things from her father, but she had never gotten them, no matter what she did. It was difficult to believe it would be any different in the future. She'd rather not be disappointed.

Angus tilted his head, looking at her uncertainly. "Ye want a wee bairn some day, dunnae ye?"

"Well, yes," she admitted and peered down at the ground, feeling foolish.

"Then ye need a man," he crowed.

She drew her gaze up to his. "Not just any man. I want a man who will truly love me."

He waved a hand dismissively. Marriages of convenience were a part of life, she knew, but she would not marry unless she was in love and her potential husband loved her in return. She would support herself if she needed to.

"The other big problem with a husband for ye," he continued, purposely avoiding, she suspected, her mention of the word *love*, "as I see it, is yer tender heart."

"What's wrong with a tender heart?" She raised her brow in question.

"'Tis more likely te get broken, aye?" His response was matter-of-fact.

"Nay. 'Tis more likely to have compassion," she replied with a grin.

"We're both right," he announced. "Yer mama had a tender heart like ye. 'Tis why yer father's black heart hurt her so. I dunnae care te watch the light dim in ye as it did yer mother."

"I don't wish for that fate, either," she replied, trying

hard not to think about how sad and distant her mother had often seemed. "Which is why I will only marry for love. And why I need to get out of England."

"I ken that, lass, truly I do, but ye kinnae go through life alone."

"I don't wish to," she defended. "But if I have to, I have you, so I'll not be alone." With a shudder, her heart denied the possibility that she may never find love, but she squared her shoulders.

"'Tis nae the same as a husband," he said. "I'm old. Ye need a younger man who has the power te defend ye. And if Sir Frosty Pants ever comes after ye, you're going te need a strong man te go against him."

Marion snorted to cover the worry that was creeping in.

Angus moved his mouth to speak, but his reply was drowned by the sound of the supper horn blowing. "God's bones!" Angus muttered when the sound died. "I've flapped my jaw too long. Ye must go now. I'll head te the stables and start the fire as we intended. It'll draw Andrew and Peter away if they are watching ye too closely."

Marion looked over her shoulder at the knights, her stomach turning. She had known the plan since the day they had formed it, but now the reality of it scared her into a cold sweat. She turned back to Angus and gripped her dagger hard. "I'm afraid."

Determination filled his expression, as if his will for her to stay out of harm would make it so. "Ye will stay safe," he commanded. "Make yer way through the path in the woods that I showed ye, straight te Newcastle. I left ye a bag of coins under the first tree ye come te, the one with the rope tied te it. Neil will be waiting for ye by Pilgrim Gate on Pilgrim Street. The two of ye will depart from there."

She worried her lip but nodded all the same.

"Neil has become friends with a friar who can get the two of ye out," Angus went on. "Dunnae talk te anyone, especially any men. Ye should go unnoticed, as ye've never been there and won't likely see anyone ye've ever come in contact with here."

Fear tightened her lungs, but she swallowed. "I didn't even bid anyone farewell." Not that she really could have, nor did she think anyone would miss her other than Angus, and she would be seeing him again. Peter and Andrew *had* been kind to her, but they were her father's men, and she knew it well. She had been taken to the dungeon by the knights several times for punishment for transgressions that ranged from her tone not pleasing her father to his thinking she gave him a disrespectful look. Other times, they'd carried out the duty of tying her to the post for a thrashing when she'd angered her father. They had begged her forgiveness profusely but done their duties all the same. They would likely be somewhat glad they did not have to contend with such things anymore.

Eustice was both kind *and* thankful for Marion teaching her brother how to read, but Eustice lost all color any time someone mentioned the maid going with Marion to Froste's home after Marion was married. She suspected the woman was afraid to go to the home of the infamous "Merciless Knight." Eustice would likely be relieved when Marion disappeared. Not that Marion blamed her.

A small lump lodged in her throat. Would her father even mourn her loss? It wasn't likely, and her stomach knotted at the thought.

"You'll come as soon as you can?" she asked Angus.

"Aye. Dunnae fash yerself."

She forced a smile. "You are already sounding like you're back in Scotland. Don't forget to curb that when speaking with Father."

"I'll remember. Now, make haste te the cliff te leave yer cloak, then head straight for Newcastle."

"I don't want to leave you," she said, ashamed at the sudden rise of cowardliness in her chest and at the way her eyes stung with unshed tears.

"Gather yer courage, lass. I'll be seeing ye soon, and Neil will keep ye safe."

She sniffed. "I'll do the same for Neil."

"I've nay doubt ye'll try," Angus said, sounding proud and wary at the same time.

"I'm not afraid for myself," she told him in a shaky voice. "You're taking a great risk for me. How will I ever make it up to you?"

"Ye already have," Angus said hastily, glancing around and directing a worried look toward the drawbridge. "Ye want te live with my clan, which means I can go te my dying day treating ye as my daughter. Now, dunnae cry when I walk away. I ken how sorely ye'll miss me," he boasted with a wink. "I'll miss ye just as much."

With that, he swung up onto his mount. He had just given the signal for his beast to go when Marion realized she didn't know what Neil looked like.

"Angus!"

He pulled back on the reins and turned toward her. "Aye?"

"I need Neil's description."

Angus's eyes widened. "I'm getting old," he grumbled. "I dunnae believe I forgot such a detail. He's got hair redder than mine, and wears it tied back always. Oh, and he's missing his right ear, thanks te Froste. Took it when Neil came through these parts te see me last year."

"What?" She gaped at him. "You never told me that!"

"I did nae because I knew ye would try te go after Neil and patch him up, and that surely would have cost ye another beating if ye were caught." His gaze bore into her. "Ye're verra courageous. I reckon I had a hand in that 'cause I knew ye needed te be strong te withstand yer father. But dunnae be mindless. Courageous men and women who are mindless get killed. Ye ken?"

She nodded.

"Tread carefully," he warned.

"You too." She said the words to his back, for he was already turned and headed toward the drawbridge.

She made her way slowly to the edge of the steep embankment as tears filled her eyes. She wasn't upset because she was leaving her father—she'd certainly need to say a prayer of forgiveness for that sin tonight—but she couldn't shake the feeling that she'd never see Angus again. It was silly; everything would go as they had planned. Before she could fret further, the blast of the fire horn jerked her into motion. There was no time for any thoughts but those of escape.

About the Author

USA Today and #1 Amazon bestseller Julie Johnstone is the author of historical romance novels set in the Medieval and Regency periods and occasionally modern-day times. Her novels feature fast paced plots filled with political intrigue, intricate world building, and complex characters.

Her books have been dubbed "fabulously entertaining and engaging," making readers cry, laugh, and swoon. Julie is a graduate of The University of Alabama & Springhill College. She lives in Birmingham with her youngest son, her snobby cat, and her perpetually happy dog.

In her spare time she enjoys way too much coffee balanced by super-hot yoga, reading, and traveling.

Sign up for her newsletter here:
www.juliejohnstoneauthor.com

Manufactured by Amazon.ca
Bolton, ON